For Alexis ♥ Ethan
Enjoy the Read
From your cousins
Kevin

Publisher's Note:

Thank you for purchasing this book. It began as an idea, was shaped by the creativity of its talented author, and was subsequently molded into the book you have before you by a team of editors and designers.

Like all EDGE books, this book is the result of the creative talents of a dedicated team of individuals who all believe that books (whether in print or pixels) have the magical ability to take you on an adventure to new and wondrous places powered by the author's imagination.

As EDGE's publisher, I hope that you enjoy this book. It is a part of our ongoing quest to discover talented authors and to make their creative writing available to you.

We also hope that you will share your discovery and enjoyment of this novel on social media through Facebook, Twitter, Goodreads, Pinterest, etc., and by posting your opinions and/or reviews on Amazon and other review sites and blogs. By doing so, others will be able to share your discovery and passion for this book.

Brian Hades, publisher

ENDLESS HUNGER

Kevin Weir

EDGE SCIENCE FICTION AND FANTASY PUBLISHING
An Imprint of HADES PUBLICATIONS, INC.
CALGARY

Endless Hunger

Copyright © 2018 by Kevin Weir

This is a work of fiction. Names, characters, places, and incidents are the products of the author's imagination or are used fictitiously and are not to be construed as real. Any resemblance to actual events, locales, organizations, or persons, living or dead, is entirely coincidental.

EDGE SCIENCE FICTION AND FANTASY PUBLISHING
An Imprint of HADES PUBLICATIONS, INC.
P.O. Box 1714, Calgary, Alberta, T2P 2L7, Canada

The EDGE Team:
Producer: Brian Hades
Acquisitions Editor: Michelle Heumann
Edited by: Heather Manuel
Cover Design: Lynn Perkins
Book Design: Mark Steele
Publicist: Janice Shoults

ISBN: 978-1-77053-178-9

EDGE Science Fiction and Fantasy Publishing and Hades Publications, Inc. acknowledges the ongoing support of the Alberta Foundation for the Arts and the Canada Council for the Arts for our publishing programme.

Canada Council Conseil des arts
for the Arts du Canada

Library and Archives Canada Cataloguing in Publication
CIP Data on file with the National Library of Canada
ISBN: 978-1-77053-178-9
(e-Book ISBN: 978-1-77053-177-2)

FIRST EDITION
(20180524)
Printed in USA
www.edgewebsite.com

Acknowledgments

For Mom, Dad, Erin, and Bryan who tolerated me while I hid in a fantasy world for months at a time and motivated me to create. For the friends who inspired me and helped me keep moving; Nick, Leah, Darci, Caralee, Ella, and everyone I may not have mentioned but I can't forget. Thank you.

Chapter 1

"Name and date of birth?"

"Kraft. August 12, 2105."

The Unemployment Office was bustling. While most lines steadily rolled people through, my line had not moved an inch in the last ten minutes. If the looks from the crowd behind me could kill, I would be dead twenty times over. It may have been my fault.

"Kraft?" The large middle-aged woman working the desk looked at me with a half-cocked eyebrow over the rims of her thick glasses. A picture of a fat white cat sat on her desk, and "Delores Briar" was projected on the glass separating us. So far, the conversation had been circular, third time she'd asked me for my name and DOB. I was going hand over hand up Jacob's ladder. She pursed her lips and frowned at me. "Sir, for the last time, I need your full name."

"Just put quotations around it. It'll come up!" I can't stand my full name, and I can't stand bureaucracy. All I needed was open water to create a trifecta of hatred.

The UO had a special way of getting under my skin, always filled to the brim with grime, bodies, and mediocrity. Worst of all, it had a weird almond smell; I pretended it was cyanide pumping into my lungs. Poison seemed a better end than death by boredom. Or death by starvation if I couldn't figure out why my unemployment check hadn't shown up in my account this month.

"Hurry it up, laghole! I got things to do!" The insult came from the quickly growing line behind me. The semi-reflection of the divider showed a gaunt-faced man with a greasy skullet hairstyle. *Northsiders.*

"Steps back, Skullcap," I said, staring into his reflection. "You'll get your dome polish."

Skullcap shoved me hard enough that my hat flipped off my head when my face hit the divider.

I spun around and shoved two fingers against his chest. "Shut it before I shut it for you!" I forgot about lagholes; trifecta of hatred, here I come.

Skullcap growled at me, showing off a gap where a tooth should have been. He was either too cheap to get a fake, or thought it was cool. *Let's see how cool you feel with them all missing.* I stepped closer until I could smell the sweat on his stained hoodie. His gaze flicked to the security guard leaning against the sickly green-blue wallpaper in the corner. The guard tapped his stun rifle. Skullcap receded like his hairline and began looking at pictures on his phone.

I picked up my baseball cap. It was a little dirty, but not any worse for wear. I brushed the dirt off the *HARDWIRE* logo and put it on. Satisfied I'd showed Skullcap who was boss, I turned back to Delores. "Just put it in, alright? Then we can both carry on with our meager little lives. Don't forget the 'K'."

Delores rolled her eyes and turned to her screen. The light reflected in her glasses indicated her thin glass monitor had turned on. I stretched to see around the metal screenback that gave Delores her privacy, but the glass divider kept me from seeing the screen. What I could see were her fingers typing K-R-A-F-T into the red light-projection keyboard.

She arched one of her eyebrows. Barely a second had ticked by. Evidently, something came up.

"I'll be damned, here you are. Kraft." *It's like she didn't believe me.*

"Wonderful! Now can I *please* get my check?" I rapped my index finger on the counter, attempting to convey "hurry up."

"You've been canceled." She yawned and clapped her hand on the desk. The light in her glasses disappeared and the projection keyboard shut off.

"Canceled?" I balled my hands to prevent myself from tearing out my own hair. "Why would they cancel my unemployment? Who can cancel my unemployment?"

"Your employer."

"I don't have an employer! Hence the unemployment checks I've been getting from you for the last year and a half!" I placed both hands on the window's ledge and put my face as close to the glass as my hat brim would allow. A red warning flashed. PLEASE STEP BACK.

"Well, apparently someone hired you." Delores looked around me and waved for Skullcap to step forward.

I'm a little ashamed to say I threw a small hissy fit, flipping my green thigh-length canvas coat around to no desired effect. I took a deep breath and pushed all anger and annoyance down to my feet. Cutting Skullcap off from the counter, I swept off my hat and put on the sweetest smile I could muster. I was sure removing my hat left a mat of shaggy brown hair, so I mussed it up into something somewhat presentable. "Ms. Briar — er — Delores, if I may?"

"You may not." She crossed her arms.

"Fine. Ms. Briar, I don't work for anyone. I did work for someone, but now I don't. Once again, hence the unemployment checks. To that end, there must be some glitch. Are you sure you have the right file?"

Delores narrowed her eyes, seemingly attempting to use them to burn through mine. My charm had been ineffective.

"There is no one else in the system with only one name, *Mister* Kraft." She stood as though she was a giant. "You should feel lucky you had it for a year and a half as is. If you have a problem with your situation, I suggest you take it up with your employer, Glowing Future Technologies."

With that, the glass divider displayed a large, screaming red text: MOVE ALONG. I suppressed the urge to unleash every curse word I knew, dropping my hat back onto my head. Glowing Future Technologies. I knew exactly who to talk to. The only man at Glowing Future that had a score to settle with me. I spun around and smacked Skullcap's phone away before leaving. *Showed him.*

———— «» ————

Glowing Future Technologies' head office was not far from the southern edge of Montreal Island, in the coincidentally named Glowing Future Tower. There were no short buildings outside the train's windows, only dozens of glass skyscrapers scattering light. I hopped off the train in the center of the Lighttech District, where most — if not all — the key developers of Lighttech-based technology were stationed. Stairs brought me to the streets where fleets of people bustled around south New Montreal.

"Sir!" A stick-thin vendor cut through the crowd. I lengthened my strides, but he slid through the mob like a snake through grass. "Are you in the market for a new screen? I have the Infitex Neo."

"I have a phone." I hurried to cross the street. The DO NOT CROSS light came on and the crosswalk lines turned red. I halted at the curb and did my best to ignore the screen vendor I was now stuck with.

"Perfect, I suppose. If you want to deal with a tiny screen." He pulled up his sleeve to reveal a wristscreen. "This is great for on-the-go data management. I also have flexile, optic and the ol' reliable solid body."

I stared at the second-tier street a dozen stories up, trying everything to show my disinterest.

"I can see by looking at you, you're worried about the price. Well, it's nothing to concern yourself over. These are cheap, brother. In cost, not quality."

See by looking at me? My coat was a little faded, my jeans a little worn, and my stubble was a few days beyond the normal shaving schedule, but I didn't think I looked homeless.

"Don't tell me you're one of those Lighttech-bashers. Neo-Luddites are out of fashion these days. Look, brother, we're talking about the fastest connection to the Network here. Check out the net, update your status, even start your car faster than you ever have before."

I had to take a second to comprehend that. "You... You can't be faster than instantaneous. It's not possible. Or at least not worth it."

"Not possible is not a word to me, brother! This is the hardware the transit line uses to manage all those trains and buses."

Now he was straight-up lying. The hub that New Montreal Transit uses to communicate with the Network is the size of a small car. NMT isn't even the biggest transit line on the planet, so he definitely wasn't trying to compare his dinky screen to a place like London, Mosgrad, or Nuevo Tokyo.

The crosswalk turned white again and I started to cross, vendor on my tail. Glowing Future Tower had an impressive pavilion out front. The kind of display you'd expect from New Montreal's key producer of Lighttech. The head office was a full ten stories taller than any other building I could see and had twin videos playing on either side of its front door that expounded on every screen, hub, and receiver chip made by them. *A gleaming tower among many more gleaming towers.*

Suffice to say, with my ball cap and dirty coat, I stuck out against the polished architecture.

"You're not going to want to pass up these deals," the vendor said.

I had almost forgotten he was still shadowing me.

"Look at me, man." If I was going to be confused with a vagrant, I might as well abuse it. "Does it look like I have money to throw around?" I pointed at a group of people huddled around a table. One of them was playing something on his tablet. Their badges identified them as interns. "Try them, maybe they're looking to upgrade."

The vendor charged off toward his new prey. "Brothers! Are you interested in some top-of-the-line Lighttech?"

I never liked the word "Lighttech." It seemed far too obvious. Then again, there does seem to be a distinct lack of subtlety with these corporations. Or maybe everyone needs a pavilion and I just missed the memo.

With the vendor gone, I was free to return to the problem at hand, Glowing Future. Through the doors, I marched across the spacious glass and marble lobby. The entire first floor was a painfully cavernous void. A few chairs against the distant walls, but other than that, it was depressingly sterile. I pulled my black Gloves on as I approached the security area. A skinny security guard with an upside-down name tag, Daniels, sat next to a white bot. Daniels looked to be in his early twenties and was repeatedly trying to fix the knot in his tie. I tapped the gate as I passed, the circuits etched into the Glove's fabric pulsing slightly as I did.

"Hey, y—" Daniels started to say something but stopped in his tracks as I swept through the scanner. No sound, not even the slightest beep, molested my stalk.

"Uh, alright, sir."

The guard returned to his seat, satisfied by the scanner's result. I scoffed inside my head at the lame guard. They were taught to trust the equipment. Unfortunately, the equipment didn't always work for them.

I arrived at the admin desk and knocked on the counter. The clerk across the desk took one look at my unshaven mug with my *Righteous Beer* tee-shirt and stuck up a finger in a "one-second" gesture. He turned back to his phone.

He had an Acog Theory phone. Acog made fairly secure devices, but "fairly" isn't always enough. I tapped a few icons on the back of my right Glove. Not even a second later, the clerk's prattling about his weekend plans stopped. He frowned at his phone. CALL FAILED blinked on the screen. With a sweet smile, I gently knocked on the desk again. "I'm here to see Mr. Godwin."

"He... uh, do you have an appointment?" the clerk asked, barely looking away from his phone.

"Oh, he's expecting me."

— «» —

The elevator played repetitive synthesizer music that drowned out all of my thoughts. I let it play for thirty seconds before touching the wall and shutting the song down.

"*Name not found, Kraft,*" an overly cheerful voice said. "*Do you find yourse—*"

"None of that." I shut off the advertisement just as quickly.

It had been a long time since I had gotten to hack anything with my Gloves. Back with the Information Bureau, I was constantly putting them through their paces. These days, I'm lucky if I get to break into my apartment when I forget my phone.

I mentally slapped myself. Thinking about the charms of a spook's life was pointless. Warren Godwin was waiting for me at the end of the elevator ride. The clerk had rung him, so he knew I was coming. *Who knows what kind of show he's planning to put on for me.*

I exited the elevator with the *ding* and approached Warren's office. A screen next to the door read WARREN GODWIN: HEAD OF NETWORK OPERATIONS. Warren was twenty-nine, only a few months older than me if I remembered correctly. Some say it's impressive for someone as young as him to be the head of anything at a company as large as Glowing Future. I say the impressiveness diminishes when your father is the company's largest shareholder. And your job could be replaced with a sign that says "DON'T FUCK UP."

I peered carefully into the dimmed office. Warren Godwin leaned back in his large leather chair, chewing on a fat cigar. A video projected onto the wall from the small cube on his desk. A smooth female voice talked over black-and-white images of war and destruction.

"It's been one hundred years since the Third World War destroyed much of our world. Tens of millions dead from the biological warfare, with tens of millions more deaths to come from the fallout. It was a setback, technologically and sociologically. The remaining population seemed unlikely to survive, forced to abandon the land poisoned by biological weapons. And yet, humans are not only surviving, but thriving."

The images changed to views of New Montreal and the laboratories of Glowing Future Technologies. Smiling scientists and citizens filled the screen. I rolled my eyes and stepped inside, shutting the door behind me. Warren was showing off, acting as though he didn't know I would stumble upon this video.

"The Lighttech Boom has revitalized a dying world and Glowing Future Technologies stands at its helm. They are ready to push the United Americas into the future. Lighttech and smartglass will be—" The video froze. The last syllable repeated until the system gave up and shut down. I had heard enough of it. The office was left substantially darker.

Warren touched the display on his desk to bring the lights back to full. He paused for a long second, blowing twisting smoke into an outflow vent on the ceiling. Only once the last wisp disappeared did he turn to me. "Kraft, what a surprise."

"Nice digs, Warren." I leaned against the doorframe, motioning to the extravagant room that surrounded me.

Warren smiled and followed my motion. "I think it has its charms."

The office was mostly wood with a regular interspersion of screens. Like a glass factory had thrown up in a farmhouse. It was much like the lobby far below though. Too much wasted space.

The massive bookcase to my left brimmed with information on everything from virtual intelligence to post-Third World War rebuilding, but it was purely aesthetic. Warren Godwin was not the kind of man to waste his time reading, and if he did, it would be an ebook. An office bookcase was a vestigial ideal from times long past to give an impression of scholarly aptitude. Most of the pages were probably blank.

Warren chuckled to himself, moved the projection cube into a desk drawer, and stood from his chair. He adjusted his expensive looking pinstripe suit and ran his hand over his heavily slicked black hair. I've seen this act a dozen times from business types. He wanted to sell me something. He dropped his cigar into an ashtray and sauntered toward me.

"When did you start smoking?" I asked. "Weren't you the guy who brought salad every day?"

"It's the style." He showed off the dark vest beneath his jacket. "Pre-war retro. You need to advance with the times, not... wear the same coat for two years. Your green's starting to fade."

"At least I don't look like a target, rich man."

Warren gave me an unsettling wink and turned back to his desk. "In university you occasionally wore sweaters."

"I'm surprised you even noticed me at school. What with your nose so far up the faculty's collective asshole." I pushed off the doorframe. Warmth radiated off the heaters in the slate gray carpet. It was pleasant compared to the November chill outside. But I would be damned if I let Warren know I was happy in any way.

I nearly leaped out of my skin when I saw the hideously large portrait of Warren — smirking his bastard smile and holding his suit's lapel like some pretentious Napoleon wannabe — next to the door.

"I always had an eye for potential, Kraft." Warren leaned on his desk, brushing a slight amount of dust off the surface. "I am to assume you hacked the scanner downstairs?"

"Yes." I had to tear my eyes away from the portrait's discomforting expression. I was sure it was a total coincidence that it was perfectly positioned to be seen from Warren's side of the desk.

"In that case, I am also to assume you are armed?"

"Very much so." I tapped my coat where it covered my hip. The hard bulge of my revolver met my hand with each motion. Staying armed was an old habit from my days at the IB. I'm not a fan of a firefight, but I wouldn't want to be lacking in firepower if one came up. Still, I prefer to win before the first shot.

"Why?" Warren slid his hand along the desk as he walked. The CALL SECURITY icon moved with him.

"Because I can. Your security sucks." *He doesn't really think I'm going to shoot him, does he?*

"Just because you can beat it does not mean it sucks." Warren shook a playful warning finger. An elegant bar spun out of the wall as he approached. A screen rested inside. The CALL SECURITY icon followed him to that screen. Grabbing various unlabeled bottles from the rack, he began mixing a drink.

He put up a strong wall, but cracks were starting to show. A tremor was apparent in his hands as he poured the spirits, even as he tried to hide it by turning away. He told the UO he hired me so he could show off? No way. Something was eating away at him. And it wasn't my gun.

"You know, even with all of our recent advances in robotics, there is nothing quite like a hand-mixed cocktail," he said as he rattled the shaker.

"If you did all this just to get me drunk, then you are sorely overestimating our relationship," I warned. I crossed my arms, casually putting my hands in clear view and far from my revolver.

Warren shook his head, never losing that strained smile. *He put that employment flag on my file for a reason. What's got him so worried?* He finished shaking the ingredients and then poured them into two crystal tumblers. An orange-red liquid covered the single sphere of ice already waiting in each. He held one drink out as he crossed the carpet.

"Here, try this," he offered. "It's my own creation. A Godwin, I call it."

I accepted the glass to push the conversation forward but did not show a sign of gratitude. "You know why I'm here, Warren, my UO file—"

"You know." He grabbed my free hand, inspecting the Glove. "If you let my scientists here take a look at those we could probably whip up some implantable version. Some cybertech firms would kill for the blueprints of a device like that."

I yanked my hand back.

Unrelenting, Warren looked the Gloves over from a distance. "It's some sort of induction weaving, obviously. But how you can do it touching anywhere on a device is astounding. Not to mention intercepting wireless signals."

"Warren." I snapped my fingers to bring him back to the real world. "The government barely tolerates me having them. They're not going to let them be mass-produced."

"The government is always changing policies." He gave a knowing smile that sent shivers along my neck. "Besides, they liked it enough to give you a job at the IB. Why wouldn't they want more?"

The Gloves were without a doubt the only reason the IB accepted me and kept me around for so long — even though most of my time there was spent telling superiors I wouldn't tell them how they were made or how they worked. The government had enough power as it was. I didn't mind keeping a little counter-response to myself.

They didn't agree. When I made them, police tried to arrest me a bunch of times or confiscate them. However, the Gloves' existence were merely a gray area in the law, since all devices *technically* send and receive Network signals — have to thank my lawyer for that one. Eventually the government did the next best thing and gave me a job.

Now I have to deal with the IB's constant eye on me, as though I'm going to walk into a bank and walk out with everyone's money. I mean, I could do that, but I probably won't.

"I'm not here to talk about what I did or did not make." I sipped the Godwin. A fruity drink. I could barely taste any alcohol. Made sense. "I can't get my unemployment check because, apparently, I work for you."

Warren sipped his drink and motioned for me to follow him back to his desk. He tapped his back wall and the once opaque surface became transparent with piercing sunlight. Another building blocking my sight soured what could have been a breathtaking view of New Montreal. I could see my city stretching into the distance at the edges.

I sat across from Warren. He wiped away the open windows displayed on the smartglass that covered his massive wooden eyesore of a desk. Some project he didn't have time for now.

"Did you catch any of my movie before you shut it down?" he asked. "We're coming up to the VDay centennial of the Final War, you know. We need to find some way to capitalize on that."

"It's corporate pandering," I growled. "Now, about my money—"

"Of course, of course. You really are one track, Kraft."

"Warren!" Warren had a habit of drawing out conversations. Maybe being a pain in the ass came with being a businessman.

"No need to get sharp. I have a job for you. Something special for your techno-talents."

"I don't need a job; I need you to tell the UO you didn't hire me." *That's a weird sentence.*

"You could fix it yourself if you really put your mind to it."

I gave him my best death glare. "That's illegal."

"Since when do you care about legality?"

"I care about legality when it's as obvious as hacking into an account at the UO. Might as well be flying a flag outside my window saying 'look at me, look at what I can hack into.'"

Warren let out a loud laugh. I nearly jumped out of the chair.

"It's exactly that kind of discretion I need!" he shouted. "So, your job—"

"I told you, I—"

"I'm paying five thousand eurodollars."

"You have my attention."

The tremor in Warren's hand stopped. "I'm worried someone has accessed our systems. I want you to run a trace — do that magic that you do — and find out if there has been any kind of leak." He swirled his Godwin.

"Any money gone?"

"No."

"Sensitive information finding its way to the media?"

"Not at all."

"Then what?"

"Just some... oddness."

"Oddness?" I stared at Warren, searching for the joke. The well-dressed man's face betrayed nothing but sincerity. Cologne covered sincerity. "Are you kidding me? This is a job for tech support! Or, hell, with your funding you could hire some IB analyst yourself to chase this little game. Jesus Christ, Warren, I've helped take down terrorists! What is this joke?"

"I'm not interested in the IB, Kraft. You were their best analyst anyway. Before they fired you, of course."

"They let me go." I slammed the tumbler on the desk. Small amounts of orange liquid splashed onto the glass.

"Oh please." Warren tossed me the kerchief from his breast pocket. "I'm surprised they kept you around for as long as they did." The kerchief flopped between us. Warren sighed and reached across the desk to clean the drink spill himself.

"What's that supposed to mean?" I eyed Warren as he wiped the Godwin from the desk. A hydrophobic coating kept any liquid from touching the glass.

"Kraft, you've always been a little, well..." He spun his finger beside his head. He tossed the kerchief at me and motioned to the garbage can. "Glitchy. You were always into ghosts and supernatural mumbo-jumbo. There are hobbyists, then there's you. I heard you once tried to convince your supervisor zombies were in the sewer."

"I had a reason for that." I fastball pitched the kerchief back at Warren, who tossed it into the garbage himself. "Are you keeping tabs on me?"

"Research. It was a kind of... pre-interview. And it was not easy. You're working hard to stay incognito."

"I like my privacy. I'm not one of your bright-eyed interns who will bend over backward for a job in your stupid lab."

He shook his head. "*Tut-tut.* You're nearly thirty. Don't you think this disheveled rogue persona has run its course? You hate the students for being so enthusiastic, you hate the experts for being so confident, you hate the poor for whining, and the rich for complacency. Kraft, where exactly do you put yourself in this wide world of ours?"

"In my apartment. If you're trying to convince someone to take a job you may want to think about not insulting them. But I guess you did flunk out of business school."

Warren raised his hands in surrender. "True, I apologize. Only wanted to point out you don't have many options these days. Unemployment Insurance will only hold you for so long. Especially when the IB stops pulling strings for you."

I drummed a beat on the desk. An old rhythm to help me concentrate. *Tap, tap, tap-tap.* Warren wanted me to get upset. I would lose focus and bargaining power. Seem weak. I would take the job but Warren would have the upper hand. Business bastard.

"I want you onboard," Warren continued. "The money is real, and once you're done I promise to explain the whole misunderstanding to the Unemployment Office. Simple."

Nothing is ever *simple*, not when corporations come into play. Warren still wasn't telling the whole story. *Keep your calm, Kraft. Analyze, don't antagonize.* His tie was done in haste, or while he wasn't paying attention. Not in a perfect double Windsor a men's magazine reader like him would normally tie. Small clumps of concealer sat beneath his eyes. The image of Warren putting on pressed powder in the morning made me chuckle. It was clear he was trying to hide the signs of sleep deprivation. He had been losing sleep over this. It was about more than just a little leak. He wasn't going to fool me. "You got some nasty things in your system you don't want the IB to see, don't ya?" Warren's face ticked. That was a *yes*.

"We do have some... less than legal projects in our database, yes." His jaw firmed up. "I need this dealt with before the boys upstairs catch wind and get scared. We are so close to finishing a new codec that could increase data transfer five-fold, no loss in quality either. It's a huge money-maker and could seal my career. But the Board could put a halt on all projects if there's a risk that one of our... other ones are found out. They can't think our system is compromised."

"Sounds like your system *is* compromised."

"Please, Kraft." He gave me the most puppy dog look his tired eyes could manage.

"Well, I do believe the markets are in flux, Mr. Godwin. With these changing trends in business, I have to say my price has just gone up. Ten thousand eurodollars is the new deal."

"What! You—"

"Alright. Well, I can tell when I'm not wanted. You have fun when the bosses see their dirty little projects all over the deep net. Ta-ta!" I started getting up from my comfy leather chair.

"Wait!" Warren cried.

I settled back into my seat. "Do you have something to say, Mr. Godwin?"

Warren clutched his crystal glass until his fingers turned white. He wasn't the smartest businessman, but he could tell when the wall was against his back. He looked for a long time at his blank desk screen. "Fine, ten thousand it is." He leaned forward, shoving a finger at me. "But I'm not talking to the UO, and you don't see a dime until you fix this."

"Half before and half after."

"How about none before and you do it quickly?"

I narrowed my eyes at Warren. I placed my hand on his desk. My Glove pulsed and I projected the system information out of my other one. Warren's eyes widened.

"Biotech?" I said, never looking at Warren. "The government has been a little down on that ever since the — oh, you know — biowar. You remember that? Scorched earth, billions dying from bioengineered poison."

"How did you get through the firewall?"

"If your desk is through the firewall, I'm through the firewall." I stood from my chair and held out the projection detailing biotech experimentation.

"Look, the government doesn't even know how it feels about biotech." Sweat was already glistening on Warren's forehead. "They let Medioxyl through because they deemed it beneficial to society. We aren't doing anything evil, we just need to prove the benefits before we can bring it public."

I couldn't care less about his rationality, or the government's stance on biotech. I only cared about leverage and paying for dinner. "Half before. Half after."

"Fine!" Warren brought out a cash stick. I swiped my phone over the thin metal. FIVE THOUSAND EURODOLLARS TRANSFERRED read across the screen.

"Happy to do business with you, Mr. Godwin." I offered my hand.

Warren reached across the desk and shook my hand — the kind of shake one would share with the relative they would rather not spend time with. *Ah, the joys of negotiation.*

"I'll tell security you'll be by tomorrow. Someone I can trust. Or control." He wiped his hand on his pant leg. "Let's say two? It's better you come on Saturday so I don't have a fleet of snoopers wondering what you're doing. We'll talk more then. Only tell security what they need to know."

"I only ever do." Smiling, I clapped Warren on the shoulder and slammed back the last of my drink. It was definitely vodka. *I'm pretty sure this is just a Screwdriver.* I headed out, leaving the man substantially more upset than when I entered.

There was a fluttering tightness in my lungs. It had been a long time since I had any work like this. Even if it was simple, it felt good to be getting something done.

Chapter 2

Northwest of the Lighttech District's gleam, I rode the train to the concrete borough of Laval. I leaned my head against the window, watching the trees zip by. As the train exited Laval Preservation Park, the split-city eclipsed the horizon. Deep in this towering maze was my humble apartment.

I had spent most of my life in a little ground-level apartment in south New Montreal, so Laval's sight still upset me at times. Atop the field of apartment towers was an upper street level, which had even more towers rising out of it. It looked like some kind of spiked beast ready to devour me. The PR name for the housing set up was "bi-level residences." Probably because "Maw of Stone Death" didn't test well.

I hopped off the train and pushed through the evening crowd to my building's elevator. I was fortunate enough to have a mid-quality apartment in the lower borough. Someone unemployed usually wouldn't have any luck affording a place in Laval; they would be stuck on the north side of the island in some place like the Block. I secured my apartment as a sort of severance package from the IB.

I flopped against the elevator wall. My head groaned at me like an ancient dying computer fan. There's nothing like a day filled with bureaucracy and old faces to turn your brain into mush. I preferred an afternoon of video games and television.

The lift dinged at my floor — good ol' thirty-one. I stepped into the hallway and headed home. The thick wooden door unlocked itself as I approached, my phone vibrating to let me know my apartment was waking up.

I grabbed the handle. A door opened and closed down the hall. My elderly neighbor, Ms. Heidecker, toddled out of her apartment. Leash in hand, no dog at the end. She spotted me as she meandered down the hallway, her large paisley muumuu swinging with each step.

"Hello, Sigmund!" she called.

"Hey, Ms. Heidecker," I replied as politely as I could manage after such a long day. She didn't deserve my frustration. Sigmund was her son. I saw him once but, apparently, he doesn't visit very often. "What are you doing out?"

"I'm taking Richmond here for a little walksie," she said, and motioned to the limp end of the leash. "Oh! Sigmund, I saw this program the other day on ghosts. Do you believe in ghosts?"

Heh. "Maybe a little."

"Well you should! There's more to this world than you can see. Ghosts and demons taunt us every day!" She swung her hands wildly. The end of the leash whipped around the hall. Good thing a dog wasn't attached.

I nodded, deciding to play along. She was kind of right.

"You enjoy your walk, Ms. Heidecker." I grabbed the handle of my door.

The woman waved goodbye and wandered down the long corridor, leash dragging on the carpet behind her. Once her phone transmitted that she was on her way out, her aide worker would come find her. I put Ms. Heidecker out of my head, turned the handle, and entered my apartment.

A few lights brightened into their low setting, enough for me to see in the dying sunlight reflected into Lower Laval. I ran my hand along the crack in the drywall from where I had once swung the door open too hard. The crack led all the way to a wall mount where I placed my phone. I tapped FULL on the screen and the rest of the apartment's lights flicked on. I kicked my boots off across the room and toward my bed. The floor heaters radiated into my feet. They weren't as soothing or as smoothly distributed as the heaters in Warren's carpet, but they were still nice.

I shut the door and ran my fingers along the runic circle carved into the wood. The dead bolt kept the people out — the circle kept out things more... unearthly. If Ms. Heidecker was worried about ghosts, it's one of these circles she would want to invest in. It's crazy, but there are worse things than hackers in the world.

People have a habit of ignoring the more fantastical elements around them. I made sure there were no cracks in the protection circle, and I wished I could ignore the elements, too. No one wants to deal with vampires and trolls while also trying to keep a job. To think, Warren called it a hobby.

Maybe that's why I was excited about Warren's job. I'd had some run-ins with the things that go bump in the night. It's not something I can talk to people about. The police don't know, the IB doesn't know, most people don't know. It was nice to deal with something that was normal, instead. I understand technology. I can control it. I have a weird life.

I tossed my coat haphazardly onto the floor. The cool air, reminiscent of years working near tech cooling systems, massaged my skin. I took off my Gloves, gently laid them on the stained stone island in my tiny kitchenette, and looked across my home. The wall screens twinkled like stars across the room, my own little constellation. The only annoyance was a red blinking message. TWO NEW VOICEMAILS. *Shit.* My phone was on silent at Warren's office. I had forgotten to switch it back. I dug the heel of my palm into my forehead to force the day's headache from my skull. I tapped the prompt and spun to the bathroom.

"First message from... Millie Kraft," the female robotic voice echoed throughout the apartment.

"Stop turning off your cell when you go out." My sister's voice followed me as I entered my bathroom. *"I think I can get you a job doing some basic administration at my hospital. I know it's nowhere near as exciting as working at the Intelligence Bureau, but there is less public-relation-type work so hopefully you won't have similar... problems."*

I shook my head. My sister worried more than most because of the whole supernatural thing. *You'd think she'd believe her own brother when he tells her about the monsters.* I'm "paranoid and crazy" to her. To most people, actually.

I was still wearing my gun holster. I ran my fingers over the worn leather — years of wear and tear had taken its toll. My hand felt the loops that held specialty rounds and a pouch for dual speedloaders. All currently empty. They'd been empty for a long time. I guess that's a good thing.

"Just call them before immediately deciding you hate it."

I slid the holster from my belt and tossed the latter into the main room. It was a ritual — new job meant inspecting the hardware.

"Alexis wouldn't want you to be like this."

I winced.

"The Bureau was one thing, Kraft, but it's how you are every day. You have to move on... or some self-help bullshit like that. Just call me back this time. I thought we could visit Mom and Dad together next weekend. You've missed the last two years."

Millie would always call going to their graves "visiting." Annoying term. *What kind of sister reminds you of all the dead people in your life in one message?* Millie was never one to completely think things through. She couldn't handle the monsters in my life. It was better to keep it to our monthly "hellos."

I looked hard at my revolver, an ExS SA40. Inspecting it was better than dwelling on the dead. I moved my fingers over the cold, black metal barrel, touching each nick and scratch. The barrel sat low, firing from the bottom chamber rather than the top. Apparently, it reduces recoil or something. Not being a "gun guy," I had to take my gunsmith's word for it. The revolver was indispensable when I was with the IB. "A field analyst needs a weapon as much as they need a screen," my boss used to tell me.

"I have to get back to work. And I assume you're off hunting ghosts or something. I better see you this month."

"Message end." The robotic voice was back. *"What would you like to do with previous message?"*

"Delete." I pushed out the swinging cylinder. It stuck slightly but moved. Only three out of the six chambers had rounds in them. *Shit.*

"Next message from... Regis Baudin."

"Kraft." It was the unmistakable French accent of my old supervisor from the IB. A rage bubbled just underneath his

words. *"My boys are telling me that you are still piggybacking off our access."*

I put the revolver on the bathroom counter next to the sink. Piggybacking off governmental Network access wasn't an ideal tactic for most hackers. Really, it's the IB's fault for giving me two weeks notice. You spend eight years with something and it's hard to let it go. At least with the access, I didn't have to touch everything to hack it. I pulled open the mirror and grabbed an auto-injector syringe of Medioxyl. I popped the cap off and took a seat on the lid of the toilet.

Regis wasn't making a sound. I imagined him sitting at his desk, rubbing his eyes and trying to decide what to do with me.

"Most people have adjusted to civilian life after a year and a half, and maybe you're taking longer than most, but you can't keep using our codes. Maybe some of the bosses are giving you leeway because of what you know, but you're not going to leak sensitive information that can hurt people. That's what I know. I'm going to give you the benefit of the doubt here because we worked together for so long, but if my techs catch you again I'm going to report you. You have to stop."

Or be subtler, I thought as I pressed the auto-injector against my inner arm. I touched the button to activate it. The needle shot out and tore a hole, piercing my veins and flooding them with the palliative within. My vision blazoned with white and a solemn ecstasy surrounded me. Prickling warmth traced through my nerves. Like the sun setting, the blooms subsided, and I became aware of a voice repeating:

"...ould you like to do with previous message? What would you like to do with previous message?"

"D-delete." *I can feel my eyes.* The floor was closer than before. *Funny walk.* The walls melted. I followed the road.

Such a beautiful room. Empty. The dark smell of insulation. *There should be paintings on these walls. I like paintings. Bed.* Sinew pulled under my skin. *This is hitting hard. Couch. Table. Ceiling. Money. Warren. Death. Not good.* My bed was a sea of marshmallows. My shirt was gone. *And hat.*

The lights fried my brain. My thoughts became omelets. *Why did she have to die?* GOODNIGHT MODE. *Why?* The lights slept. Darkness. *Why?* Lamps glowing from outside. Monsters crawled in my walls. *I have a weird life.*

──── ‹‹ ›› ────

The cold woke me first, a chilled blanket that fell across my body. I like cold; I hated this. I wanted to roll over and go back to sleep. It was the feeling that got me second. The feeling one gets when someone is watching you. Someone close. Someone I recognized.

"Jack," I muttered. Every joint cracked and popped as I moved to sit on the edge of the bed. The hit from Medioxyl is always stronger when you're tired — the body doesn't burn it as quickly. That was the biggest one in a long time. "Jack of Frost."

I had hoped I was still coming down from my high and imagined the presence. No such luck. He perched on the balcony railing outside my window, a tragically thin figure. The streetlights showed his deathly pale skin and the blue-white mop of hair on his head.

Jack of Frost. The Minor Spirit of Winter. Outside my apartment. *I do have a weird life.*

He hopped off the railing and rapped the glass with one finger. "Kraft," he said. "Open the door."

I grumbled a curse, but, nevertheless, I stood. Piles of clothing littered the area around my bed. I grabbed a heavy sweater from one of them. It was about to get very cold.

"Come in," I said, as I unlocked the sliding door. "Do you never visit at a reasonable time?"

He moved with a fluid gait, bringing a supernatural chill in with him. His tunic and slacks were torn and ragged, with a constant lining of snow along the bottom hems. He was the one from the legends. Spirit of Cold. Trickster of Snow. Prince of Ice. I slid the door shut again and turned to face my unwanted guest.

"A reasonable time means nothing to the timeless. You know this, Kraft." He padded on bare feet across the carpet, leaving melting snow patches where he touched. I had forgotten to set "turn off floor heater" as part of the bedtime program. I had been meaning to do it for weeks now, but it kept slipping my mind every night. Obviously, the heat was uncomfortable for Jack as he hopped across the carpet and leaped to a seated position on my kitchen island.

"I'm not timeless. I'm *very* mortal and *very* tired. I let you into my house willingly, and that was a courtesy."

Jack gave a self-righteous smile. "How strong do you think your threshold is? You cannot create a home if you never feel at home. And that" — he motioned to the circle carved in my door — "will keep ghostly callers from coming through your walls, but when a daemon crashes through your door you're going to be found wanting."

I've only met Jack a few times, but he loves to point out the holes in my knowledge about the Dark. I know it's another dimension, of sorts. I know to get from there to here one has to cross the Fade. I know that Darklings can't enter a house uninvited without giving up a lot of power; the stronger the sense of home, the harder it is to enter the house. Other than that, it's rudimentary magic and whatever I can scratch together from folklore.

"What's your point?" I eyed Jack warily, leaning against the armrest of my couch. My mind still strained from the Medioxyl cooldown. Standing for too long riddled my head with vertigo.

"My point is that you are a little fish in an exceptionally large pond. It would, quite frankly, behoove you to make some friends."

"Friends. Now, Mr. Frost, I thought we were friends."

The comment made Jack smile, but the meaning of the grin was clear. Not quite friends.

I was far too tired to deal with Jack's crypticness. Conversations with spirits were never fun. They didn't age, so if it took them four hours to say "hello" it wasn't a problem for them. Rubbing the bridge of my nose, trying to squeeze the want of rest from my eyes, I said, "Get to the point, Jack. It's been a frustrating day, and you're only making it worse."

"It's getting cold out," replied Jack, looking into the night out my window.

"It's November."

He didn't say a word. He just cast me a sidelong glare.

"But of course you wouldn't say that unless it was important."

Jack nodded. "The power of the ice and snow is... unwell. I believe some ill wind has been cast upon it, scattering its domains."

"Dost thou require aid for thine... hath... hither..." I muttered in some mocking Shakespearean gibberish.

"This is serious, Kraft. Someone has intruded upon and rerouted the very soul of Winter."

"And you can't figure it out? What is it with people not being able to deal with their own shit today?"

"There are rules. The matter has to be brought to the Well. Even Father Winter is subject to them and the Laws."

Jack couldn't fight the Dark's ruling council, the Well of Time, any more than I could fight the courts. They created the Laws and ensured the world kept a modicum of peace — or at least that's what I had gathered from some broken conversations on the subject. It seemed those who knew of the Well weren't keen on letting those not in the fold in on the secret.

"Speaking of frosty and crotchety," I said, regarding Father Winter of course. "Does he know you're here?"

"Not exactly."

"Then why are you here? What can a 'little fish' like me do?"

Jack sighed and turned his head away. It was clear he wasn't thrilled to be asking me a favor. Favors are big things for the denizens of the Dark, considering they don't exactly go around paying for things in cash. I had owed Jack a favor for a long time now. Something to do with a golem and a goblet — I was helping out a friend. I couldn't go to the IB about it. They would have laughed me out of a job and into a psychiatric ward. Instead, Jack swept in and introduced himself. Only a moron would think that was a coincidence. Still, I owed him. It was not a good position to be in, under the thumb of a capital 'S' Spirit. He probably wanted to call it in for something big. His hesitance told me he wasn't sure if this job was good enough. That was excellent news for me.

Sure, it was worrisome for Jack, but not enough for him to immediately try to pawn it off. Maybe it would be something easier than he thought.

"Kraft," the Winter Spirit said. "You are not bound by the Laws. The Well works slowly, and I fear what will happen if Winter's energy is left in this unstable state for too long. At the very least, you might give me some insight for when we do get the Well's permission."

I pushed off the armrest and took a few steps toward Jack. "You misunderstand. I mean, why do you want *my* help? Why not some other poor soul who owes you something?"

"You are not a known entity in the supernatural community. You have no reputation, no stink. Less chance of someone finding out what you're doing."

"You want me because I'm eight-bit?"

"If you wish to say it in such terms, yes, you're green. Also, you have a knack for seeing things others don't. Don't you, Seer?"

I groaned and rubbed my eyes. Jack wanted me to use my ability, Beyondsight, to see Dark stains. Around every Darkling is an aura, signifying them crossing the Fade like a stamp on a passport. I focused intently on Jack. A flurry of scratchy characters, like the kind in old computer code, appeared around him. They danced like flakes in a snowstorm. The visual representation of Winter energy, or at least how my brain rationalized it.

"I'm already on thin ice with the wizards." I blinked until the code faded away. "Apparently *seeing* Dark energy is too close to *using* Dark energy for them. They don't like Seers."

"I know they don't." Jack ran his hands through his hair. "This isn't ideal for me, Kraft."

A spirit wanting the help of a nothing mortal? Because only a nothing and a mortal could do it. No wonder the trickster was "all serious" for once; I would never let him live down asking for such a favor. I was reminded of Warren. They both wanted someone else to do the work they could not, but didn't want their bosses to find out. *Guess the Dark's not so different from the Light after all.*

I scratched my head and moved into the kitchen. I grabbed a cup from the cupboard and dispensed some water from the fridge. I could void Jack's favor with this job. Break any hold he had over me. That was better than any paycheck.

"I'll do it," I said and took the water down in one gulp. "But I don't exactly see why someone would steal your power just to drop an early winter down."

Jack shook his head. "The oncoming frost was not caused by whoever stole the power. It's happening *because* someone stole the power. It's a side effect. If not curbed, it could freeze the entire city."

"You could start with that next time. But it's nice to know you care about what happens here."

Jack narrowed his eyes sharply. It spread goosebumps over my skin.

"I understand," started Jack, "that you of this Light like to think that the Dark is a place of absolute evil. You imagine two separate worlds at odds, when we are, in fact, one entity, and we no more malicious than you humans."

"I can't help but think of Darklings that take joy in brutality and violence. Or do I have to remind you of vampires and ogres? They seem rather malicious to me."

"I have been around for millennia, and I have seen you humans cut swaths through each other. Only a hundred years ago, you burned out most of your planet. Even my kind can't survive the poison you left behind."

He had me there. It was wholly humanity's fault we began the Final War and ended it with the massive dropping of biological bombs. Even a hundred years later, the scars refused to heal.

"Any leads you think I should take a look at?" I said, deciding a change of subject was needed.

"I have some ideas," replied Jack, apparently agreeing to keep things amiable and move on. "But to tell you would be to go directly against the Laws of the Well. At this point, I'm merely bending them."

"Fantastic," I muttered under my breath. Jack was trying his hardest. Adherence to the Laws was less of a good idea for spirits and more of a facet of their nature. A spirit must be neutral. By breaking a Law, they would become tainted and in time succumb to a darker nature. This usually ended with the Well dropping some righteous hell on them. That would be how this current Jack of Frost got his Spirit of Winter position in the first place; the previous one broke a Law and got blown out of the water by the Well. "How about some tips then?" I asked. "You're allowed that, I know. Just think of it as a riddle."

"Right you are." He dropped off the island and stepped quickly across the warming floor to the counter closer to me. "Cold will always stick to its kind."

I waited for more. Jack shrugged. "That's it?"

"It's a riddle."

Fair enough. I paced around the kitchen island. If cold always stuck to its kind, then wherever the Winter energy was must be covered in it. "So I find the coldest place in the city."

"Maybe you'll find who's been taking Winter's power."

I clapped Jack on the back and frost puffed out. I crossed my apartment to the balcony door where he had entered. "It's something at least," I said as I moved. "Don't forget, I do this and we're even."

Jack nodded and moved swiftly from the kitchenette to the sliding door. He bolted back into the chilled air and once again crouched on the balcony's railing. "Be careful, Kraft," he said, looking back. "If someone is willing to throw nature off kilter they can't be up to anything good."

"Thanks, Jack. It's almost like you care."

He gave me a half-hearted smile and a backward wave. With that, he dipped forward off the side of the railing. His body burst into thousands of small snowflakes that twisted with the winter winds and swept into the night.

I closed the door once again and locked it. I considered flopping back into bed and passing out, but the whole exchange with Jack of Frost had left me wide awake. If Jack was right, then New Montreal was on the path to a new ice age. It wasn't something to procrastinate about. I would need to get started on some way to measure the temperature within a massive area, an entire city. I did have an idea.

Moving past my bed, I tapped the bedside table to WAKE UP. Even without the lights on, the ambient gleam from the streetlights did enough to illuminate the room. The interior lights just filled in the darker corners.

My apartment technically had a bedroom, but what was supposed to be my room had been converted into a tech-cave, of sorts. I entered my Cave through the door by my bed and the lights inside glowed. All the windows were blacked out to preserve the projections. It had been a while since I had to use my Cave. Most problems could be solved in the field with my Gloves, but this one was going to take some serious brainstorming.

I clapped my hands and rubbed them together to get some heat into my extremities. "Let's get started." I slapped the wall closest to me.

The lights cut out, leaving me in darkness for a second. Soon the hundred small projectors set into the walls glowed.

"Let's start easy." Sometimes I talked to the Cave. "The city."

The system responded, giving me a perfect 3D display of New Montreal and its surrounding areas. I was looking at every building, every street, every back alley displayed in an aerial view on the adjacent wall. If only the satellites I was getting the footage from had heat sensors, I would be done already. Seeing as thermographic scans weren't a priority for many companies, I had work to put in.

I raised my hands toward the projection and twisted my wrists until my palms faced the ground. The projection spun, and I was hip-deep in New Montreal.

"The satellites do have the right idea though. I need to be high when I scan... or maybe better to be closer to the center? No, wouldn't matter how in the middle of the city I am if I can't reach high enough. Aim for height over positioning then. Show me the highest building in the New Montreal area."

One of the skyscrapers to the north of Montreal Island flashed red and the view zoomed in until I was eye-to-window with it. It was the tallest building by a large margin. Tartarus Securities.

If I wanted to have an accurate read, I would have to do it from the roof of the most well-respected security firm in the United Americas. The same firm that did all the Network security for the New Montreal Police Department, and kept their own private army of mercenaries for "foreign interests." I would be lying if I said I wasn't excited to take a crack at their home base. I could feel my blood rising as dozens of plans rushed through my head. Getting on top would be one thing. What to do once I got there would be a whole other game.

"Put the city away." Tartarus Tower disappeared, leaving nothing but the glow of the projectors. "To get the entire city I would need one strong thermal scanner. If I only need information, though, I could probably just overclock a sensor bomb's thermal imager."

The system was listening and replied by bringing up a projection of a small, spherical device. A sensor bomb.

"Good job," I said to the system. "Keep this up and I'll figure out that name I promised you."

Sensor bombs are used by lawmen to gain an instantaneous recon of a room before breaching. They just roll a sensor bomb inside, it "explodes," and gives law enforcement a complete overview of the room — suspect positions, hostages, even who is and who is not armed is downloaded into a datapad or neural hub. Quicker than the blink of an eye. That much immediate demand on a system means the sensor burns out after one use, hence its name, sensor "bomb." I could take one and suppress every function except for thermal tracking. Without all the other capabilities, I could risk boosting its range.

"But I would need to get it even higher than Tartarus Tower's roof." I ran my fingers over the coarse stubble on my chin. "Some kind of propulsion."

The projected sensor bomb flew up, then back down into what looked like a mortar cannon.

"Good idea, but I don't exactly have access to that kind of weaponry." I tried to rub the sleep from my eyes. I just got going and I was already feeling fatigued. But there was no point in stopping before I figured it out. A mortar would obviously be perfect. If I didn't have access to one, I could always make my own. "A potato cannon."

The mortar changed into a cruder tube and stand. It was as if the system was making fun of my potato cannon. I may have invented a virtual intelligence with sass. The potato cannon launched, but the sensor bomb didn't get anywhere near as much lift as I would need. Instead, it popped out and rolled depressingly across the virtual ground.

"Granted, a regular aerosol propellant probably isn't going to give us the acceleration necessary. But let's say I use Fyrex. And so as not to lose any fingers, instead of a lighter I'll whip up a stomp plate with some flint, ah?"

A welder's chemical like Fyrex would definitely get the lift I needed. Normally a welder would spray it on two pieces of metal and hit it with a spark for a quick weld. At the very least, the explosion from the fumes would be exciting.

The display shimmered for half a second and the sensor bomb launched again. This time, rocketing straight through the roof, accompanied by some virtual ceiling rubble raining down on me. *Awesome.*

I clapped my hands in excitement. "Boom! There we go!"

Instead of an affirmative from the system, it merely replayed the launch, followed by it zooming in on the sensor bomb surrounded by floating question marks.

"You're saying that once launched, the bomb is going to sail off somewhere? And, if I'm breaking into a place to do this, I shouldn't leave evidence laying around that could trace back to me? Good point." Another roadblock, but one I could solve fairly easily. "I'll attach some heat-resistant cabling to the bomb and the other end to a retractor underneath the tube. Bolt it down to the roof and it'll come shooting right back into the muzzle. I'll unbolt it, pick up the entire unit, and I'm off."

That got me a few virtual fireworks from the system.

"Oh, thank you. Thank you very much, you're too kind." I smiled at my success and slapped the wall again. The projectors shut off and the normal light of the room resumed. I turned the lights off, shut the door, and returned to my main room.

There wasn't an inkling of sunlight reflected into Lower Laval yet. With the whole Jack of Frost situation, I had never actually checked the time. I glanced at the digital clock on the fridge across the room: 3:54 AM. I didn't have to be at Glowing Future until the afternoon, so if I slept now I could still get a few hours.

That seemed like a kind enough idea to my body, so I tore off my sweater and jeans and jumped back into the warmth of my bed. I turned GOODNIGHT MODE back on and let the light dim away.

Flopping onto my back, I rested my hands behind my head and looked up to the bare ceiling. I had Warren and Glowing Future to deal with, and now I had to find time to look into the whole "Winter's missing power" fiasco. Peek into Glowing Future's system and then infiltrate the highly guarded Tartarus Tower with a sensor-launcher. Going to be a fun weekend.

If I was going to build a super-potato-gun and get my hands on a sensor bomb, I would have to hit up my contact, Scoundrel. I had been meaning to go and stock up on some ammo anyway. Hopefully, I wouldn't need it. Everything seemed to be going extremely easily so far.

I hope it stays this easy.

Chapter 3

The afternoon sun reflected off the skyscrapers and turned the Lighttech District into a brilliant display of traversing light streams. I had woken up at half past noon and rushed through my morning shower and breakfast, but made it to Glowing Future in time. Daniels, the same skinny security guard from the day before, stood with Warren by the scanner.

"Welcome back, Mr. Kraft," Warren said through a smile.

"That my babysitter?" I nodded toward the lanky, awkward guard. "I'm amazed you didn't stick a synthetic with me."

"Right. I would leave *you* with an *electronic* guard. Mr. Daniels is only here to keep you company."

Daniels nodded to me, confused but eager.

"Company. Perfect." It was more likely that Warren thought I wasn't to be trusted alone in Glowing Future's system. "Come on, show me the Network hub."

Warren motioned to the elevator bank near the empty admin desk. I slid around the scanner and headed to the elevators.

Daniels finally found his voice. "Uh, Mr. Godwin? Protocol dictates that everyone who comes into the building is subjected to a scan." The poor guy could barely make eye contact with Warren. "He, uh, he has to go through the scanner."

Warren turned back and looked between the scanner system and me. "That won't be necessary, Mr. Daniels," he said, continuing his walk to the elevators.

I gave a small smile from below the brim of my cap to the increasingly perplexed guard and followed after my employer. Warren arrived at the bank and called the elevator to go down. The doors opened and Daniels was just able to catch up as we stepped in and Warren pressed B3.

"Take the next one," Warren said as the doors shut and the elevator started sinking.

"You're confusing the hell out of the poor man," I remarked.

"We needed privacy."

"Of course. So, what's this 'oddness'?"

"Just some minor things that I'm hoping will stay minor." He pressed his thumb on the screen, stopping any advertisements before they could start. "Some files get moved around. Unapproved access by users that don't exist. One employee complained about a frightening pop-up. Someone is messing around and I want to catch them before they do any harm."

It sounded like a computer poltergeist. "And before someone learns about your dirty laundry?"

The elevator came to a stop a couple basement levels down. The doors slid open.

"Yes. That too," Warren growled, and stepped out.

In sharp contrast to the aesthetic of the upper floors, the sub-basement was cold — in both looks and temperature — with only gray concrete and pipes as decor. I followed Warren through the narrow, dingy passages. The sounds of our footsteps echoed infinitely into the maze.

Far behind us came the resonating ding of another elevator as Daniels made his arrival. I bundled my coat tighter around me.

"Why is it so cold down here?" I asked. The frosty climate of the sub-basement exceeded my tolerance level.

"We used to house an impressive number of servers at this level." Warren's breath puffed out visibly when he spoke. "The basement was built with shielding in the walls that was meant to absorb the heat and disperse it up through the building. A cost-effective way to heat the above areas and keep the servers down here cool. But once the Lighttech Boom hit, the multiple servers were gone and replaced with... Well, you know this. Without their heat, this place is like winter all the time."

"Makes sense," I said, zipping up my coat to my chin.

I followed Warren through the maze of pipes and power lines. We came to a metal door with the placard that read: Server Room 1.

Warren placed his thumb on the handle's scanner and the lock popped open. Inside the room was a lone metal rectangular box with numerous cables reaching from it like tentacles to the ceiling and — one would assume — to the rest of the office building. The space around the hub was empty. Hidden beneath the scent of dust and grime was the hint of citrus. Someone had tried to freshen it up with an air freshener.

"What are you going to do?" Warren asked.

"Pretty simple. I'll see if I can trace these intrusions to an access point. Hopefully it'll be as easy as seeing which one of your employees was playing around in the system." *Simple would be nice.*

The sound of footsteps alerted us to Daniels's trek through the tunnels. Warren shut the door. "One of my employees?"

"I highly doubt that a company with a firewall like yours on its system could be hacked through from the outside."

"Are you complimenting my security?"

"Well, it's excellent. Against someone who isn't me, of course." I jabbed Warren in the shoulder then donned my Gloves.

Warren rolled his eyes and opened the door. Daniels stood on the other side, dressed in a heavy coat. He was ready for the weather.

"Just let me know as soon as you find anything. And you—" Warren motioned to Daniels. "Keep an eye on what he's doing." He gave me one last glare then disappeared back into the labyrinth of a basement.

I didn't wait another second after Warren left, I was already crouching at the hub. I unzipped the zippers on each coat sleeve at the wrist and flipped them up. My Gloves projected the red display on my forearms. I located the screen on the Network hub and placed my right hand against the glass. Despite the thin layer of frost, the Glove's induction weave worked perfectly, and the back of my hand lit up a display. I could feel Daniels peering over my shoulder to try to see what I was doing. I tapped the calibration icons and synced to the Glowing Future system.

"Mr. Godwin said you're working on our systems?" the guard asked.

"That's right, skippy," I said, only half-listening.

The quicker I did my trace, the quicker I could get my money — both the paycheck and my unemployment. I twirled and sat with my back to the hub. Lights across the surface of my raised palm jumped to life, projecting a representation of the system. Daniels watched in amazement as I scrolled through the data.

"How do you know Mr. Godwin?"

"University." Daniels was like a small dog, yapping away. It was nice though; the basement would have been much creepier without someone else there. "Then later he was part of the correspondence team that was bidding to supply the bureau I was with."

Someone accessed the system then added something to it about a week ago. I started a trace and my program began sorting through the thousands of employee codes.

"And you helped him get the bid through?"

"Oh, God, no. I fought vehemently against it," I said. "We went with the better choice in the end."

"Oh… What bureau were you with? My cousin worked for Foreign. In office only, of course."

"Intelligence."

"Really!" Daniels exclaimed. I almost thought he was going to jump on me. "That is awesome! So, this computer stuff is all natural for you. What did you do with them?"

"Tech support."

"That's… interesting too, I guess." He was obviously disappointed I didn't say secret agent or something.

"Daniels, never underestimate the joys of a normal job." If only I could forget about all the supernatural madness I have to deal with.

Tech support was enough of the truth. I didn't feel like explaining the intricacies of the IB to him. It's impossible to comprehend what the IB does specifically. Intelligence gathering is such a broad field that the IB roster consists of everything from analysts to covert snipers. Really, any crime that piqued an agent's interest could become the IB's jurisdiction. Sometimes, if the case seemed like something beyond the local police's capacity, they would send an agent in to help.

But, me? I was a field analyst. I wasn't a sledgehammer. I wasn't a cloak and dagger. I was sent to figure out what was wrong and — if I could — fix the problem. Tech support.

The scrolling stopped. My program found a matching ID with the employee "Michael Harman." I opened Harman's files and was greeted with the smiling face of a forty-something-year-old man with a thick mustache.

"Do you know this guy?" I asked Daniels.

"Thousands of people work here. I can't know them all."

I leaned against my knees, staring into Harman's smiling mug. His profile was solid, and wholly bland. Yet, something seemed off.

"He's been employed here for three months. But he didn't show up for work yesterday," I recited from the file. "I'll run a facial ID." I closed my hand then gave Daniels a quick scan out of the corner of my eye. "What did Warren say about what I'm doing?"

"Uh, that you're going to find some possible intrusions in the system, and I'm not to tell anyone about it."

"He trusts you?"

"He made me sign a contract."

"Fair enough." I tapped my right wrist to project the Intelligence Bureau's database. I needed to make sure Daniels wasn't going to blab about me using the IB's catalog. If I knew Warren, that confidentiality contract would take Daniels's kidneys if he broke it. Michael Harman's picture was uploaded and the database jumped into action.

"We have all his information in our system." Daniels stepped closer, until his knees were almost touching my shoulder. I subtly slid away.

"Not quite. They get a shot of your face and they can find your likes, dislikes, search history, high school grades, and best friends. All that info for whoever is watching the monitor screens. And those bastards are watching."

"That's a little paranoid, don't you think? I'm sure whoever you're talking about has better things to do than spy on everyone."

"Mostly? Yes. But it's out there. If it's in the internet, it's in the Network. Forever. And trust me, once you've been on the other side of the glass you know who's looking through."

I noticed the concern on Daniels's face. I obviously put some worry into his bright little life. It would only be courteous to throw him a bone. "There is a way around it though."

"How?"

I tapped the hat brim that shadowed my eyes. "No face. No trace."

The projection from my Glove blinked and drew my attention back. "No match," I read. "Apparently he doesn't exist."

"That's impossible. We do a background check on all our employees." He seemed more offended than worried that someone beat their system.

I shot back to the employment info and checked which sites the background checkers looked at. I brought them all up in different windows and extended my arms to project them to the adjacent wall. *Page Not Found* across the board.

"He gave himself a false history then removed it before anyone noticed." I shut off the projections.

"Oh, man."

"I don't think Mr. Harman will be back on Monday." Warren was dealing with a simple case of corporate espionage. "Do you keep the footage from the cameras?"

"We do a dump onto an external drive each week. I would have to ask the security chief to get at it."

"That's fine. I need all footage that includes Michael Harman. I'm sure you have a program for that, ah?" I stood and paced the server room. The basement's chill made my body numb, so I hoped some movement would keep me from freezing. I delved back into the system files.

"What are you doing?" Daniels kept step behind me, nearly taking my boots off with his proximity.

"If I can't find *who* did it right now, I'm at least going to find out *what* he did." Lights flashed before me as I zoomed through the code.

"You learned how to do all this stuff doing... tech support?" Daniels rubbed the back of his head.

"Yeah, sure, why not?" A clever guard would have been interested in the fact I could access the system by touching it. A genius guard would have been interested when I then mirrored the entire system. Daniels was evidently not a clever or genius guard. A discrepancy stood out among the thousands of lines and I stopped. Most people might have shot right past it. But I'm not most people.

"Here we go," I said, stopping so abruptly that Daniels nearly crashed into me. I was right. Someone put a virus in the system, but something else was strange.

"What is it?" Daniels squinted, as though it would help him comprehend the language in front of him.

"They hid a file. A video." It could be the virus. But the fact it was a movie file was weird. The whole situation was starting to get eerie. I've taken apart a few sickos' computers, and nothing good is found in a video. My common sense begged me to stop, and my uncommon sense screamed at me to stop. But my curiosity was stronger. The file name was FEAST.AVC. I opened the video and projected it onto the wall.

Daniels stepped closer to me, and we stared into the initially black video. A tightness enclosed around my heart as the seconds ticked by and the video projected the blackness. The basement seemed to freeze in anticipation.

The image of a dissected human body on a dinner table assaulted my sight. A family sat around the table, smiling like they were at some kind of macabre Thanksgiving feast. The picture changed. I watched in horror at the grotesque and disturbing images that flashed across the screen. Dismemberment, mutilation, and indescribable acts of torture. Each time there was someone different there. Smiling at the camera.

"Kraft, turn it off." Sweat rolled down Daniels's face.

It was as if I was hearing him through water. I was in a terrifying mesmerization with the video. It was disgusting and terrible and I felt sick to my stomach, but my body would not respond. No matter how horrible it was, I was locked in.

A piercing screech emitted from the hub and the lights began flickering. It was chaos. I thought the world was going to rend at the seams, as though the earth would split beneath me and I would be swallowed whole. I would fall into the dark and it would be me, watching someone else. And I would be the one smiling.

The video stopped on an image. It was of a man. The image was blurry, and I couldn't make out his features at first. *Brown hair maybe? Something was on him. Paint?* The image came into focus. It was me. Naked from the waist up and completely covered in blood. He — I stared right into my own eyes. Not at the camera lens. Somehow, I felt like he was seeing me. His expression twisted with some orgasmic hatred.

The screech intensified until it was a drill boring into my skull. A presence seeped from the walls and surrounded me, as though the other me's glare was coming in from all angles. He reached to his neck and dug his fingers in deep. He pressed hard. Blood flowed as his nails tore through the skin.

"Kraft!" Daniels lunged at me and yanked my arm down, shutting off the video. The screeching disappeared and the room seemed to brighten. I inhaled deeply and dropped to my hands and knees, coughing at the sudden intake of stale basement air. The oxygen turned to acid in my lungs. *Had I not taken a breath the entire time the video was playing?* Steadily, I controlled my coughing fit, and I stumbled back to my feet.

"Wh— What happened?" I asked. My head pounded out of control.

Daniels was bone-white. When he spoke, his hands shook incessantly. "It was that video. Those... images. You started shaking and growling and..."

I needed to get out. I needed wind against my face. I needed the blooms.

"Just... call me when you get that footage," I said through deep puffs of air. I shoved Daniels aside and staggered to the door.

"What about—"

"Just do it!" I yelled as I crashed through the server room door.

My stomach turned as I forced my way through the hallways. I followed the signs leading me to the elevator but each concrete corridor bled into the other. My breathing picked up and the walls began to spin around me. *Everything looks so damn similar!*

The passage opened into a room. The elevator bank waited in front of me. I stumbled to call the elevator. The bell dinged after a few seconds, and one door barely slid open before I threw myself inside. My legs couldn't hold me anymore. I dropped, shaking, into the corner.

I dug into my inside coat pocket and pulled out an injector of Medioxyl. The liquid flooded my system and the familiar blooming filled my sight. *Elysium.*

The door's maw opened to an empty existence. *Stone. Stone. Glass.* I didn't move. It shut again. Metal clicked. Heavy silence. Hum of the lights. *Soothing.*

So much for a simple job.

My body burned through the Medioxyl in record time. It was the most peculiar feeling. My brain felt fractured. Overclocked. An infinitude of thoughts. So much so, it was impossible to focus on one. So, I focused on none. Joyously numb. That feeling didn't last forever. The Medioxyl cut the anxiety somewhat, but I wasn't going to be passing out like yesterday. Too much adrenaline. It always hits harder when I'm tired. *I'm anything but tired.*

I sat in silence for what might have been several minutes after the initial high was gone, before I pressed the door-open button and left the elevator. *Why is it so empty?* I had to focus on what I knew. Pushing down the experience, I pulled out my cell phone and called Warren.

"Hello, Kraft. How—"

"Who are your enemies?" I asked.

"What are you talking about? What did you find?"

"Someone put a virus in your system. A Michael Harman went through the trouble of creating a fake history and worked at your company for three months to do it. This is an attack against you. So, I ask again, who are your enemies?"

"I've never heard of a 'Michael Harman.' We have plenty of corporations who are threatened by us, people who hate us. It could be anyone."

"Think harder."

The phone fell silent. "Orion Industries. They're our biggest competitor, and there has been some heat thrown around. Remember that codec I said we're close to finishing? Both us and Orion are rushing to release a new one first."

"There's nothing like competition to bring out the worst in people." I exited Glowing Future Tower. The cool November air was a relief on my face. *Cold. Beautiful.*

"Did you find anything else?"

The gory images bubbled up and flashed through my brain. *Blood.* "No." I ended the call.

It was starting to stink more and more like something from the Dark was involved somehow. They love to mess with people's heads. Watching yourself tear your own skin off seemed right up their alley. A treat for anyone shoving their nose where it didn't belong. But I wasn't ready to take the job as a paranormal incident. *Was I? No. Maybe.* Even if I was, I had no idea what could do *that*. Maybe a spirit of some kind, but I couldn't be sure.

I considered going back down to the hub. I could use my Beyondsight and get a glimpse into the energy behind the virus. At the least, it would confirm whether or not it was something magical. My chest tightened at the mere thought of returning to that freezing maze.

Could have been a very twisted prank on whoever was foolish enough to open the movie file. I could have imagined the guy at the end looking like me. The mind can play some terrible tricks when it's afraid. *Wrong.* I was fooling myself, making it seem more mundane than it was. I didn't want to face what lay in the Dark today. *Or any day.*

Orion's head office was a few streets down. Maybe I could get a meeting with the CEO. The walk gave me time to get through the Medi cooldown too. Until overwhelming evidence told me otherwise, the case was still about corporate espionage and not the Dark. I dug my hands into my coat pockets and started for Orion Industries.

——— «» ———

The CEO of Orion Industries was Helga Dubois. I found her marching through the atrium entrance of her business's head office. She looked just as angry as she did in her employee photo — and just as pretty. Great columns stretched up on both sides of the hall, imitating Greek architecture. I jumped out from behind one and blocked her path.

"Helga, right?" I asked, hand extended with a goofy smile stuck on my face. I kept my hat low so none of the cameras would get a clear shot of me.

"Ms. Dubois," the woman corrected as she pushed past me.

"Of course, Ms. Dubois. I'm Hank Pym with the New Montreal Gazette. I was just wondering if I could ask you a few questions?" I tapped the fake reporter's ID I had forged long ago for another job. *Lie.* I was still on the tail of my cooldown. Fractured thoughts were slipping through. I could manage. Ms. Dubois looked at the ID briefly without stopping. I followed closely after her wide steps.

"I'm not exactly up for questions right now."

She appeared to be looking at emails on her screen as a way to ignore me. New accounts, meeting requests, nothing pertinent for me. "Is it normal for a CEO to work on Saturday?"

"We pride ourselves on being anything but normal, Mr. Pym."

"Hank."

"Hank Pym?" she clarified, making eye contact with one of the security officers. He typed furiously on his wristscreen.

I now had two minutes until security realized that it was a fake name and I would be quite forcibly ejected. "I really won't take long, ma'am."

Helga rolled her eyes and I followed her into the elevator already waiting. She motioned for two security guards to follow her in, but I wasn't interested in eavesdroppers to my conversation. I brushed the elevator wall and the doors slammed closed.

"Whoa!" I exclaimed. That was a little more violent than I had thought it would be. The elevator started rising shortly after. Now she and I had some privacy. "That was odd, wasn't it? I was just hoping to get your opinions on Glowing Future Technologies."

"They are a fine company." She saw that she wasn't getting out of this and decided to play it cool. Eager reporters weren't a new opponent for her.

Now that she'd stopped fleeing, I was able to take her in. Her black hair lay loose across her shoulders. She was one of those middle-age women you knew was a heartbreaker in her day. Hell, she might still have been one. The business suit she wore held to her body in all the right places; certain ones I may have lingered on longer than I should have. I like to believe I have a very professional mind, but every so often, the human in me creeps in. *Boobs. Damn.*

Her lips pursed together in anger, paling against her dark skin. I had to be as inviting as possible without being a pushover. If she felt threatened she would shut right up, and I'd find myself on the inside of a jail cell quicker than a flash.

"I heard that you two are in a pretty fierce competition for a new codec," I said. "It must be frustrating to have such a high-profile company fighting with you."

One minute, thirty seconds left.

"It happens. Companies race to new technologies all the time." She kept both eyes on the counter that ticked up the floors.

I leaned forward to put myself in her view. "Apparently someone has put a virus in their system."

"That is terrible, but I do not see what it has to do with me." She stood solid as a stone.

"If anything happens to their system you can bet all their current projects are going to slow down considerably."

One minute.

"What exactly are you accusing me of, Hank?" She shot a death glance in my direction. *Danger.* My heart leaped into my throat and before me the woman's appearance shifted. A dark pit grew in her eyes. Spirals of code twisted from her shoulder blades. My Beyondsight was warning me, granting me a glance deeper into Helga Dubois. Any questions I had fell out of my brain. A chill shot up my spine. *Danger. Run. Shut up.*

"Are you alright, Mr. Pym?"

Forty seconds.

I was out of time and thankful for it. "Well it has been nice talking with you, Ms. Dubois," I said, keeping the words as even as I could manage. I touched the wall to stop the elevator. The elevator ground to a halt, and I touched again to open the door. Nothing happened.

"Must have shorted out the power," I muttered. Technology was finicky at times.

I gave Helga an awkward smile and began forcing the doors open manually. Her eyes widened. I pushed the two doors open, but the elevator wasn't quite at the next floor yet. I scrambled up into the hallway and waved back to the shocked Helga before hurrying away. I crashed through the emergency exit with a loud *bang.*

As I took the stairs down two at a time, my phone rang. "Hello?"

"Hey, Mr. Kraft? It's Daniels from the security desk," the voice said. "I called the security chief, but he said he wouldn't be able to come in to get the footage off the drive until the early shift tomorrow."

"That sounds perfect. I need to go, though; I'm kinda in the middle of fleeing."

"What?"

I ended the call and hit the exit door into the alleyway. An alarm resounded through the Orion offices.

Exiting the building was a huge weight off my shoulders. I grabbed my revolver from where I had hidden it earlier behind a dumpster and turned left down the alley, toward where I could slip back onto the streets without anyone seeing me. A cold wind took my coat, flipped it around, and cut deep to my bones. It could also have been what I had just Seen hitting me. My right hand was shaking persistently, so much so I had to grab it just to keep it still. I kept flashing back to what I Saw when I looked at Helga Dubois.

She wasn't human.

Chapter 4

Spotting something with Beyondsight is never peaceful. It's the brain rationalizing the irrational. Even if I know what the aura means, it sends a blade across my nerves. When I see one in a shape of something I can't recognize, that's scary on too many levels. There are Darklings I've heard of that I wouldn't want to tangle with. I needed some info.

I waited in a Taco Hut for the only guy who might know what was going on with Helga. I adjusted my coat, draped across my lap to hide my revolver. People get antsy about firearms even if you have a license. Absolutely reasonable reaction, of course. Before society recovered from the war, it was common to see people walking around with all sorts of weaponry. That habit was starting to fade, but it wasn't gone yet.

I looked down at my half-eaten beef taco and hash brown clumps — I had to resist the urge to go all out with my new cash or I would be broke yet again. If my contact didn't arrive soon, I might dig back in out of sheer boredom.

A creak and slam brought my attention to the front door. Caleb Brennan looked unearthly slender in his fitted, black peacoat and matching gloves. I'm not fat by any sense of the word, but I looked practically rotund next to Caleb's "stick with arms and legs" physique. His dark hair swept across his brow in a stylish cut. That's what Caleb was all about — looking good.

He saw me after a quick scan of the room. He hurried over, pulling off his gloves and smoothly opening his peacoat. Every movement he made seemed practiced and exquisite, as if he tried his motions in front of a mirror before public display. He slid back the chair after draping his coat-scarf combo over the backrest.

"Ya rang?" He sat down across from me, smiled, and lightly drummed the table with his fingers.

"So, how's the NMPD?" I might as well start with small talk before getting into the heavy things.

"Oh, it's doing quite fine." His Irish accent pushed through his words, turning the *i*'s to *oy*'s, and the *th*'s to *t*'s. "Crime is still crimeing and all that. This burner came in yesterday and took a lunge at my throat. Fortunately, his equilibrium was all wonked on account of the Emerald Eyes in his bloodstream, and he ended up passing out on the floor instead."

I smiled and laughed a little at the image of some druggie trying desperately to keep his footing.

Caleb grabbed a clump of my hash browns and popped them into his mouth. He cleaned the unexpected grease off his fingers with a napkin. "But ya certainly did not invite me here to make small talk about my day. What's going on, Kraft?"

"Maybe I just wanted to see you?" Unfortunately, a meeting with Caleb usually meant I was out of my depth with magic. It's been that way for several years, ever since I got assigned to his serial killer case that ended up being a spirit stripping people's skin. I would have died had Caleb not come in and blown the spirit away with a well-performed ritual.

"Ya never want to see me. Ya *have* to see me. Usually about something Dark." He gave me a smug grin as he pulled up another chair and rested his leg on the seat.

I leaned back, resting my hands behind my head. Caleb was always ready to pass on his knowledge — and he wasn't as patronizing as Jack about it. During the flesh-ripping spirit case, he learned I had Beyondsight and took it as a sign he should pour everything he knew into my head. People who know about the Dark are limited — those willing to talk about it are even more so.

"I saw an aura I didn't recognize today." I opened the drawing app on my phone and tried to sketch what I saw around Helga. "It was as if wings flared out of this person's back."

Caleb made a silent *ah* motion with his mouth and chuckled slightly. "That's a faery."

I had to take a second to make sure I heard him right. "A faery? Like, small people with wings? I've never seen one before. They're real?"

"Those aren't faeries. The small things are pixies, about *yey* tall," he explained, holding his hand about six inches above the table.

"And pixies are real?"

"Of course pixies are real! How do ya know about daemons but not pixies?"

"I had an unusual upbringing," I snarled. My first encounter with the entities from the Dark had been when I was very young, but my worst encounter was a few years after. Research told me it was a raven daemon. Not something I enjoyed talking about.

"No kidding." He settled himself into the uncomfortable plastic chair. He took a look around as if to make sure no one was listening in. "Faery is a broad term. One kind is beautiful, radiant, and just a straight pleasure to look upon. Those are sidhe, faery royalty, essentially. Your common, or lesser, faery is called a spriggan. They also can be beautiful, but that's only a magic glamour they cast on themselves; beneath that they are ugly and green. The nastiest of the spriggan have a habit of eating people. Spriggans are also some of the most bountiful spirits of the Dark; I'm really amazed ya went this long without seeing one!"

"I thought crossing the Fade was hard?" The line between worlds isn't impenetrable, I knew that, but it still exists.

Caleb rocked his head side to side. "Well, the thing about the Fade is that it is much more efficient at keeping out the bigger things. The harder something hits it, the harder it becomes. Small things can sneak through. I swear I told ya this before."

"You probably have." I rubbed my eyes. My history with the Dark involved dealing with things when they were here, not worrying about how they got over. Usually it was a ritual — either gone right or wrong — or something that started on our side — like a vampire. All this ignorance was starting to catch up with me.

"Anyway," Caleb continued, eating another hash brown, "the problem lesser faeries have is that, because they are so weak, they can't keep that glamour up for too long. Their power just drains away, and they're left without any faery magic to tap into. They have to run off to a nest called a faery circle. It's a place where they connect across the Fade to their own domain and feed off the energy to keep their guise up for another three days." He spat the second chunk of hash brown into a napkin. "Whose wings did ya see?"

"Helga Dubois." Faeries. I had heard a little about them. Seemed too silly even for my life.

"*Shite*," he muttered. "She's the CEO of Orion, ya know? It's not exactly common for a faery to stick around long enough to be a CEO; they're usually in and out. Are ya sure?"

"Yeah, I was there. And, yeah, I saw the wings. I guess she's a... faery." The word felt strange coming out of my mouth. If they really did eat humans, then I guess I was the fortunate one in the elevator that day. No telling whether or not she would have shown her nature once we hit the top office.

"There are a couple of tribes too, but I doubt you care about that."

Fair enough, I didn't. If they died the same, I could handle it. "What was that sidhe you mentioned?"

"They're treated like royalty, but, as far as I can tell, they're a completely different species," he explained. It was scary how much I was starting to understand. "Very beautiful, very powerful. Look just like us, though. You'll come to find what we call 'looking human' is a rather common template."

"The sidhe wouldn't have to replenish their power then? No guise to keep up?"

Caleb nodded in affirmation.

"Maybe Helga Dubois is a sidhe. She wouldn't have to disappear every three days. What does it matter if she's a sidhe or spriggan, anyway? When it comes down to it, a dead monster's a dead monster."

Caleb bowed his head in contemplation. "A spriggan is one thing, they're base and understandable. If a sidhe lady has spent this much time placing herself at the top of a company such as Orion, then we have a problem. A sidhe won't do anything unless they're getting something huge out of it."

"Like what?"

"Power, usually." Caleb paused to let a worker sweep the area around our table. He only continued once he was out of earshot. Caleb doesn't like being looked at like he's glitchy. "The Sidhe Courts aren't like monarchies. Each one has a queen, but everyone else is fucking or fighting to the next step up the rung. A sidhe lives or dies on the number of humans they have under their thumb."

"You think she's here gathering favors?" Something about that didn't sit right in my stomach. There are easier — and less public — ways to get people in your debt.

"I'm here dispensing information, not opinion."

"And if you were to give your opinion?"

"Stay away from the faeries." All hints of a smile dropped from Caleb's face. "Especially if they could be sidhe."

I mumbled a curse under my breath. "Can't do that. I've got a job to do for Glowing Future and it's gotten kinda weird. Orion's my only lead."

Caleb cocked an eyebrow. "You're working for Glowing Future?"

"I'm working in the general vicinity of Glowing Future."

Caleb ran his thumb over his lips. It's what he always does when something upsets him.

"Okay, I'll bite," I said. "What's your problem with Glowing Future?"

"It's just…" He snapped his hand away from his mouth. "Nothing is good when those big corporations are involved."

I already knew that. Caleb likes showing off what he knows, and yet he was keeping his mouth shut on this. It was weird — but I had bigger shadows on my horizons. "Unless you're going to convince me it's a coincidence that Glowing Future is having problems and that it just so happens that their biggest competitor is run by a faery, it's the only lead I have."

Caleb laid his hand over his thumb, but I could see it rubbing the table's edge.

"So, faeries," I said. "How does one deal with them?"

"Cold iron. Just as with any fae. Purer the better, but anything with iron in it will do," Caleb explained. "Even a steel rod would work. You've dealt with ogres; it's the same thing. They're both fae."

"Yeah, but ogres are..." I was going to say scarier, but that was hardly a reason against faeries existing too. "Fine, I should've known faeries are real. My bad. I have some iron shopping to do. Let's assume she's a lesser faery — uh, spriggan — that means I have to find the — what did you call it?"

"Faery circle."

"Right, *faery circle*." *How could I forget?* "I have to find that."

Caleb let out a chuckle. "There is a reason you keep me around," he said. "Word is a faery circle exists in an old microchip factory south of the city. Only five minutes out."

"That's not far from the Dead Zone."

"Of course not, the creepies love abandoned places. But some faery *is* using it."

"You haven't shut it down?"

He shrugged. "It's live and let live in this world, Kraft. Some Darklings are just looking to stick around. Others..."

"Maybe you should tell wizards about the whole 'live and let live' thing." To a wizard laghole it's more like "live under my rule or don't live at all."

"Maybe you should give wizards a break, you know? I've seen you do some magic."

"Rituals and runes, yes." I had to keep myself from ranting about wizards. I didn't have the few hours it would take to get my feelings out. "It's not about magic. It's about how they go around acting like they're the rulers of the universe. And I shouldn't have to mention how they feel about a Seer like me. Remember that flesh-ripping spirit? Well, not soon after that I had one of the High Circle's Sentinels nearly bust down my door and tell me they're gonna kill me if it seems like I'm using Dark magic. They're just like the cops after the Gloves. Treating me like a criminal even though I haven't done anything."

Caleb rolled his eyes. He was always too trusting.

"Don't trust people in charge." I spied the fast-food workers looking at me over the counter. I lowered my voice. "Their first goal is always to keep themselves at the top."

Caleb raised his hands in defeat and slid lower in his chair. "I just hope you don't someday need help from the High Circle."

"Me too." But I had already dropped the subject. I was thinking about the microchip factory where the faery circle was. I could think of one in that area, the result of scanning ruin charts out of boredom. I stood up from my seat, pushing the chair across the linoleum with a squeak. I swept my coat on. "There's still some daylight left. I'm gonna take a look at that factory."

Caleb put his gloves back on.

"You're not going to stop me?"

"I haven't seen anyone do it yet." He still refused to make eye contact. "Just stay vigilant."

"I'm only scouting." I clapped Caleb on his shoulder. "What are the chances of the faery being there?"

"Don't taunt Fortune, she can be cruel."

"Thanks for the tip." I curled my mouth. "What would I ever do without you?"

Caleb stopped putting on his coat and gave me a flat gaze. "You would die."

I jabbed Caleb's arm. *True enough.* His demeanor about the faeries caused a pit in my stomach. If he saw what I did in the video at Glowing Future, would he be as apprehensive?

I left the Taco Hut and Caleb. I could already feel the temperature dipping for the evening. I zipped my coat up right to my chin and dug my hands into the warmth of the pockets. In my left pocket, I felt the fabric of my Gloves. In my right, the reassuring bulge of my revolver on my hip.

Caleb had wanted nothing to do with this excursion. I was glitchy to walk into it willingly, according to him. But how bad could it be? We were only talking about faeries, after all.

Chapter 5

I caught the train a few streets down from where I had met Caleb. The train shot away, hovering above the rails, making a smooth and silent ride. If I could see the Dark energy at the faery circle, I could match it with Helga's aura. Then I could trap her when she came to recharge and make her talk.

First, I was going to have to get there. I had the misfortune of deciding to go during rush hour. The bodies crammed around me ignited my irritation for public transportation.

A joyously fat man's belly rubbed against the small of my back for fifteen grueling minutes. He pushed past me when his stop came. It was times like these I wished I made enough to own a car. As the commuters cleared out, I was able to get myself a place on a bench seat that lined the side of the train car. More bodies disappeared. A cute redhead wearing a white, weather inappropriate tank top caught my eye. She gave me a small smile when she caught me looking. I returned a smile. The exchange raised my mood and my self-esteem. Unfortunately, she too left at a stop close to the edge of New Montreal. I was headed southward.

The train had mostly emptied by Mohawk Hills Station, so I slid my Gloves on and set myself up to do some quick research. A projection in the middle of a train car would attract unnecessary onlookers. I didn't need some techno-geek grilling me about my Gloves. I displayed the info on my phone and began researching Helga Dubois. She had a history, and an impressive one at that. She graduated with honors from the University of Montreal with a Masters of Business, managed a few small businesses, then two years earlier she became the CEO of Orion Industries. The database failed to mention she was an otherworldly monster. It was a justified oversight. *Did this faery really spend a couple decades leading a normal human life to become a CEO?*

I had exhausted the public channels and took to the private ones. My Gloves cracked the wall, but I kept the info on my phone. Still, she seemed legit. She had even been arrested once when she was seventeen for public intoxication. Prettiest mugshot I ever did see. It was possible that some hacker could have tampered with the public records, but it would have been harder to alter the private bank records and police reports.

The speaker above me dinged. *"End of the line. Isidore Station. Thank you for using New Montreal Public Transportation."*

I put my phone back into my pocket. The train had an eerie, empty feeling to it. I was the only one who had ridden this far down the line. A shiver hit my body. *What in the world am I doing?* I stepped from the train to Isidore Station.

The sun hadn't set yet, but it threatened to in the next hour. There was enough light to take in my surroundings. The area around had been bulldozed years ago. City Hall constantly talked about expanding New Montreal. That was why they built the station, but no one had stepped up to take the job. It was probably seen as too much of a risk. When I was young, I remembered some kid getting poison in his lungs, and the city council freaked out. Now they give the Dead Zone a wide berth.

The St. Rémi Industrial Area rippled along the horizon. It's far enough back from the Dead Zone that I wouldn't need a respirator. Even a hundred years on, the bioweapons from the Final War hung around. It's no wonder a faery would place its circle there. The Fade is weak in places of sorrow, and the Dead Zone is one hell of a sorrowful place. Of course, any closer to the Dead Zone and the faery risked poisoning itself. There are not many things — even from the Dark — that can survive in those tracts of land. We humans make some wicked toxins.

I drew in a few slow, steady breaths. I could feel a rumbling in my veins. Now I was dealing with faeries. *It was a simple job.* My face grew hot. I screamed and kicked a dent into a trash can.

"Fucking damn it!" I punted the dent again.

Even a job that was supposed to be a normal computer gig turned out to be magical. Nothing I ever do can be normal. *So sick of this Dark crap.* I attacked the trash can until I lost my breath and the dent was nearly touching the other side of the can.

"Let's get this over with." I shut my eyes until the rage was hidden deep inside.

The train was long gone as I left the platform. I closed my coat and flipped the collar up against the wind. As long as it didn't start snowing, it would be an easy walk. If Jack of Frost was right about the early winter, then there was no telling what the weather would do. I groaned. I had almost forgotten about my second job. Faeries on the one hand and a Spirit of Winter in the other. At least I'd be fulfilling a favor with Jack's job, a stress reliever in and of itself. But that was a concern for later. I had a faery circle to investigate.

The cloudy sky was able to hold in most of the snow, though I did see a few flakes when I arrived at the first decrepit building along St. Rémi's northern edge. About a dozen stories up, the top half of one of the taller buildings had broken off. Like a massive redwood snapping. The debris blocked my path. I checked my map. The connection was weak but I got some reception. The blue of the projection cast ambient light all around me and made weird shadows in my peripheral vision. The factory was right past the ruins. The Dead Zone's edges were where the monsters came out to play; I didn't want to waste time walking around the barrier. I took to climbing.

The cracks in the building were well spaced for an ascent, and spikes of rebar jutted out to give me handholds. I only made it up twenty — maybe twenty-five — feet before I discovered what seemed to have been a window, now broken and creating a large hole in the wall. The cold of the rebar permeated my Gloves and I braced myself. My free hand projected a steady beam of white light, which I used to sweep the room.

All the desks and chairs had tumbled along what used to be the floor into a large pile to the right. I had to blink hard to get my brain wrapped around the orientation. The room seemed to barely hang on to its structure. About two feet below me was the wall, now a floor. I traced a potential path with the light across to another window on the other side. My exit.

The dust that kicked up when I scrambled through the hole nearly choked me. A heart-stopping groan accompanied me putting my weight on the wall-floor, but it held. I switched the Glove light into a lantern and shuffled onward. Each movement creaked and cracked the drywall beneath my feet. The light illuminated decaying posters and empty picture frames until the wall stopped. What was once a hallway was now a pit. I shone my light and was able to just see the bottom — a wall with a frame that had probably held some picture that had long since rotted away.

Ten feet across the pit was the rest of the wall-floor. Not an incredible jump, but still one I would have to put some effort into. I took a couple steps back, suddenly wishing I had tried harder in gym as a kid. Or as an adult. If I was going to be doing this stuff, I really needed to start working out again, like when I was with the IB. Too late for that. I bolted forward, throwing my body with as much force as I could muster. The darkened pit flew by beneath me, and I cleared the other side with inches to spare.

There was a cracking sound like a gunshot, and the ground fell out from beneath me. My stomach flew into my throat as I tried to reach out and grab for anything to save me. A sharp pain shot through my jaw as my chin struck the wall-floor. I tried to get some kind of traction with my hands on the drywall, but it might as well have been smooth glass.

A tilted office blurred through my vision. My back screamed as I landed. The next surface held for a second before the familiar cracking sent me falling through another hole.

The surroundings exploded out into another hallway. I sped toward a window, jagged glass lining the edges. I was about to be shredded. I pulled my knees closer to my chest. The glass rim shot by me; I could almost feel the cutting edges reaching out for my skin.

I hit dirt ground. My breath disappeared from my lungs on impact and a fiery pain enveloped my right side. I couldn't decide whether to clutch my throbbing jaw or my now heavily inflamed shoulder. Instead, I didn't move at all. I just lay in the dark, small crawl space-like area beneath the fallen building.

I didn't know how long passed before I risked a movement. I wiggled my toes, praying I hadn't broken my back with the tumble. I felt them rub against the inside of my boot. I breathed a sigh of relief and used my good left arm to sit up. There was just enough room to sit comfortably, the ceiling a couple inches above my head.

Light from the dying day crept in a short distance from me. The opening was to St. Rémi's interior, no less. *Lucky me.* I shut off the Glove light. Using my good arm, I awkwardly half slid, half crawled out from beneath the building. It was slow, my jaw and arm hurt like hell, but I was eventually able to get into the St. Rémi Industrial Area. I had made it across the building, albeit not in the way I had intended.

I gently touched my right shoulder. The area immediately flared up, and I pulled my hand back. It didn't feel dislocated, fortunately, but I was going to be black and blue for a while. My jaw ached and I couldn't open it more than halfway without a sharp pain. I was lucky I hadn't shattered it. I swore at myself for using the last of my Medioxyl at Glowing Future earlier. It wouldn't heal the bruising, but it would dull the pain.

I'm sure, back in the day, the buildings were easily marked to tell them apart. But whatever had been used to distinguish them had long since worn away, leaving a labyrinth of gray towers and warehouses. Thankfully, I knew how to access the system, and the ruin charts were kept to tell each building apart. The Network signal was even weaker still. Without the ambient power in the Network or solar energy, my Gloves were relying on my body's bioelectricity, and already stored power, to have any function. It wasn't nearly good enough. If I wasn't careful, I could find myself without power. I checked the map then switched the Gloves into power-saver. The microchip factory was only a few more blocks south.

My right arm would be useless for shooting, so I unbuckled my belt and moved my revolver to the left side.

I'm not as accurate shooting offhand, but part of my IB training was to learn to be at least competent with either. I guess that place did have its benefits.

I sighed and started walking south. If I'd come this far I might as well go all the way. I wasn't going to get any clues by going home and sleeping. What made me think I'd be done in St Rémi by sundown, I'll never know. My shoulder pulsated, as though some invisible giant was rhythmically squeezing down on it. I rolled it occasionally to get used to the soreness. The pain dulled by the time I arrived.

A large warehouse lay before me. It had two floors from the look of it, probably a warehouse level and a level of some offices above. The ruin charts said it was going to be used by one of the forerunners for Lighttech, some company name that escaped me.

A metal door was propped open with a cement block. I instinctively reached my right hand to where my gun was normally, but the pain made me wince and feel like an idiot. I flipped the left side of my coat behind the grip of my revolver. The look made me feel like one of those old Western gunslingers from the movies. I took a few bowlegged steps and chuckled to myself. I became instantly aware I was very much alone.

I shook off the feeling and moved to the door, keeping my hand resting on the firearm. I pressed against the wall and peeked into the warehouse. The sunlight had almost disappeared and the interior of the building was full of pitch shadows. If something was inside, they'd get me before I'd see them. I'd have to flush them out. I moved my hand from the revolver grip to hover just inside the doorframe. I flashed my light into the building, then whipped my hand back to my firearm.

A long minute passed. I held my breath. Nothing inside reacted to my light. No sound but the wind whistling through the ruins. I risked a breath and slid into the darkness.

I popped my right Glove to life at my side, and its light filled the area in front of me. I drew the revolver from my hip and lightly tapped it against my thigh — a nervous tic I developed a long time ago. The reassuring beat against my leg helped me focus.

Tap, tap, tap-tap.

I stepped deeper into the warehouse. It was strangely uncluttered. The owners must not have had much time to move their stuff in before the bombs dropped. Either that, or scavengers picked the place clean. Metal shelves littered the floor with only a few still standing. The rest of the area was filled with various machines, no doubt used for microchip manufacturing.

I moved from the first room into another area. The space was long, like a hallway, but the entire left side was open with sills that I guess used to have glass in them. Through the windows, I could see St. Rémi disappearing into the horizon. I approached a sill and looked out into the evening. Directly across from the building I was in was another warehouse — gray paneling just like all the rest. In between the two I could just make out the impression of tire treads in the gravel. I couldn't tell how long ago a car had been there, but if Caleb was right I could assume anywhere from one to three days.

I flicked a shard of glass out of the frame. No signs of a circle so far, but I was just getting started. There was another door a few meters down the hallway. I wasn't going to find anything by standing around, so I headed deeper inside.

I walked through an interior corridor, peering into the small rooms on either side, each piled high with garbage, or littered with beer bottles. Nothing signifying a faery infestation, though. I hoped I wasn't on some phantom hunt. The next large area had to be nearly the center of the building. If there was a faery circle, that was where it would be — it was the furthest from prying eyes. All the iron-based items in the room had been pushed to the walls. The center was open; not even a dust coating on the floor. I figured that was a solid indicator of a faery infestation.

I shut my eyes and took a few deep breaths. The feeling that overcame me was impossible to describe. I just felt... different. Like I had immersed my body in water. I opened my Beyondsight. The room was flooded with code. It covered the walls and flowed like water to the center of the room where it rose up like a fount, spiraling into a mass of twisted letters and numbers. The code nearly touched the ceiling.

Code was just an easy way to describe the aura, though it looked nothing like any computer code. Sometimes it was merely rapidly changing numbers and letters, sometimes a word would appear. No matter what it looked like though, I could always understand it somehow. Call it magic.

It isn't a real code anyway, it doesn't have to make sense. Beyondsight shows you things that are beyond human comprehension. Code is just the way my brain rationalized the information it's given. I haven't met anyone else who shares the talent as of yet, but Caleb told me once each person sees it differently. Apparently, he once met a guy who saw everything as fire. Seemed pretty terrifying to me.

This code screamed at me the same thing that Helga's aura did. Faery. But this one felt as though it was written by a different hand. It was a faery, but it wasn't Helga Dubois.

The distinct sound of a car engine and tires on gravel yanked me out of my contemplation. I snapped my Beyondsight away, turned off my Glove, and spun toward the sound. Headlights scanned across the hallway exiting the room. They were coming from the tire tracks I saw earlier. It could be a scavenger, but I wasn't ready to bet my life on that.

The headlights shut off, and I bolted for the rubble farthest from the entrance. A few shelves were shoved close to the wall, but far enough away that I could easily scoot behind them for cover.

My arm and jaw painfully reminded me of their wounds, but I held my breath. I steadied my heartbeat and listened carefully. Footsteps. A distinct *click-click* of heels echoed down the hall and into the great room. Someone dressed fancy with little care for stealth. They obviously assumed no one would be in their safe place.

The *click-click* drew closer, and I peered between the shelves' slits. The woman who entered was pretty, very pretty in fact. She was probably in her mid-thirties and dressed in a nice, gray business jacket and skirt. On anyone else, the suit might have looked plain and drab, but on her, it might as well have been a slinky evening gown.

She stopped a few feet inside the room and stepped out of her heels. I clicked my Beyondsight on and watched all the code drop from the fount and flow outward to form a perfect circle. I blinked the Beyondsight away, and the code became blue light. Magic taking form.

The woman reached to her hair and pulled a needle from the tight bun. Her strawberry blonde locks elegantly dropped into a perfect trail down her spine. She worked her hands on her suit jacket, unbuttoning quickly but methodically. She gently folded the fabric and placed it on the floor next to her.

Completely practiced, she undid the buttons that held the white-collared shirt together. The layer came off and revealed a generous bosom pushing against a simple, beige bra. *You have got to be kidding me.* The gentleman part of my mind was telling me to avert my eyes, but I kept looking... for research, of course.

She folded the white shirt and laid it next to the gray suit jacket. Next came the skirt. She unzipped the side and pushed it down, working it along her legs until it was off, and she was down to the barest she could be without full nudity.

As she reached for her bra clasp, it became apparent she intended to go further. At that point, I felt much too voyeuristic and perverted. I succumbed to my gentleman brain and averted my eyes. I could barely hear some scuffling and two faint sounds of fabric hitting the floor as I focused on my feet. She had to be a faery, that or some very freaky nudist. I wasn't going to learn anything while making firm eye contact with my shoes, however.

The blue light circle brightened and I looked up. If this woman was astounding clothed, she was breathtaking nude. She had been blessed with perfect curves and walked as if she knew it. The blue light reflected off her snow-white skin and cast soft shadows from her cute face to her flattering waist, across her exquisite backside, and down her drool-inducing legs.

Then the freak show started.

Chapter 6

There was a moment of absolute silence, then the veil — or glamour, as I guess it was — dropped. Where the perky blonde once stood was a green and vile looking creature. Its hair ran stringy and barely covered its scalp. Its face was smitten with a pig nose and cracked lips over rotting fangs. The once silky, white complexion was replaced with leathery skin marked with spots of moss. It had gained another bend in its legs and a reverse knee — like a cat's — just below the forward bend. At the bottom of the legs were hooves, of all things.

So, this is a spriggan.

I guess the change took me by surprise, because I involuntarily snorted — or almost threw up. Honestly wasn't clear. Whatever I did caught the spriggan's attention. It snapped its eyes to me. They perfectly reflected the ambient light from the magic circle, a silvery-blue, unblinking hollowness. An unearthly howl split its lips. The ritual stopped, and darkness fell upon the room.

I drew my revolver and aimed through the shelves. I held onto the image of the spriggan hunched in the center of the room. Distance from the shelf. Distance from the wall. Half a heartbeat passed. I snapped on the lantern light on both my Gloves. The spriggan appeared, flying at the shelves that lay between us. Its fangs oozed drool and bile, bared open to bite something off of me. Its talon-hands reached forward, ready to slip between the shelves and tear my throat out. The revolver roared and kicked back. The bullet tore through the faery's throat. I was aiming for center mass, but my left hand was less accurate.

Another cry, this one of pain, and the spriggan came crashing into the shelves. I awkwardly dove aside, so as not to injure my shoulder further. The shelves and faery slammed into the wall where I once stood.

The spriggan screamed even louder. The sickening smell of burned flesh filled my nostrils. It thrashed off the steel shelves, smoke rising from where the metal had touched its bare skin. Iron-aversion. Just like Caleb said. I took my chance and fired another round into its back. My aim was better this time. The bullet found its mark where a human would have a heart.

Evidently, not a spriggan. Or maybe a heart shot didn't matter for them. The spriggan returned to standing too quickly for my liking. A green ichor dripping from its back and neck stained the ground. Under its snarling expression, the neck wound was almost fully closed. I could assume the back wound would not be far behind.

I raised my weapon for a third time, then froze. The night before, I had checked the cylinder. There were only three bullets. One in the throat and one in the back. I was down to my last.

The spriggan saw my hesitation and lunged. I grabbed one of the shelves that was still standing and pulled it down between us, my bad arm screaming in reply. The spriggan hit hard, and I had to leap aside to avoid being crushed as the creature's tackle pushed the shelf forward.

My injured shoulder struck the ground. Fire shot through my right side and blurred my vision. *This is nothing compared to what this faery will do,* I kept telling myself so I could stagger to my feet. The exchange was not going well. I was surviving but not winning. If I kept taking that thing on with a fair fight, I was going to lose — and lose badly. The faery had entered through the same hallway I had searched. Somewhere down there was that line of broken windows. The perfect escape. I memorized the path, shut off the lights, and burst into a sprint.

The spriggan snarled behind me, but I didn't look back. Darkness wouldn't protect me if it had low-light vision — so I wasn't slowing down. The moonlight through the broken windows gave me a target to strive for, and I pulled out everything my muscles would give me. When the window was close enough I jumped, tucked my knees into my chest and held my elbows close. The sill flew past me, and I hit the ground with both feet. I tumbled forward with the momentum, rolling over my back, and hopping up into an awkward run. A gymnast I am not.

The sun was just below the horizon now. The temperature was dropping rapidly. It kept me from overheating from the sprint. The spriggan could come lunging into my back at any second. No time to think about it. I dug each step into the gravel.

Another building lay across the street. The one good thing about ruins is that most of the windows are pre-broken. I vaulted inside through the closest one.

The place had obviously once been a factory floor for some heavy-duty manufacturing. Huge machines surrounded me on all sides. It was a death trap for humans, more so for an iron-adverse fae. There was no way it would follow me in.

Someday I may get tired of being wrong. I turned back to the window. The creature was in a dead sprint straight for me. It coiled its powerful legs and hurled itself like some macabre rocket. *This thing's getting to be a pain.* I bolted around a machine and hightailed it deeper into the factory. Behind me was a resounding gong and screech as the spriggan crashed into the iron machine. The faery was either really stupid or really aggressive — with my luck, probably both.

The gargantuan mechanisms gave me plenty of choices for a hiding place. The high windows blessed me with enough light to maneuver in without having to reveal my position from the light of the Gloves. A massive bucket elevator stretched all the way to the catwalks a couple dozen feet above. The struts that held it up left a small gap beneath the belt. Just enough to hide me. I slid under and pressed myself against one of the solid stands that sat on either side. It was dusty, cramped, and the machine's power cord dug into my back. The choking scent of rust and old machine oil threatened to suffocate me, but a single cough would give away my position. I held my breath.

Silence. Horrible, horrible silence. Then the padding of soft feet. I pulled myself carefully forward and peeked through the space between the buckets and the stand to see the spriggan back in its glamour.

It called out, "Oh, mister."

I swear it looked like it was thirty-something back in the first building, but as it sauntered through the warehouse floor it looked twenty. *Damn faeries.*

"Please come out, mister. The scary monster is gone. You scared it away, and I need to thank you."

Its voice dripped with sexuality. It ran its finger from its thigh, through its cleavage, to its mouth, and hung off the bottom lip. It bounced with each step, and further bounced with each bounce. It probably thought I was just some poor soul out exploring in the ruin and happened to stumble onto its faery circle. I was more prepared though. Not as prepared as I should have been, granted, but still more prepared. *Been a long time since I had to worry about ammo.*

"Please, mister, I have so much thanks to give."

It was getting ridiculous. It was as though the spriggan learned everything about humans from a porno. Which it actually might have, the more I thought about it.

It kept the sexpot act going as it turned the corner and left my sight. I allowed myself to release the air I'd been storing in my lungs. If it didn't find me, it was entirely possible it would write it up as a loss and go on its way. Even if some guy came forward ranting about a woman who became a monster, it knew no one was likely to believe him. They'd call him another crazy and shunt him off to an institution somewhere. Most of us humans are like that. I just had to wait until it got bored and went home.

I held onto that idea right up until I heard the sound of a snarl from past my feet. Looking down, I could see the spriggan — still beautiful and naked in its glamour — on all fours at the other side of the crawlspace.

"Oh, mister, I found you," it purred, a venom hiding behind the sex. "Please come out, it's so dirty under there."

It put an emphasis on the word "dirty." Subtle. Caleb warned me about the manipulative nature of faeries, and this one was going all in. I bet its act lured many men to their deaths. Sirens had the right idea with the beautiful woman routine. However, I've seen too many beautiful women turn into horrifying creatures in my time.

"Fuck off, faery." I kicked some dust into the spriggan's face. *I'm classy.*

It was strange to see someone so beautiful growl so deeply, but that's what came next. A tremor flowed through it, and its monstrous true form was back. It must have decided the ruse wasn't worth it. It was probably going to rend me to shreds. *Much better.* The deep-set eyes stared me down as it crawled forward, taking care not to touch the iron on all sides.

I slammed the revolver back into its holster and used the motion I had remaining in my right arm to touch the power cord digging into my back. The circuits pulsed as my Glove grazed the cord. My Glove dumped its electrical charge.

The elevator roared to life and began turning. I used my left hand to grab one of the buckets and braced my feet against another one further down. I waved sarcastically to the faery as the motion dragged me first away, then upward.

The screech of ancient machinery nearly drowned out the spriggan's howling fit. The charge that kick-started the elevator died out, and I hopped onto the steel catwalk above. The faery wouldn't be able to touch this area, much less walk on it.

The faery charged through the factory floor and back out from where we had come. *Maybe it was leaving?* More likely, it was hoping to lure me down into someplace it could grab me.

I used the time to look over my right Glove. I had spent all of its power on making my escape. Hopefully the faery would give up so I didn't have to stay out in the wastes all night with one dead Glove.

On the bright side, I did find the faery circle. Unfortunately, it didn't belong to Helga Dubois. I can't imagine I would have fared much better if it were hers. How would anyone interrogate a thing like that? That was the million eurodollar question I would have to answer before confronting her for real. That's if I survived the night. I was rash and jumped in without thinking. *Idiot. I used to always have a plan.*

Motion caught my eye, and I returned my attention to the ground level. The faery was back, glaring up at me with those perfectly reflective eyes. A — thankfully — full moon cast light down on it. There was something odd on its legs. I strained my eyes against the shadows until I could make out what it was. The creature had grabbed its shirt and suit jacket, wrapping both around its hoofed feet.

Oh, hell, no.

Its leg muscles coiled again and with one otherworldly leap, it flew two dozen feet up and onto the catwalk before me. The impromptu shoes were protecting it from its iron aversion. A grotesque smile cracked across its bladed teeth. It took a single step forward.

I didn't wait for it to charge. I spun on my heel and took off in the other direction. The faery's footsteps resounded against the steel. I wouldn't be able to straight outrun it. I had to play it smart. The only way down from the catwalks I could see was a lift. Still at ground level.

If I couldn't play it smart, I had to play it reckless. I aimed for a field of chains over the edge of the catwalk. Behind me, the pounding of the faery's feet against steel warned me of its approach. I gritted my teeth and spring-boarded off the guardrail into the mass of chains. My hands found purchase. My shoulder screamed in reply, but I held on.

I tightened my grip as I found myself gliding away on a rail the chain was attached to above. I braced my feet as best I could on the links as the chain swung back and forth, striking me against the others.

The faery was not taking no for an answer and lunged over the railing. Its knife-like fingers reached eagerly for my throat. The floor was still far below me. I took a deep breath and let go.

Its talons whipped past my head; I could feel the wind brushing the top of my hat as it's failed grasp went by. I fell nearly ten feet before I was able to grab back on. My shoulder screamed again. I thought it would fall right off. But my Gloves protected my hands from the rough links.

I slid down the rest of the chain and dropped the final few feet. The faery cried and cursed above me. I looked up and saw why. It had hit the group of chains and become entangled within the iron. The smell of burning flesh joined the scent of old machines as the creature thrashed. It twisted so violently that chains broke from their holdings and crashed down around me. The spriggan gave one final jerk, kicking its feet downward. It snapped one of the chain links that held its left leg. That was enough to dislodge it and it dropped — for about six feet. Its descent came to a vicious halt when the remaining chain wrapped around its neck pulled taut.

A sharp crack cut through the constant sizzle of flesh. The faery went still.

I stared at the swaying body. All of St. Rémi froze in anticipation. I could feel my heart squeezing in my chest. My jaw ached, my shoulder burned, and my lungs felt like I was breathing acid. I prayed I wouldn't see the spriggan move.

Its hand twitched. My breath caught in my throat. It reached for the chain around its neck and grasped the links. Blood oozed from the thing's mouth. Its body had to be burning.

"What the hell?" I growled. This thing had taken a beating and come back from two mortal wounds.

I grabbed one of the chains that had fallen. A carabiner was attached to an end link. I looped the carabiner around and made a simple noose. Even with its skin melting, the faery was almost serene in its attempt to take the chain from its neck. That made it easier to toss the chain-lasso up and yank it tight around one of the faery's cloth covered legs.

That got its attention. Its silver eyes fixed upon mine. The blood rage had subsided. Now I saw confusion and fear. It didn't know what I was doing but it looked worried. That worked for me. If it was afraid, it meant it could die. I managed a small sneer and continued with my plan.

I had to work fast, before the faery escaped from its bindings. It was once again trying to get out of the noose around its neck — more frantic this time. I drew on whatever adrenaline or instinct was keeping my body going and sprinted. I slid the loose end of the chain under a nearby press and out the other side, toward the lift that ascended to the catwalks. I tied the loose chain tightly around the railing of the lift and looked back to the faery.

I could see it just over the press. The chain around its neck was tangled fiercely, but it was methodically trying to loosen the bit around its throat. The leathery skin of its neck and hands had turned a smoldering black, as if it were dead. My skin itched looking at it.

I used the light from my Glove to find the lift's generator. My right Glove was still dead from starting the elevator. I couldn't risk it not working, so I pumped every ounce of juice from my one good Glove into the power source. The lift groaned and started to rise, pulling the chain tied to it.

A smile risked its way across my face, and I ran back to where the faery was suspended. It had worried so much about the chain wrapped around its neck, it didn't think about the one tied around its leg. The press acted like a pulley, transferring the upward lift motion into a downward pull. Now there was too much pressure pulling on its leg to even try loosening the loop.

The tugging on its leg hauled the top chain hard on its throat. Newton's third. Any work on freeing itself had been undone. Both chains grew taut and strained apart. The lift wheezed and cried as it worked against the tension. The faery hung at an odd angle, one leg being pulled almost forty-five degrees away.

"Human!" it cried, choking through the words. "I will f-feast on you!"

"Just hang out and die." I turned away.

"Obasin will taste your flesh!"

That's new. The lift creaked and risked giving out soon. I spun back to the spriggan. "Who is Obasin?" I yelled.

"The Great Devourer!" The faery could barely force words out at this point. "Feast, feast, feast!"

The lift strained and cracked. It wasn't going to make it. I considered briefly letting it fail, so I could interrogate the spriggan more. It kept chanting *feast, feast, feast* over and over. The words had a weight to them, like a pressure pushing down on me. I felt tired. So tired…

It had to be faery magic. I couldn't let that thing beat me. The lift would break. It would get the noose off. It would eat me. *Feast. Feast. Feast.*

I squeezed my eyes shut and cleared my mind. It was my mind; I could control it, only me. I took my gun in my hand. *My mind.* I opened my eyes and found my target. I squeezed the trigger.

The gun roared.

The round hit its mark. Best shot I've ever made offhanded. It tore through the spriggan's throat again. Green ichor rocketed from the hole, and the pressure of the chains did the rest. Flesh ripped, sinew tore, and the head went the opposite way of the body.

"I have yet to meet a creature that can survive that," I mumbled to no one in particular.

The head had flown off into the shadows of the warehouse; I had no interest in finding it. As a Darkling, it would turn into ectoplasm before long. Dead monsters don't normally leave bodies. The rest of the faery grotesquely dragged across the concrete floor, leaving a dark stain behind it. The lift finally reached the top and left the cadaver partially dragged under the press.

I gave myself a minute to catch my breath — a minute more to get over the gore of the situation. I composed myself and turned on the detective side of my brain. I moved to the headless form and began untying the suit jacket from one of its legs.

I had looped the chain around the leg that was wrapped in the button-up shirt, so the jacket was easy to remove. I had thought the creature's skin was leathery, but up close, it looked almost like moist bark, like a rotten tree after a rainstorm. The smell of blood was thick over its form. Nothing really smells quite like blood. Coppery and metallic. Spriggan blood was different. The metal smell was still there, but something else mingled with it. Like a deep forest grove. It wasn't enough to overpower the gross copper, but it was present.

I decided to ignore whatever else about spriggan biology might surprise me, and focused on the jacket. The two outside pockets were sewn shut. In the left inside pocket, I found a half-empty pack of Lumos brand cigarettes. They're specially designed to exhale rainbow-colored smoke, very popular with club goers. Maybe the faery had a less business-style weekend life. I put the pack into my coat and dug into the other inside pocket.

This one proved more helpful. I felt flat, cold plastic and withdrew an ID card with a metal clip:

Diana Forsyth
Personal Assistant
55th Floor
Level 1 Access

The left side was covered with a picture of the faery's glamour, looking stoic as many do in their identification photos. But she also looked incredibly attractive, even without any emotion. Behind the words on the right was a watermark. A man holding a club above his head and a shield before him. Orion Industries.

What a coincidence. I tucked the card away. The fifty-fifth floor was the top floor of Orion Tower. Level 1 access was the top access. It was safe to say Diana Forsyth was the PA for Helga Dubois. The plot thickened rapidly. I had no idea if Helga Dubois was related to the goings-on at Glowing Future, who Obasin was, or what stake the faeries had in all of it.

That was a tomorrow problem. I needed to rest.

Chapter 7

I found the keys to "Diana's" car still in the ignition; she wasn't worried about anyone taking it for a joyride. She drove a high-end silver Benz that smelled like pomegranate on the inside. I felt woefully underdressed just sitting in it. It was the kind of car I only dreamed about owning. I wished I could have kept it, but driving around in a missing woman's ride wouldn't be the smartest thing to do.

The electric engine ran quiet. There was the soft drone of a system meant to replicate the sound of twentieth and early twenty-first century gasoline engines, so pedestrians could hear a car coming down the road. The high-end luxury cars had quieter engine replicators, and this one was nearly silent. I had to find a rock station on the radio to kill the stillness of the ride.

My hands shook on the wheel. A crawling feeling encircled my chest. I'd seen death before. I'd investigated some of the worst crime scenes in New Montreal. It's not something you get used to. That wasn't what got to me. What twisted my stomach around was how outclassed I was by the spriggan. I got lucky, and my nerves reminded me of that. My shoulder and jaw further reinforced it. *What am I getting myself in to?*

I choked down whatever vomit or emotions were trying to work their way up my throat. The situation wasn't going to get any easier, might as well steel my stomach lining.

I parked the car back at Isidore Station. They weren't going to find her body. Where her car was didn't matter. But I couldn't risk any biological evidence of mine being found in her vehicle. That wouldn't look good for me.

I tossed the keys onto the passenger seat and stepped into the night. As soon as I had crossed the threshold of the car door, the artificial atmosphere left me. The pomegranate fragrance was replaced with damp dirt, along with the temperature dropping ten degrees. My Gloves had charged since being back in the Network's coverage; not much, but enough for what I needed them to do.

I placed my hand inside the car. The Glove flashed a deep red and left behind a slight burning smell. Biological negator, a wavelength that disintegrated most biological residue. It wouldn't dust a full person but hair, skin cells, and body oils are all fair game. A dry cleaner's favorite tech. I had adapted it for my own, illicit uses.

Confident that the NMPD wouldn't be knocking on my door anytime soon, I walked to the station and waited for the train.

It was one transfer and a ten-minute walk to the medium-sized building hidden underneath an overpass — a seedy looking mechanic's shop known as Total Care Auto Body. It was just after eleven when I arrived. They would be closing up any minute.

The glass door to the service desk had a huge crack spidering across the surface and creaked when it opened. A lone man leaned on the counter, a cheek resting on his palm and his fingers lazily flipping through a guitar magazine.

"Francois, I need Scoundrel," I said as I stepped in.

The man jerked his head toward the service floor. I gave Francois a nod as he returned to his magazine. Francois was a quiet man, but a good man. He was most likely in his thirties but obviously took care of himself. I didn't know much about him other than he had been working with Scoundrel for as long as I could remember. The head jerk was the most I was going to get from him, so I went through the metal door into the repair bay.

A few vehicles spread across the room, blocking my view of anyone who could be inside. I ran my hand over the hood of a deep red sports car. Cars were never my thing, but that Benz was an invigorating ride. Perhaps there is something to be said for the high-quality death traps I see everyone cruising around in. As I came around the front of the sports car, I saw two legs sticking out from underneath the next over Forta sedan.

"You gonna say something or just stand there all creepy-like?" came a voice from beneath the car.

"Scoundrel."

She slid out on a dolly, grinning through synthetic chemical stains. With the frumpy coveralls and dirty face, she was one of the prettiest sights I'd seen all day. She wore a greenish cadet-style cap that held up her black hair. I extended a hand for her. She grabbed it and leaped up, wrapping her arms and legs around me. "It's good to see you, Mr. Kraft."

"Down girl," I said, as I pried her off me and set her back on the ground. She made it a point to keep her hips close to me as she dropped, only stepping back once she had both feet on the ground. Then she socked me in the ribs.

"What was that for?" *Good thing she didn't hit my right side.*

"You're slow." She swung again.

I jumped back and her fist went wide. "You're mean."

I had known Scoundrel — Selene, to the layman and the lawman — for just over two years. She had been an informant for the IB on a chop shop ring case just before I was let go. Apparently, she found me "interesting." After the case was closed, she somehow got my number out of the IB systems and began calling me. I knew it had been her, because I hacked her number out of the system and had it programmed into my phone. In case I wanted to call her. It's not creepy if you're stalking each other.

"What if a Gravel junkie tries to jump you in an alley?" she asked, putting two fingers on my chest and pushing me back.

"I'll tell him very politely that drugs are bad."

Selene rolled her eyes and turned back to the car. She kicked the dolly across the shop floor to a dark corner.

"How's the car?" I tapped the Forta's hood.

"Some problems with the wires. Information isn't reaching the entire system, you know?" She turned a sly eye back to me and took a step closer. "Now you didn't come by to make small talk about work, did you?"

"I'm in the market for some violent supplies if you're selling."

"Oh, baby, you know my language," Selene said with a wink. "Alright, let me see it. Where's little ebony?" She beckoned with her hand.

I handed my revolver off to her. "Did you name my gun?"

"Stopped being your gun when you let me inside her." She ran a hand over my coat sleeve as she spoke. She looked over the revolver, pursing her lips. "What did you do to it? Pistol-whip a brick wall?"

"I'd like you to stay out of my business between me and those walls."

Selene smirked and walked across the shop. Her hips swayed perfectly, obvious even in the overalls. "Come on, funny guy. Let's talk in my office," she said over her shoulder.

Selene stopped at the back wall of the shop and slid a camouflaged panel aside to expose a screen. She tapped in her code, and a chunk of the shop wall opened to reveal a secret room filled with Lighttech and weaponry. She placed the revolver on her workbench and peeled off the top of her coveralls, letting them hang down, and showing off her slim figure and fitted tank top. She fixed the bra strap hanging off her shoulder and leaned against a loading bench displaying a disassembled assault rifle.

"What are you looking for, exactly?" she asked.

"Just some ammo."

"Just some ammo? Or some of my special rounds?"

"I'm not looking to start a war; I'm just working on something that doesn't quite feel right." I grabbed an armless chair, wheels squeaking across the concrete floor, and took a seat. I stole a glance around Selene's workspace.

One wall was covered in prosthetics of varying materials, hanging like a macabre limb display. Screens littered the counter behind me, many with their rims broken open and internal components spilling out. There was a constant hum from the cooling unit that kept Selene's Lighttech system from overheating.

Selene frowned, her nose crinkling in a cute way I would never describe to her. She pushed herself from the counter and dropped down onto a small leather office chair.

"What have you gotten yourself into, Kraft?"

"An old friend asked me to help him with some computer troubles."

"Computer troubles?"

"Yeah. Mysterious virus, employee betrayal, corporate espionage. Computer troubles. I just want some extra protection." *Lots of protection actually.* "Throw in some special stuff, and uh, do you think you could make iron rounds?"

Selene raised an eyebrow. She swept off her hat and threw it on the loading bench behind her. Empty bullet casings surrounded a reloading press. Color-coded casings used for her special rounds hid among the regular ones. I didn't know how she found anything with it all scattered about. Her hair fell to about her chin and she roughed it up out of contemplation. "Like steel-core rounds?"

"Yeah, those should work." Selene wasn't "in the know" about the magical. I didn't feel the need to worry her with the facts. People aren't known for taking it well.

"You have some armor you need to be piercing these days?"

"You never know when you may need to take down a rampaging giant robot."

Selene laughed — my flippancy was nothing new to her. "Fine. But you know I am more than willing to teach you how to make this stuff yourself if you share some of your hacking tips and tricks." She motioned to my Gloves.

"And what exactly do you want to crack you can't already?"

"Protectorate Manufacturing got a new, very strong firewall. One of my associates started working for them and I have a sneaking suspicion that they stole my designs on modifying their Model 72 to fire fifty caliber rifle rounds. It's only one at a time, but good for a handgun."

I couldn't tell if she was serious or not. "Well, I promise I'll look into it. Why don't you stick to the more material stuff and leave the data to me?"

Selene stuck out her bottom lip in a playful pout. "Fine again. I'll get you an ammo and specialty package for the very reasonable price of, let's say, one hundred eurodollars."

"Sounds good, S." As my eyes wandered over a security wristscreen on her desk, I remembered my second reason for being there. "I was also wondering if I could use some of your supplies to build something?"

"What cha makin'?"

I projected the super-potato-cannon.

Selene whistled. "You're making a mortar?"

"Potato cannon."

"Potato mortar." She spun in her chair and looked over her domain. I could see the gears working in her head. "You're going to need a tube with an ignition site, some legs to keep it upright—"

"The feet need to be able to be bolted down."

"Can do. Simple supplies, I have it all here, but you'll have to get your own potato."

"Actually," I said. This was where it would get awkward. "I need Fyrex... and a sensor bomb."

A silence dropped over the room; only the soft, ambient hum of the lights above us and the cooling system could be heard. Selene turned back to me with a soft squeak of her chair.

"You know," she said, "someday you're going to have to let me into the secret world of Kraft."

"It's very boring, you should know."

"I highly doubt that." Leaning back in her chair, she stared me down, arms crossed in a way only she could. "I do have some Fyrex and some sensor bombs."

"How much?"

"You can have them for free if you tell me what you're doing."

"How much?"

"Alright, you can have them for free if you promise you're not doing anything illegal."

"How much?"

Evidently, she wasn't finding this as funny as my other jokes. She dropped her head back and shut her eyes, taking in a few deep breaths. Even if I told her I was breaking and entering, she would keep pressing me to tell her why. And then what? I say that an embodiment of winter wanted me to find out who's been stealing their power? She'd only get even madder at me for "lying." People never believe. There's always an explanation for the supernatural; drugs, the wind, and gas leaks are all common excuses I've heard to distance oneself from the truth.

When it comes down to it, most people would need a vampire to slap them in the face with a leprechaun before they'd start to feel something was wrong.

"Just," she finally said, "promise you'll be careful."

"I always am."

I got a hard look in return.

"I will be this time."

"You left your equipment bag here. I take it you'll be needing it since you're apparently working again."

I nodded, but couldn't make firm eye contact with her. Part of me wished I could tell her everything. I knew she would worry more not knowing. But I also knew it's better to not know what's hiding in the dark. I wish I didn't.

"However, since I am doing all this for you," she spoke as she slid her chair closer to me, pinning my knees together with hers. She placed her hands on my legs and leaned forward. "You are bunking over tonight, mister."

"Oh, am I?"

"*Mmm hmm.*" She leaned in and softly kissed my cheek. "How could anybody say no?"

She gave a sly smile and slid herself off her seat and onto my lap. Her legs pressed slightly on either side of my hips as she draped her arms over my head. Using her nose, she knocked my hat off. I moved my hands up her canvas covered legs to her waist. I could feel her warm skin through the fabric.

She smelled of synthetic oil, a strange plastic smell. I didn't mind. She brought her head down until her nose touched the tip of mine and her chin-length dark hair brushed my cheeks.

Her hips shifted across me, searching for where we both wanted them to be. The movement put strain on my right side. The throbbing returned to my ribs. I bit my tongue so as not to be too loud. It didn't work.

Selene narrowed her eyes and drew back. "Oh, come on, I'm not that heavy," she said.

Her position had not changed. The throbbing increased on my wounded side until it felt as though I was being beaten with a bat. I tried my best to hide the discomfort, but she could see it. She stood and folded her arms once again, glaring at me.

"What did you do?" she asked, never looking away.

I favored my right arm and avoided meeting her eyes. Whatever I told her wouldn't calm her down. Still, she was going to stare me down until I spoke.

"I fell," I murmured almost inaudibly.

"You what?" She took a step closer, her arms somehow crossed harder, and her stare got sterner. She was frightening for such a tiny girl.

"I fell," I replied at a normal volume, still not meeting her eyes.

"From how high?"

"I don't know. A wall kinda broke my fall."

"Oh Jesus!" She buried her face in her hands. I knew it was out of anger rather than worry. The two emotions were pretty close for her.

I pushed myself to standing. Selene stepped forward into my chest without removing her hands from her face, and I wrapped my arms around her.

She didn't return the hug but melted slightly into me. "I assumed when you were fired—"

"Let go."

"—you wouldn't be in anymore of these situations. Now this and the potato—"

"What situations? For all you know, I fell doing everyday things."

She looked up from her hands and shot me a death glare. "Okay, not this time, but it could happen."

She returned her head into her hands.

I squeezed her closer. Funny how my side was splitting, and yet I was the one who felt like the jerk. We stood like that for about a minute. I could hear the faint sound of the reception door close. Francois had locked up.

"I just need some Medioxyl and I'll be fine," I finally said.

Selene pushed back from the hug. "You're not supposed to use that for everything. You need Tylenol." She opened the desk drawer and tossed me a white bottle of painkillers. "Or a hospital."

I looked the bottle over but didn't open it. "It's not that bad."

"Nothing is ever that bad with you, is it?"

"Selene, I don't work for the IB anymore. Dangerous situations aren't in my plans."

She sighed and turned to her loading bench. She picked up a firing pin from the assault rifle and looked it over.

"Say something," I said.

"Dangerous situations." She didn't look back. "I'm beginning to feel as though you can't survive without them."

"What are you talking about?"

"It's just..."

I can't survive without dangerous situations? I rushed into St. Rémi without a plan. Was I getting rusty? Or was I looking for something dramatic to happen? *No way. It takes someone with something seriously wrong with him or her to want to deal with what I deal with.*

Selene let out a puff of air. She dropped the firing pin and spun around. A smile spread across her face. "Never mind." She poked me in the stomach and hopped away. "I'll grab you some water for your pills. Go upstairs, take your pants off."

"Oh. Okay," I said. "Should I leave the gun on your table?"

Selene was already gone. She was definitely still mad.

But, even with the faeries, everything turned out better than expected.

Chapter 8

~ ~ ~ ~ ~

A dark cavern. The earth stretched on forever until it joined the shadows in the distance. I was alone. Yet some... thing was with me. No. Surrounding me. It watched me from all sides. It engulfed me. It was coming closer! I tried to run but my legs gave out. I fell. A metallic taste filled my mouth. Warm blood poured out as the entity tore into me. Only pain...

~ ~ ~ ~ ~

I jumped awake with such force that I almost threw myself out of bed. My hands reached for my gut, but I found no wounds.

"Jesus Christ!" Selene yelled from her side of the bed. A lamp turned on, casting an eerie glow throughout her bedroom above the auto body shop. "What the hell?"

"Sorry." My throat had gone dry. Each breath felt as if I was sucking through a filter.

Selene laid a hand on my bare back. "Kraft, you are freezing cold."

"Just a little nightmare."

"You're telling me. I'll get you a glass of water," she said, as she tossed off her covers. Out of the corner of my eye, I could see her nude form bathed in the lamp light. She really was beautiful. She pulled on some underwear and a tank top as she walked and flicked on the bathroom light.

I clenched my hands together, willing them to stop shaking. The sight of that dark cave never left. That presence that surrounded me still felt heavy on my body. My side and jaw ached, as though the injuries had just happened. I wanted to think of something else, be pragmatic about the situation, but every thought twisted back into an image of those endless shadows. *This is not normal.* That much I could figure out.

Selene returned with a cup of tap water. I took it and sat on the edge of the bed, blanket wrapped tightly around my waist.

"Thanks." I drained the cup in no time.

"I've never known you to be the night-terror type," she said.

"Happens to the best of us." I was finally able to get my thoughts in order. I racked my brain for what creatures can interact with dreams in such a way. Germanic mara have been known to sit on sleepers' chests and induce bad dreams to feed. *I would have sensed something Dark being so close.*

Selene kneeled across from me. "Back when my dad died, I used to have these terrible nightmares. For years afterward, I would see him in my dreams and, even though I loved him, they scared me."

Is the Sandman real? Could he do this?

"Is it... is it Alexis?" she asked.

"What are you talking about?"

"Alexis. Your old girlfriend."

I licked my lips. They were painfully dry. I turned to look out the nearby window. The lights of downtown New Montreal glittered in the distance. *That pressure I felt in the dream feels familiar.* "Why do you think it was about her?"

"I dunno. She died, didn't she? I mean... I don't mean to sound harsh..." She rested her hands on my knees.

"No, it wasn't about her." The lamp light glowed across Selene's messy black hair, creating a half halo across her form. *The pressure was the same as what I felt when "Diana" chanted.* "I'm starting to worry about this job. It's... distressing."

"Maybe you should stop then."

I don't think that will help at this point. That faery must have done something to me. "What time is it?"

Selene tapped the bedside table. The red light projected into the air: 3:01 AM.

"Christ. You should get some sleep," she said.

"The early shift at Glowing Future is six," I said, as I grabbed my boxers off the floor. "I made plans to meet with the security chief and get some footage. I need to make my potato cannon and get over there. I want to get this job done as quickly as possible." I donned the rest of my clothes while Selene brought the cup to the bathroom. I placed my lucky cap on my head and felt Selene's hand against my back.

"Your gun is in the shop." She circled to my front, never letting her hand leave my body. "I laid out some speedloaders and specialty ammo, so don't forget that. I also picked out a few scraps you could use for your little potato mortar."

"When did you have time to do that?"

She shrugged. "Sleep's a waste of time."

I nodded and stepped around her. Selene grabbed my arm. She pulled back and stretched up for a kiss. Her lips pressed sweetly against mine for a second before breaking.

"Try not to die. Then I would have to follow you to hell and kick your ass," she murmured without opening her eyes.

I smiled. The kiss gave me the energy to push the darkness to the back of my mind. I was going to figure it out. I had to.

——— «» ———

The morning fall air was crisp as I wandered through New Montreal's neon-lit streets. The odd car zipped by, but in general the roadways were empty. I adjusted my bag of tricks, tightening the strap so it was firm against my back. It — along with the super-potato-cannon swung over my shoulder — made me feel a whole lot more prepared for whatever was waiting for me.

The buildings around me stretched higher as I got closer to the Lighttech district. A few had walkways spanning between them. The elevated highway sounded busier than the road below. Signs in English and French cast their glow across my path. I took care not to stare too long into the darkened alleys. Every place the shadows touched twisted in my head and reminded me of that cave.

Dreams have a power to them; it's our minds allowing the magic of the world to interact with us. Sure, some dreams are nothing more than our minds telling us what they want, or the acting out of our deeper fantasies. I haven't dreamed since I was young. It was something I never did, or at least never remembered.

I'd heard that most dreams fade after you wake, until you can't remember them at all. The cave never left my memory. It was seared into my brain. The details were perfect but limited. It was dark, just dark. The floor was like a smooth granite or marble — maybe a hall. Still, "cave" seemed to fit the feeling it gave — a never-ending expanse of lightless space.

I whipped out my phone without breaking my stride. If that faery cast something on me, there must be a connection between this "Obasin" it mentioned and the dream. Blue light danced across the screen, and I opened a search engine. I tried the word "Obasin," but nothing pertinent came up. "Great Devourer." Nothing.

Most powerful beings had some kind of impact on folklore, and nothing weak had followers as devoted as "Diana" was. *What is Obasin?*

I returned the phone to my pocket. As I drew my hand back, I felt the ammo belt on my waist. My fingers played across the colored specialty rounds set in the loops on my belt. Small engravings on the casings let me know what each bullet was through touch. "White flash, red incendiary, green sonic, blue EMP," I mumbled over and over, keeping my mind focused on the material.

So intent on my mindless task, I didn't realize I had arrived at Glowing Future. Back to the job. I had to see some footage of this "Michael Harman" — the man who put that video into the system, then disappeared. I flipped my coat back over the ammo part of my belt and knocked on the glass.

Inside, a large man stood at the security desk. As he came closer, he got even larger. When he finally arrived at the entrance, he dwarfed me, standing a full head taller. My height isn't anything to scoff at either.

"Mr. Kraft?" he bellowed through the door.

God, he's big. I nodded.

The giant pressed his hand to the glass. Small lights flashed, and the door clicked open.

"I was told you would be coming by for the footage. I'm Rick," he said.

When he shook my hand, his fingers wrapped entirely around mine. His gaze drifted to the super-potato-cannon on my back.

"Oh." I swung it off my shoulder. "It's a long story, I have another job I'm working. I can leave it in the corner." I leaned it against the glass wall.

Rick cocked an eyebrow, a strangely intimidating gesture coming from a man his size. He had a kind smile, though, and he began leading me across the lobby. The guy was built like a brick wall. He wore a nice suit, and I could see back muscles flexing through the fabric. He could snap the legs off anybody who tried anything in his building; I was sure of it.

Rick unlocked the door behind the security desk, his thumb barely fitting the scanner. The room beyond was disappointingly uninteresting. A large piece of glass had feeds from the various cameras on it and a monitoring desk below it. A water cooler bubbled in the corner. The rest was cold, gray plaster and a stained carpet. The majesty of what lay behind the scenes.

"Sorry, I was just having breakfast," Rick said.

At the monitoring desk was Rick's breakfast. A full steak sat on the plate.

"That's a hearty breakfast," I said.

"Steak's good any time of day." He ducked under the monitoring desk. "Come in."

Next to his steak, I saw a small bottle of lemon air freshener. The kind that made the same citrus smell I noticed around the Network hub.

"Rick?" I asked.

Rick popped his head up from beneath the desk.

"Did you use this to try to make the Network hub room smell nice?"

He chuckled and put a scanner-sealed lockbox on the counter. "Some of the techs were complaining about it smelling like mold and dust. Thought it would be nice if they had something else to smell."

Rick seemed like an odd man. I shook my head and approached the lockbox.

Inside was a black rectangle with some ports on the back. A hard drive. The only way to keep something completely secure was to separate it entirely from the Network.

"I'll hook it up," Rick offered.

"No need." I pulled my Gloves from my pocket and slid them on. I placed my hand against the surface and copied the footage to my system. This would be much faster than any program they had. I clapped my Gloves and pulled them apart. The space between them filled with hundreds of windows.

"I'm going to have to ask you to delete all those once you're done," Rick warned.

"Yes, yes, of course." First, I discarded all the windows that didn't detect Michael Harman's face. A few hundred screens dropped off. I looked at the time stamps and laughed.

Rick gave me a sideways glance. "What's so funny?"

"Michael Harman's file says he worked here for three months," I said, chuckling.

"Yeah?"

I showed him the projection. "These videos only go back a week."

He dropped his head into one massive hand. "You're kidding."

"You guys are on the ball, aren't cha?"

I got myself under control and went back to work. "Michael Harman" was using a face that was not his own. There is nothing that can replicate a face without some flaws. I set a program to look for the most common ones. Then it was about waiting.

Rick let out a massive yawn. Deep bags sat under his eyes. I never liked getting up early, so I could feel for him.

"Tired?" I asked, trying to alleviate the awkward silence with some small talk.

"Bad dreams." He stretched and cracked his neck.

For a brief instant, I was back in the cave. *You have no idea what bad dreams are.* I shook my head right, reminding myself I was awake.

"How is this going to help you catch this guy?" Rick asked, rubbing the sleep from his eyes.

"Before I find him I need to find out exactly how he kept himself hidden. So I'm running a program to look for any irregularities."

"Irregularities?"

The program dinged. "Yeah, like this." I slid the projection to one hand. The hundreds of screens had been whittled down to one. It was a frozen image of Michael Harman exiting the bathroom. It seemed normal on first look — but on close inspection of the face, it was obvious what was wrong. All of his features had become squished into the center of his face, as though some invisible man was squeezing his cheeks together.

"What is that?" Rick asked.

"A glitch. Mr. Harman was wearing a hologram collar." I could feel a smile growing on my face.

"He's smart."

"I'm hoping he thinks he is." I dropped the projection and began heading out. "Where is his desk?"

"Twenty-third floor, station forty-three," Rick replied after consulting his wristscreen.

And then I was gone. I speed walked to the elevator bank and headed to the twenty-third floor.

I was so close to finally getting a break in the case. The elation sent adrenaline through my system. I almost forgot it was six in the morning. If I could figure out what this mysterious infiltrator did to the system, I could figure out what was haunting me. *Faeries and daemons be damned, this is my world.*

The elevator glided up the floors with barely a sound — only the wind running along the outside of the glass could be heard. I stared over the waking city. My reflection half-showed on the glass. Even one night of bad dreams was enough to start bags forming under my eyes.

I had to push the thoughts away. The back of my mind was getting full. The elevator doors opened with the usual ding, and I stepped onto the twenty-third floor. Lines of desks filled the center of the room, each set into an interconnected pod of three — like pie charts with a hole in the center.

"Thirty-six, thirty-seven, thirty-eight," I counted off, peering at the numbered placards on each desk. "Forty-three!" I spun into Michael Harman's desk chair. The desk was almost bare. Twin drawer-sets laid at a forty-five-degree angle beneath the tables to either side. When I sat on the chair the screens around me jumped to life. The three low partitions before me projected a calming video of the sea, blocking my view of the two other stations at that unit. The low sound of waves lapping a rocky beach began. A way to boost morale and keep workers happy. A screen slowly rose from the wood.

WELCOME.

Moment of truth.

I raised my hand as though I was playing a marionette. Red light shone from my Glove and touched every surface across the desk. Small dots appeared all around me. On the counter, the drawers, the chair, everything. Fingerprints from everywhere Michael Harman had touched.

"I love dumb criminals who think they're smart."

Chapter 9

I spent the next few hours talking things over with Rick. He seemed like a nice enough fellow, with a huge appetite for steak, apparently. The topic of what exactly I was doing for Warren and Glowing Future never came up. Rick was perfectly content in keeping to his own business.

A name did kick up when I ran the prints, though not Michael Harman's of course. Milos Ravinich. A small-time thug.

Mr. Ravinich's file described him as a frequent club-goer who only went out at night. He would have to wait. I still had a full day that I intended to use working on Jack of Frost's job. I said so long to Rick and headed to the subways. It was time to break into Tartarus Tower and get out from under Jack's thumb.

Tartarus Tower was all the way to the north, across the St. Lawrence and on Tartarus Island. It was going to take over an hour on the subway line to get there, transfers and all. I utilized that time to come up with a firm game plan. The fiasco with "Diana" had reminded me of the importance of thinking things through.

Their firewall was far too heavy for me to be able to walk in as I had at Glowing Future and Orion. And a Sunday meant a reduced working staff — I would stick out even more if seen. But even a company as private as Tartarus Securities had to have their floor plans on file with the city. That I could get my hands on. Using my Gloves linked to my phone again, I wormed into the Building Code Office's online files.

Tartarus was locked up tight as a drum. Still, it was nothing me and my bag of tricks couldn't push through. The tunnel between Forsyth and Charlemagne Station ran right beneath Tartarus Island. The island was artificial, built out of rocks excavated for New Montreal's Metro expansion. The basement should run directly above the train line. I could make my way inside from there, similar breach to a job I'd done in London. It might not be as hard as I had thought.

I jumped off the subway line at Forsyth Station and waited for the platform to clear. Soon it was me and a snoozing homeless man.

I counted three cameras in the station with only one pointed at the northbound tunnel. I pulled my hat down low over my eyes and sauntered toward the exit. Once I was beneath the security camera I stopped and went to work. *God, this is exciting.*

It was a simple "City of New Montreal" CCTV camera — the kind I've dealt with on numerous occasions. Working legally didn't always translate to acting legally, which seemed to be the unofficial slogan for the IB. I could feed the camera looped footage, but it would be easier and quicker to disrupt its outgoing signal and hightail it into the tunnel. I'd used that technique so much I had programmed a shortcut into my Gloves.

A quick scan of the Forsyth Station system gave me the identification number of the camera. Using that, I put up a virtual wall for its video signal. It would have five seconds of black. By the time the camera was back online, I had dropped off the platform and ducked into the darkness of the tunnel.

I waited until I was a good few meters into the tunnel before striking up my Glove light. The beam cut the dark and revealed the dirty, gray stone of the subway tunnels. *The cave.* My breath caught in my throat. *I'm awake.* I exhaled in pieces and forced myself to keep walking. It wasn't long until the next northbound train would come roaring through — I did not intend to be there when it did.

I walked until the GPS marker on my phone was directly under the tower. Another meter forward and to my right was a maintenance door. A more secure place to breach than the tracks.

The door was sealed with a simple electronic lock. I wasn't worried about someone coming by in the next hour and noticing my tampering, so I used the virtual equivalent of a battering ram and brought the lock down. It got the door open, but the lock's display was freaking out. It turned blue, red, flashed between green and yellow, then finally settled onto black.

The room was a closet. Some tools around, along with boxes and the odd jumpsuit. Still, large enough for what I needed it for. I'd go right around the gates of Tartarus.

In the corner farthest from the door was a ladder that would nearly scrape the roof. I set it up in the middle of the room and hung my super-potato-cannon off the side.

The easiest way to breach into a building through a wall is with controlled explosives. It's quick and *relatively* safe. The Intelligence Bureau preferred a little more subtlety at times, so they devised another way to get through walls. It was this style I had in mind. I loosened my bag strap and pulled out a coil of black wire wrapped around a small, silver container.

I stuck the black wire to the ceiling, in a circle just wider than my shoulders. I took a painting pad from my bag and spread the murky, translucent gel from the container evenly within the circle.

Ghost Goo was my favorite IB tech. With a simple electrical charge, the goo — along with five meters of whatever wall it was spread on — became permeable. As cool as it was, it had its drawbacks. I saw a guy put it on a load-bearing wall and bring down half a house. Another didn't spread it evenly and got state-flicker. Came out the other side without a nose.

Despite the dangers of the gel, blowing a hole into the basement of Tartarus wasn't an option. Ghost Goo would have to do.

I pressed on the black wire and it sent its current across the substance. Nothing too dramatic, but I could see the concrete shudder where my breath hit.

The goo was doing its work. I pulled a thin cable-cam out from the bag strap. The wire snaked up through about two meters of concrete until it breached the other side. From the feed displayed on my phone, I was looking at what appeared to be one of the basement hallways of Tartarus Tower. Tartarus might be a fantastic security company, but no one expects people to be coming in through the basement. The cable-cam zipped back into the bag strap. I swung the super-potato-cannon over my shoulder, eyeing the concrete above me. The roof still looked unnervingly solid. I tapped it with one finger and the surface quivered in return. With my breath held and eyes shut tight, I pushed through the ceiling.

Going through Ghost Goo was how I imagined it would feel to walk through jelly. I kept my hands raised until I felt air wrap around my skin. I grabbed the solid concrete outside of the Ghost Goo's area of effect. My bruised right arm pulsed as I used all the upper body strength I could muster to pull myself up and out of the floor.

Back on solid ground, I patted myself down to ensure I hadn't lost any chunks of myself in the transfer. I was still whole.

I gave the invisible hole I came through a wide berth when I crept around. The concrete would stay permeable for about another fifteen minutes. That was the life span of the electro-wire before it disintegrated. Another touch of subtly.

The hallway was dim; only every second light was on. According to the floor plan, the elevator bank wasn't too far.

I tapped a few commands into my Gloves and pressed one palm against my coat. The forest green canvas was overtaken by a flood of black. I grabbed the brim and my dark blue HARDWIRE hat turned black as well. Variable pigment cloth — a favorite for high-class socialites who wanted to change dress or suit color on demand.

I wrapped a gray bandana loosely around my neck, then pulled it over my lower face. It had a small device set into the fabric that acted as an air purifier. The entire rig had put me back a few nifty nickels, but it was worth it.

An ecstatic tremor rolled down my entire body as I tightened my pack's strap. There were no spirits. No ritual. No arcane threshold. It was base, human obstacles. Finally, I felt as though I was in control. I never knew how much stability the IB gave to my life. Since being let go — since

Alexis, actually — everything had been so ethereal. I was back in the real world.

I held on to feeling like a badass, not even trying to suppress my grin. *First stop, elevator bank.* I moved slowly, peering around each corner before entering the next hallway.

Not one Tartarus mercenary waited around any corner. For all of Tartarus's Network security, their true strength relied on the army they had stationed, ready to go. The shoot first, ask questions later kind of people. My plan should slide me past any trigger-happy merc, though. Straight up through the elevator bank.

Or rather the elevator. Eight elevators in two shafts but only one elevator went to the basement. The fact didn't derail my plan — I just hadn't expected it.

A security terminal stood out from the basement's dreary gray paint. The kind of terminal they would put in the remote areas of the building to ensure workers could contact security in case of some trouble like, *say*, someone breaking into the tower. I could utilize it for my own means. I wouldn't be able to interact with the security system itself — they definitely had thousands of redundancies for someone doing that — but it would be a wormhole into the Tartarus systems. I'd have an idea as to what security was up to.

I unzipped my coat sleeves and laid my right hand on the glass of the panel. The terminal wasn't tied directly into the security communications, but after a few minutes I was able to crack through and insert a worm into their system. The worm fed me real time insight into the security chatter. All the security messages were guard check-ins. A lot of guard check-ins. *How many guards does one tower need on a Sunday?*

The most important information I got from the panel was a clearer idea of Tartarus Tower's layout. I was right in thinking the basement was nearly devoid of cameras. The only place they appeared was around the security servers' storage area. Each server was devoted exclusively to the Network security of one of their bigger customers, such as the NMPD. If I had more time, I could sneak into each one. I'd never have trouble with a Tartarus lock again. It was an alluring prospect, but if I was caught that would give the cops a reason to confiscate my Gloves. I would never give them the satisfaction.

I moved to the elevator. My intel described an RFID card system with a camera inside. Every thousandth of a second, information was sent back to security HQ. Any discrepancies would send up red flags and bring down the gates of Tartarus. The small bright side was that each elevator was on its own circuit. I could only assume this was so someone wouldn't have control over them all by hacking one. This same feature meant I could isolate an elevator from the others and make it a ghost. The guards would never know it moved.

Triple task. I had to loop the camera inside, fake the outgoing signal, and override the ID system. *Good thing I'm awesome.*

I kept an eye on the clock as I set up the programs for each job. The camera would show nothing, the elevator would appear to be motionless, and a phantom card would trick the RF sensors into letting the elevator move. I'd unleash them all in one concentrated attack. *Deep breaths.* If this didn't work I would know immediately by the sound of an alarm blaring. *Now or never.*

I pressed my hand against the elevator's display and started the operation.

Nothing.

A good thing. The guard chatter kept right on, as though nothing had happened, as the elevator moved down to pick me up.

I only had minutes — seven at max — until the system would reset and the elevator would reconnect. That was more than enough time to get roof-side, launch the sensor bomb, and—

Bri-i-i-i-i-ing.

Every muscle seized. The alarm screeched like a banshee. Red lights flashed. The elevator door slid open. I leaped into the lift and slammed the button for the one hundred and eighty-fifth floor. The elevator rocketed up. I ensured my bandana was still in position. If the camera came un-looped, I didn't want it catching a glimpse of my mug.

The ringing of the alarm was dulled in the elevator but I could hear it passing by on each floor as I rose. I racked my brain over what could have gone wrong. There was no good reason why I should have tripped the alarm. I still had around a minute and a half before they would be able to regain control over the eleva—

Cha-chunk.

Damn it! The elevator stopped dead at the thirty-fourth floor. Security was working faster than my calculations predicted. It was as though they were ready for me. That was impossible. I didn't even know I was going to be breaking in. *All those guard check-ins. They were on high security. Why?*

FIND INTRUDER. HANDLE SITUATION. The security chatter was repeating the same message.

The elevator speakers crackled to life. "Please stay where you are so security can come handle you."

"Handle" was the exact word they used. For obvious reasons, big businesses with lots of secrets avoid using the words "kill" or "kidnap and interrogate."

I was going to be thrown into Tartarus's deepest and darkest pit. The elevator began to descend. A soft whirring emanated from the walls. A sickly yellow gas flowed from the cracks in the paneling. *Knock out? Or poison?* They could claim I was intent on unleashing the chemical agent only to have it turn against me.

I was going to be another missing person headline for Jack of Frost's request. Worse yet, there was a distinct chance New Montreal would freeze if I didn't find where that Winter energy had gone. It was time to get moving.

My bandana kept the air from choking me, though the gagging smell of rotting eggs snuck through. I found the overhead panel that lead to the elevator shaft, pushed it open with my good arm, and awkwardly climbed to the top of the car.

The lift descended at a leisurely pace — most likely to give me plenty of time to inhale that gas — so I had some time to take in my surroundings. Emergency lights lined the walls. I traced them down to the hard landing thirty floors below. Like a landing strip to my demise. The other elevators hadn't moved. They were only interested in bringing down mine. Climbing the tower seemed like a better plan considering what awaited me below.

The shaft had four elevators in it, all before me. The closest was only a few floors below. I would have to jump. The memory of that sideways building in St. Rémi made my bones ache. Another deadly leap.

"This one will turn out better," I assured myself.

I waited until it was closer, then threw myself to the next elevator. The impact of my landing sent a tremor through my bones. I stumbled forward with the momentum. A long drop waited to greet me, and I grasped for anything to keep me from tumbling over. I clutched tightly onto the solid steel of the elevator cable. A spike of pain shot through my right shoulder, but I didn't let go. Only once I got my footing did I loosen my grip and kneel on the elevator roof.

My shoulder swore at me and I swore back. I wanted to tear it off. Anything to get rid of the pain. Maybe Selene was right and I needed to go to the hospital. Nothing to do about that now.

It wouldn't be long before the guards saw the empty elevator. I wasn't about to jump into another elevator and get gassed again. I touched the elevator roof. The Glove's induction weave reached the gas trap, and I used it as a gateway into the elevator system. I commanded the elevator up.

The lift launched skyward. I didn't know how fast I was going, but it was far more than I wanted to be. The elevator should have started decelerating, but it gave no indication it was planning to stop before it crashed through the roof of Tartarus Tower — the fast approaching roof of Tartarus Tower.

I pushed another signal through the car but it was non-responsive. Bypassing through the gas release system must have corrupted something. If I was going to stop the elevator, I would have to get inside and do it from the panel.

I threw open the trapdoor into the car and jumped inside. The floor display was going wild. Maybe it was for the best I didn't know which floor I was zooming past.

I tapped like a madman on my wrist, praying I wouldn't feel the disheartening crunch of metal against elevator shaft roof. I struck the panel with a stop command.

Clunk!

The ensuing event was a brake so immediate that I was thrown from my feet and fell on — of course — my right shoulder. The pain reminded me I was alive and that counted for something. I thanked my bag's kinetic damping material, or else the Fyrex could have exploded from the fall. A sledgehammer couldn't break its contents. The door slid open and I crawled out. A sign on the wall told me it was Floor 183.

"Close enough." I forced my body to stand.

The floor was filled with offices, but no people. A look to the various elevator displays told me the floor wouldn't be empty for long. Two elevators from the right shaft and one from the left were rising, presumably filled to the brim with Tartarus agents itching to introduce themselves to me.

I didn't wait around to be the floor welcoming committee. Another elevator ride didn't interest me. I took the stairs. If the guards wanted to play, the game was going to be hide and seek.

The super-potato-cannon struck my back with each step I took. That was going to be another bruise to add to the list. The distinct sound of boot-stomps entered the stairwell below. I readjusted the bandana. I didn't want a guard identifying me.

I reached the roof access and burst into the sunlight. The frosty wind on the roof whipped my coat around and threatened to tear my hat straight off my head. Not wanting to lose my favorite hat to the November winds, I shoved it into my bag.

My hand brushed the can of Fyrex I planned to use to launch the sensor bomb. The mercs had to be only minutes behind me. I wouldn't get the chance to launch the sensor bomb if they joined me on the roof. I grabbed the can and sprayed the combustible liquid over the roof access's metal doorframe. Next came the flint and steel stomp-plate for the cannon. I held it close to the door and struck, sending sparks flying at the Fyrex.

The chemical jumped to life with such brilliance that I threw myself back so as not to be fried. The blaze traced across the doorframe, following the path I drew. Within three seconds, it had fused the door and frame together and cooled back down to a stable steel slab.

As the last flame left the door, a loud bang emanated from the other side, followed by some hectic shouting. It wasn't a perfect weld, but it would give me some time.

My heart pounded a tribal beat. As long as I was up here, I was going to make the trip worthwhile. *Jack and his fucking favor.* I whipped the super-potato-cannon off my shoulder and planted it onto the tower's roof. Selene's mini torque gun secured the cannon's feet firmly and I flipped the lid open.

The pounding at the door had stopped. In no way did I see that as a good sign. I took it as a cue to work faster.

I held the sensor bomb with the cable in one hand and sprayed the cannon full of the aerosol inferno with my other. I had only one shot at it so I wasn't stingy with the Fyrex. When I felt content, I dropped the sensor bomb inside and drove my foot down to the stomp-plate.

Pum!

It was a dull sound, followed by a much less dull six-foot-high fireball that heated the entire roof for a second. The projectile disappeared into the clouds until my only indication of its position was the cable tracing into the sky. The cable started to tilt more and more as the wind pushed the sensor bomb off course.

I could only hope I gave the sensor enough juice to catch the entire area in its scan. If it worked, I should get a good thermal readout of several hundred square kilometers.

God, I hope this works. For a moment, everything was calm. New Montreal shone in the brilliant light of the early morning sun. It was all laid out before me. That terrible, wonderful city I called home.

My Gloves picked up on the data sent down from the sensor. The electric winch at the cannon's base began retracting. I didn't have time to look over the info at this point; the unmistakable sound of a power saw cut through the air and would soon be cutting through the door.

The sensor crashed back into the roof, pulled by the winding cable. I threw myself back just in time to avoid having my head taken off by its bounce. The bomb whipped around a few more times until it was pulled back into the tube.

I unbolted the cannon's tripod and slung it back over my shoulder. The metal was warped and smelled of a smithy. Still, the job was done and it was time to retreat. I had to get off the roof, and it wasn't going to be the way I came up.

The power saw was already visible and making its way through the weld. I didn't have long. I could think of one way off the roof but it was untested to say the least. It's never fun to have anything's maiden flight be under duress. There was not a more apt time to call it sink or swim.

I reached back with both hands for my backpack and grabbed hold of another strap. I pulled it forward and clipped it to where the other harness was, making an X across my chest. The lower straps had hooks I clipped to my belt. All ready to go. *Unfortunately.*

Boom! The roof access door fell solidly to the ground. Tartarus security agents backed by white synthetics glared through, all armed with assault rifles and pissed off looks. The one with the saw tossed it to the ground and started to bring his rifle up — intent on helping me with my Swiss cheese impression. They were all crammed into a small hallway and the guard had trouble moving. It would give me the time I needed.

It all seemed to move in slow motion. The gravel crackled as I twisted my feet and drew my revolver, still working offhanded. With my good hand, I felt along the ammo on my belt until I touched the design I needed. Cylinder open. Round into chamber. Cylinder closed. The motor and sensor spun the round until it was primed to be fired.

The guard looked ready to open hell, but I was quicker. The shot went wide. It struck the doorframe. The bullet exploded into a thick smoke screen as the guard fired. *Bra-*

ta-tat! Debris kicked up as each round struck the rooftop. The trail of impact ran away from me as the guard became engulfed in the choking smog.

I let a smirk appear, only to have it disappear just as quickly when three more rifles started up. The rooftop was dirty with flying dust and machine gun chatter. Before long, one of them was going to find their mark, so I took off. I slammed my gun back into its holster and barreled with all the speed I could muster.

The south side of the building was not far but it might as well have been across the city. The New Montreal skyline was still lit up beautifully for me. If I died, at least I would have a wonderful final image.

Bra-ta-tat! Bra-ta-tat! The firing machine guns were my driving drum. I took a deep breath, pushed one foot against the lip of the tower, and hurled myself into the void.

Chapter 10

My feet kicked and my arms pumped, searching for another few steps of concrete to carry me forward. I only felt the drop and rush of wind through my hair as I fell story by story. New Montreal still stood before me, but the building tops were rising and the earth was rushing to meet me.

The experience was strangely calming. It's like they say: "It's not the fall that kills you, it's the sudden stop at the end." The fall was actually pretty wonderful, as long as I survived the stop.

I let a few dozen stories fly past me, before I reached back to my pack and pulled the cord. The fall was stopped with a yank on my belt and chest. I nearly screamed when my shoulder flared up. I peered up to the thin, bronze-colored fabric catching the air. Hurt like hell. Still — once again — I was alive.

The nanotextile parachute was thin. I could see holes starting to form through it. *No wonder this didn't get past R&D.* I chose a rooftop across the river and aimed carefully. The parachute was not cooperative with chunks missing from it. But I was able to pull on the strings enough and direct myself to the rooftop. I stumbled on the concrete and made a grab for the parachute before it could pull me away again.

A quick slice with the knife hidden on my bag and the fabric was free. I reeled it in and bundled it as small as I could — which was pretty damn small. Sirens came from across the water and a dozen black trucks tore along the bridge. The specks of distant drones shot out of the tower like bees. I wasn't home free from Tartarus yet.

The super-potato-cannon had done its duty, so it deserved a Viking's funeral. It would double as a good way to get rid of the evidence. I swung it off my shoulder and shoved the parachute into the tube. Digging through my bag, I threw my black hat back on and pulled out the Fyrex. I gave the cannon a good heavy coating before igniting. By the time the flames died, there was nothing but an unrecognizable pile of slag. The best tech in the world wasn't going to get anything from that.

Tartarus security teams would be converging on my position any second. They brought the chase into the city and off Tartarus Island, which meant they wouldn't be able to keep the cops out of their business for much longer. The NMPD getting involved wouldn't be much better. I dug my heels into the gravel of the roof and hit the door.

I came into a combined stairwell and hallway, doors to people's apartments lining one wall while the flights continued down on the other one. It was a perfect amplifier for the heavy boot-stomps that were making their way up.

Another current passed through my hat and coat to return them to their normal colors. I spun my cap around and loosened the strap on the bag so it looked more like a postman's style pack. I shoved the bandana into my pocket and pushed myself to one of the doors, making it seem as if I was trying to unlock my apartment.

"No fucking way," came a voice from down the hall. Skullcap, the jerk from the UI, threw down his groceries. He cracked his neck and approached.

No, no, no. I banged my head softly against the door. The mercs' footsteps were getting louder.

Skullcap pushed my head. "Those pacers down there looking for you, huh?"

I didn't have long until the floor was flooded with Tartarus security. Skullcap's prattling would get me killed.

"That phone cost me half a month of unemployment." He looked down the stairwell. "Aw hell, those aren't pacers, those are mercs. Can't wait to see what these guys do to y—"

I grabbed his throat. A jolt of electricity traveled from my Glove and knocked the punk out. I kicked his legs out, slammed him into sitting against the wall, and put my hat low on his head.

The footsteps of nearly a dozen men and women in full tactical gear pounded on the floor as I pushed against the door again. I breathed slowly and tried to keep my heartbeat down as they passed. I imagined hearing a shout, followed by the power of twenty highly trained mercs crashing against me and dragging me away. You don't fight a group that big, but I wasn't going to open fire on them either. If I was found, I would be taken. Simple as that.

They kept flooding by. I kept my charade of an interested onlooker going. A few shouts of protest rang out from the tenants below. Nothing accusatory toward me. With time, the stomps faded to the floors above. I finally exhaled and grabbed my hat, letting Skullcap slump to the floor as I left.

A few tenants of the complex were peeking out of their doors, trying to see what the commotion was. Not one of them paid attention to me. I looked like another Northsider punk.

I moved with purpose to the main floor. The front doors felt like a portal to my freedom. I pushed through and back into the cool air.

"Hey, you!" commanded a voice from behind me.

Of course, they would have guards posted at the doors. Stupid of me not to think of that. I couldn't risk showing my regret. Instead, I put up all the defiance I could muster.

"Turn around!" the voice yelled again.

"What cha yelling 'bout?" I replied as I turned. Two guards stared at me. One had his rifle aimed squarely at my chest while the other seemed uninterested. "Yo man! Who're you pointing that at?" *A 5.56 mm round would punch straight through my chest at this range. Instant death.* I hid any fear under miles of attitude.

The rifle guard took a few steps closer to me. A drone hovered silently a few feet over our heads, the camera focused squarely on my face. "Where did you get that coat?"

"Bought it."

My flippancy was not endearing to him. He dropped his rifle onto its strap and grabbed me by my lapel. I was less than an inch from his face. At this distance, I could count the hairs in his stubble and see the yellow lining the top of his teeth. I twisted my body the best I could, making it seem like I was struggling to get away, when in fact I didn't want him to see the revolver on my hip.

"I'm not interested in your sass, boy!" he screamed, sending spittle into my face.

"The jacket was black," the uninterested guard finally spoke up. "The perp's jacket was black in color."

The first guard looked down, apparently realizing for the first time the forest green canvas he was clutching on to. "What about that color changin' shit?" he growled.

Great. I get the one merc in New Montreal who keeps up with fashion trends.

"Does he really look as if he could afford that?" the second guard said. "Look at him."

I forgot I hadn't had time to shave that morning. First that screen vendor, now the guard. I should look homeless more often. The guard roughly pushed me back. "Get outta here," he said.

"Yeah, fuck you too," I said on my heels, with a parting flip of the bird just to cement my point. I heard the guard growl once again, but nothing came of it. I was lucky he didn't search my pockets or my bag. I doubt he would be fooled into thinking any of that was common gear for a hoodlum.

A few faces poked out from the surrounding apartment buildings. Every so often I heard a voice whoop at me, either condemning me because the guard was wrong to let me go, or congratulating me on sticking it to the pacer. *Northsiders.*

I turned at the second corner after I left the apartment and ducked into the first alley I could see. My heartbeat was returning to a normal rhythm. I leaned against the alley wall for support.

"Always getting in trouble, eh?" a voice surprised me from the other end of the alley.

I threw myself off the wall and brought my hand close to my gun, ready to fight off whomever was approaching. Sauntering toward me was the second guard, the one who spoke against me being arrested. I didn't relax. I didn't move.

He let out a joyful laugh as the wind picked up around him. Snowflakes encircled his form and the armored guard guise fell away. It was replaced with the gaunt form of Jack of Frost.

"You didn't notice it was me? What good is that Beyondsight if it's not on all the time?" He grinned widely.

I relaxed — but not too much. "You were watching that whole thing?" I asked.

"You always do put on a good show," he said, leaping up into a squat on a nearby dumpster. "I gave your little toy an extra *umph* up as well, you're welcome for that. But you didn't disappoint. I wasn't expecting you to jump off a roof, but *whoosh*! There you went. What was that shiny parachute?"

"Nanotextile. It's... not the best."

Jack howled in delight and clapped his hands. "You had no idea if it would work or not? Oh, Kraft, you are a treat for the senses. But you got what you went up there for?"

"Just about to take a look."

He licked his lips. "Show me."

I raised my hand and the projection started up, sending a map onto the alley wall.

The sensor bomb was strong enough. What we saw was a thermal display and readout that covered every inch of New Montreal and into the surrounding areas. It was exactly what we needed — with one problem.

"Shit," I muttered. *All that work...*

"What's wrong?" Jack asked, straining to understand the readout.

I sighed. Jack wasn't going to take it well. "Obviously the river is the coldest thing in the area, but we have about seven different spots that share the lowest temperature inland. And even that's not an impressively cold display."

"What are you saying?" Jack growled. He didn't look at me. He never broke his gaze with the map.

Not excited to invoke the wrath of a Winter spirit. "Are you sure the energy is in New Montreal?"

"Of course I'm sure!" he threw himself off the dumpster. The force of his jump crumpled the steel like cardboard. "Your machines are wrong!"

"Don't blame the information when it doesn't match your assumptions! This thing even took readings from under the ground! You don't get more comprehensive!" I shut the projection off.

Jack faced me and I squared my shoulders to him. The top of his head was barely over my chin but I knew better than to judge a book by its cover. If Jack wanted to, I'd be a Kraftsicle before I could blink. Still, if I backed down it would give him dominance. It was a dangerous game.

"Keep looking," he growled before whipping around and stomping off.

"Jack!" I grabbed him by his arm. His skin felt like ice. "Give me something here!"

Jack eyed my hand. I let go.

"Sorry," I said. "You're not the only big player in town these days. Have you ever heard of Obasin?"

He thought for a second, pacing the alley. "Can't say I have. Who is it?"

"I don't know." I took my hat off and ruffled my hair. "I'm guessing some sort of Dark deity. Has at least one spriggan follower, maybe more faeries. There's this virus on a company's system, but all it seems to be doing is being creepy. I think someone is trying to summon something."

"And do you think the missing Winter energy is related?"

I froze. I hadn't considered that a possibility. "Could it be?"

Jack ran his hand along his neck. "The thing about crossing the Fade is that the stronger you are, the harder it is to do. A faery can basically slip through, but a Dark deity..." His gaze grew distant. "Winter energy would be perfect for a crossing ritual. It's less chaotic than Summer energy. One could hide it somewhere until it's needed and it will merely hibernate."

I walked across the alley. Jack cocked an eyebrow in my direction. I planted my forehead against the brick wall, trying to formulate the many strands in my brain into something useful. The Fade was simple. The harder something hits it, the harder it gets. But a crossing ritual? It's a scalpel that cuts, and then tears a hole for whatever monster wants to wander through.

"How would someone steal Winter energy?" I asked.

"It would be a binding. Energy like that can't float around, so they would have to use themselves as an anchor to keep it in this world."

"Would it show in any way?"

"They could take on some winter characteristics."

"So they would be cold?"

Jack nodded. "Unnaturally so. Do you have someone in mind?"

"No." I ground my palm into my forehead. "But it's something to keep my eye out for."

"That won't always help if the culprit is already a gelid; yetis, jotuns, and some faeries are naturally cold."

"Some faeries?"

"Winter faeries. Unseelie." Jack paused. "You don't know much about faeries, do you?"

"Let's focus on Obasin."

"You want my hint?" Jack stepped gracefully closer. "Follow the humans. Darklings are always delegating jobs to you. You have freedoms."

"Like you did to me?" I pointed out.

Jack laughed and spun away without a word.

"Hey, Jack!" I called after him. "Were you allowed to tell me all that stuff?"

"I cannot reveal too much pertaining to Winter energy. This Obasin fella is different." He shrugged. "Let's just say it's a gray area."

The Well wasn't known for seeing gray. "Thanks."

Jack waved me off. With that, he was into the wind.

The cold air seemed to rise around me. I wondered what sort of chaos would appear if the Winter energy stayed missing. Surely, the Well of Time wasn't going to let anything happen. If our world went, the Dark was sure to follow. Unless Obasin crushed us first. I didn't have any concrete evidence that Winter energy was being used in a ritual. But it was better than no theory. I would have to keep my eye out for cold people.

There was an electricity in the air. I could feel it over the entire city. As though the buildings themselves were holding their breath. Whatever was going to happen, it was going to be loud, and it was going to be soon.

Chapter 11

For a Sunday night, the clubs were busy. The lineup for Sparc wrapped around the block. Of course, that was exactly where I needed to go. I had considered the back door, but it was built without a handle on the outside. Low-tech security at its finest.

I swept past the lineup, inciting cries from the club-goers. I came to the door and a meathead-looking fellow in a tight black shirt and blue jeans stepped in my way.

"Slow down, cowboy," he grunted.

"I'm just gonna stop in. You can time me if it makes you feel better." I took a step to the side of the great black wall only for it to shift back in front of me.

"Back of the line, smart ass." The bouncer shoved me back. The line of hair gel and short skirts started laughing. The bouncer leaned in close, snarling. His eyes were tattooed with jagged lines to create the image of shark teeth.

I pulled down on my hat brim and took a deep breath. *Plan B.* I lashed my arm out. The bouncer didn't flinch. I stopped my Gloved palm an inch from his face. I took one last sidelong glare at the bouncer and the laughing crowd as I sauntered around the corner.

The bouncer had pushed on my injured shoulder and it pulsed with pain. It seemed more and more likely I'd have to hit the hospital when it was all done. *I hate hospitals.* The pain would fade, I decided, so I gritted my teeth and got to work. The face of the bouncer — Horace Whitaker, apparently — projected from my Glove. The facial recognition gave me his DMV records.

BRAND: MATORO
MODEL: 2108 LEOPARD

COLOR: YELLOW
LICENSE PLATE: NR04-659

A glance into the nearby parkade and Horace's ride was apparent. A large, obnoxious canary yellow sports car parked across from the entrance. Black racing strips ran down the immaculately polished surface. I unzipped my sleeves as I approached. *This is going to be fun.* Matoro was notorious for giving its products the best anti-theft devices on the doors and windows. So I put my hand on the hood.

The vehicle roared to life. The simulated engine was deafening, a purposeful choice of decibels. Relic from the age of gasoline and machismo. I commanded the car's transmission to shift into neutral. The driver-side window opened. I took my hand off the hood and reached into the open window. I steered the car into the street. I aimed for the building across from Sparc and slapped the Matoro's hood once again. The engine revved and the tires screeched. The yellow bolt tore down the road.

I could imagine the bouncer turning to see his beloved Matoro shoot around the corner, jump the curb, and smash into a lamppost across the street. His shark-tooth eyes would widen and his perfectly shaved jaw would drop. Maybe he would even weep.

"No, no, fuck no!" I heard him cry.

I peeked around the corner. Horace was crying over his smoking heap of a car. The club's line was laughing and recording the man on their phones. My imagination wasn't too far off, after all. I pulled my hat low and corrupted the ID scanner's camera as I ducked inside the club.

Sparc was packed with sweaty, dancing bodies. Loud synth-pop blasted from every corner of the room. Multicolored lasers cut the fog and filled the air. People were crammed against the bar, tapping phones and cashsticks against screens as the bartenders threw drinks at them. The sights and sounds were already giving me a migraine and, of course, I'd picked the only club that wasn't selling headache patches. I forced my way through the pastel and neon crowd to where the booths were. Couples were going at it in most. I eventually found myself an empty seat.

Sparc was where I would find the real owner to Michael Harman's fingerprints. A criminal-for-hire type called Milos Ravinich. His rap sheet read like a pamphlet on small time crime — smash-and-grabs, muggings, breaking and entering. It was the file of someone too dumb for anything remotely high-tech. Unfortunately, also the file of someone with aggression issues. The club was listed as one of his hangouts. I hoped I'd find something here, if not Milos himself.

Out from the crowd swept one of Sparc's hostesses. A blue, neon flower design pulsated on her left temple, below pulled-back brown hair. The stem flowed down her neck and across her chest to where it twisted around three metal studs pierced along her sternum, before disappearing into her corset. Her eyes linked with mine and the flower wilted off her cheek. It unfurled along the stem until it became an eagle blazoned across her chest. *Implanted tattoos. Fancy.*

"Something to drink, sweetheart?" she asked, sweetness on her tongue.

"That looks like it was painful." I motioned to the three studs in her chest.

"Nothing wrong with a little pain."

I bet she gets tipped well. "I'm looking for Milos Ravinich. Seen him?"

"Who wants to know?"

"No one important. Can you tell me if he's come in lately?"

The woman considered. She considered wonderfully. "I'm all out of cigarettes."

"You want to trade cigarettes for information? Sorry, it's the twenty-second century and I don't smoke." I cleared the menu window off the tablescreen. Hopefully the hostess would take money.

"Then I don't talk." She gave me one last smile and pirouetted back to the crowd.

"Hold on!" I dug into my coat pocket.

She cocked her head back and I tossed the pack of Lumos cigarettes. "Diana's" gift. I had nearly forgotten. She snatched them from the air, inspected the pack to ensure it was filled, and sauntered closer.

"All yours. They were a friend's," I said. "Now your turn."

"Been around all night flexing his cash. Which is new for him." She nodded to a nondescript door on the other side of the bar. "He's in the VIP area, baby. Good luck getting in," she said with a wink. The eagle design morphed into a wicked string of barbed wire. The design curling up both sides of her face added menace to her grin.

"I have my ways."

"Oh, do you?" She slid in next to me. Her arm lightly touched mine. "That sounds exciting. What exactly do you want with Milos?" She smelled of peaches and spring days.

"It's his yearly employee review. We want to make sure he gets it as soon as possible." I gave myself some space from the woman.

"Fine, then don't tell me, mystery man."

"It's all part of my charm."

"I'd say so." Her gaze lingered as she slid away. "Well, mystery man, if you feel like talking some more come find me. The name's Harlequin."

"Kraft."

She gave a sly smile and rattled the Lumos before she disappeared back into the crowd.

I stared at where Harlequin once was, even after the ever-swarming mass of dancers swallowed her up. *Why can't Jack's job bring me to places like this?* I shook myself straight and slid out of the booth.

I pushed through the crowd once again. I had to shake off a few of the more aggressive dancers. I could practically smell the Euphoria in the air. A club-goer's favorite drug. I was able to force my way to the door Harlequin indicated. The club's cameras were conspicuously facing away from the entrance to the VIP room. There's probably not always decent things going on in there. I turned my coat beige and hat green as I inspected the lock. It was a basic electronic lock — entry would be as easy as faking the signal a phone app would send. I cracked the system in barely a second.

Last time I rushed in I got blindsided by a security team. The time before that by a faery. The dance steps weren't coming as naturally as they used to. Rather than hurrying inside, I took a few deep breaths and formulated a plan. A shiver crawled along my spine. I looked back at the crowd still dancing away. One person's body flowed into the next from the constant movement. But something was odd. Something was there. Hidden among the faces. It was bulbous and pulsated grotesquely. A fleshy blob ignored by the crowd. It was like a pound of flesh put through a blender, sweating and throbbing like a horrible growth. My chest seized. *How can they not see it? It's right there. Pushing against them.* I blinked rapidly. There was no code on that creature. It wasn't Beyondsight making me see it. Sticky tendrils rubbed damp bodies, licking up every drop of glistening sweat. It had no discernible eyes, but I knew it was staring right at me. Hungry. It wanted me.

Feast, feast, feast...

The words pounded like nails into my head. I squeezed my eyes shut and leaned against the wall. My knees were failing. Someone here *had* to be holding some Medioxyl. I could just grab some and duck into the bathroom. *This isn't real. It can't be. But if it's an illusion, other people would see it. Only I'm affected.* I just needed to hit up to calm down. I tried to tap my focusing beat on my thigh, but the rhythm was all wrong. I had to stay focused. *It's not real.* I had to breathe. *In and out. In and out...*

I didn't know how long passed until I was able to control my breathing. I dared to open my eyes. The thing was gone. Everything was right. As though it was never there.

That has to be Obasin. The same pressure from my dream. The same pressure "Diana" summoned. He was wrapped in it. The cave, the virus, Obasin. They all felt the same. All connected. He finally showed himself. He wasn't actually here. I knew that now. I would have seen the code if he was. But he made me see him. A warning, maybe? He was strong. A crushing force. That thing could be beyond me.

I swore under my breath and turned back to the door. I wasn't going to get rid of the fat bastard by sitting around crying. *Big guy showed himself. I must be doing something right.* I twisted the door handle and stepped inside.

The VIP area was a good-sized room decorated in deep purple and blue. It was a strangely depressing and dark decor to have for a hot nightclub. The centerpiece was a gargantuan burgundy couch. On it was Milos Ravinich, surrounded by two women in tight black dresses. I thought Warren was weasel-like, but Milos's pointed face looked exactly like a rodent's. His stained leather jacket and torn black jeans exuded a disheveled charisma that was all the rage. Still, I doubted those girls were there because of his natural charm. Probably more the cashsticks he was flashing.

My entrance didn't go unnoticed. There were two guards talking to a man and woman. As soon as I stepped in, they stopped their flirting and whipped around, training their eyes on me. The door clicked shut. All noise from the club was cut out, leaving only the music piped in through the speakers. *Soundproof room, excellent.*

"Whoa! This isn't the bathroom!" I laughed.

"Get out," one of the guards ordered. He made the obvious motion of tapping his shoulder holster.

"Wait. Milos? Milos Ravinich?" I ignored the guard, stepping closer to Milos. A smaller couch sat across from Milos's and I leaned against the back. "It is you! Milos! Or is it Michael Harman? I get confused."

That got his attention. "Everyone out," he said.

The guards looked at Milos, confused.

"Not you. Obviously."

A moment later, it was only Milos, his two guards, and me sharing the romantic atmosphere. Milos touched a screen on the couch's armrest and the music shut off.

"Check him." Milos scanned me up and down. He was a rough-looking fellow. A scar cut across his nose and a serious chunk was missing from his left ear. This guy was not afraid of a fight.

The two guards swept up beside me and grabbed my arms. I let them drag me to the front of the smaller couch. The armed one was stronger, judged by his grip along my neck. The second guard seemed more apprehensive. He was gentler. Gun Boy would have to go first. The gentle guard started patting me down.

"Oh, you're a frisky one," I said.

The guard stripped my revolver from my hip, handing it to Milos. "I found this."

"Oh, yes, hidden so cleverly in my holster."

Gun Boy grabbed me and pushed me onto the couch. His nose was crooked and slightly swollen. It had recently healed from being broken. *Still tender, I bet.*

Milos swiped a cashstick over the armrest. A bottle of some vodka I'd never heard of, but I assumed had to be expensive, slid out of the wall. A disruption in the solid blue of the room caught my eye. A slender, black robot guard transported the alcohol from the wall tray to Milos. Its faceplate blinked SERVING. Clubs didn't normally have robot servers in their VIP rooms, and it was a pretty expensive toy for a thug.

Milos looked over my revolver as he took a big swig of straight vodka. "ExS SA40. Semi-auto revolver. Barrel set low to reduce recoil. Slight modification to the chambers, too. Impressive."

"I just shoot it."

The synthetic stepped back behind the couch. Its faceplate went blank. *A command-based model. That could be useful.*

"Wanna see mine?" Milos placed my revolver on the glass table between us. Some large and gaudy vase graced the center of the table. Next to it were some Euphoria pills and auto-injectors of Medioxyl. I had to consciously stop my eye from twitching.

Milos drew his pistol from inside his coat. "Neo Glock eighteen. Selective fire. Seventeen-round clip. I keep an extended thirty-three-round clip for full-auto though." He acted like the father of an honor child, musing over his gun. He trained the sights to my skull. "I'm fairly sure in this case, semi-auto will work fine. Who the fuck are you?"

Two negative variables. He had a gun on me and it was a soundproof room. Two positive variables. He held the pistol loosely and the Glock looked as though it had never been fired. *He won't shoot me himself.* "I wanted to ask you a few questions about Glowing Future," I said.

"Glowing Future?" Milos leaned back into the couch. He never took the gun off me. "What are you? A cop?"

"No. I'm IT."

"IT?" laughed Milos. "IT, that's funny." He motioned to the guards. "Shoot this fucker."

Gun Boy whipped out his sidearm. Cold metal pressed against my temple.

"Whoa!" I threw my hands into the air. "We can talk about this." I had one chance to get out.

Whipping my arm back, I pushed the gun away from my head. *Crack!* The bullet fired into the armrest. My ear rang. I lunged a rising punch to the guard's face. My knuckles struck his crooked nose. The bridge cracked. Gore exploded.

I held Gun Boy's wrist firmly and grabbed the vase off the table. I hurled the vase at the other guard's head, and it shattered on his skull before he could draw his own pistol.

Gun Boy was trying to manage the blood pouring from his nose. I took his arm in both hands and yanked down. He went straight through the glass table. Drugs and shards flew into the air.

Out of the corner of my eye, I saw Milos bring his gun to bear on me. Light flashed from the barrel. The shot went wide and struck the back wall. I dove behind the couch as Milos opened fire again. My right shoulder flared when I hit the ground. The couch shook as each round impacted and tore through. I covered my head until the assault stopped.

I could hear Milos shouting, "Don't just stand there! Get him!" He must have been talking to the synthetic. I listened for the sound of the machine taking the Glock.

The heavy steps approached. I unzipped my sleeves and slammed in a control command. At best, I was guessing the synthetic's protocols. I laid in wait, my Glove at the ready. The plastic clad leg stamped into view, and I shot my hand out. I squeezed the synthetic's calf. My Glove lit up.

It froze. I stared up the barrel of Milos's pistol, waiting for it to fire. The shot never came. The robot spun to Milos. He swore. The machine fired. A vodka bottle smashed. I heard Milos scream, followed by a thump.

I jumped to my feet. The synthetic was still. I took the Glock from it and peered around the big couch where Milos had tumbled over. The poor guy was trying desperately to crawl away. I grabbed my revolver as I passed by the ruins of the table, and holstered it. The Medioxyl had almost all broken save one intact auto-injector. I slid it into my jacket's inner pocket.

Gun Boy moaned ever so slightly from the broken table. The other guard was unconscious against the opposite wall. I stalked to where Milos was crawling away. He had only gotten a few feet. A trail of blood leaked from his shoulder. I kicked the injured man onto his back and stepped over him.

"You can say I'm awesome. I know I'm awesome," I said.

"Go to hell!" spat Milos.

I placed a foot on Milos's shoulder wound. He swore and tried to pry my foot off. I leaned harder and pointed the Glock at his chest. That was enough to get him to calm down.

"You are too dumb to come up with this plan yourself," I continued, "much less have the ability or resources to pull it off. That means someone had to of hired you. Here's what we are going to do." I reached into my coat and pulled out the auto-injector of Medioxyl. "I have some Medioxyl right here; it'll fix you up right quick. Now, you can tell me who hired you and it is all yours, or I put some more holes in you and then it's all yours. Honestly, you're going to get the Medioxyl in the end, it just depends how much you want to go through for it." I leaned more on Milos's shoulder.

"Fine! Fine! I'll talk!" he screamed.

"Good boy."

"It was some suit bitch!"

"That's a very rude word. You're going to have to be more specific." I could hear a cracking beneath my foot as I pressed harder.

"Shit, man. I saw her on TV; she's some big shot at Orion!" Blood soaked the floor beneath him. Spit seeped from his mouth as he spoke.

"Well, I think I know who you're talking about, but let's see if you know." I pushed down until almost my entire weight was on him.

"Helga! Helga Dubois! Alright? She hired me to do all the systems!"

All the systems? I let up on the shoulder but didn't move. "What do you mean all the systems?"

"She... she had me put it on, like, five different hubs."

"Say them."

"Uh, Future, Infitex, Protectorate... Jesus!"

I eased off the wound more. I wasn't going to get information if he was in too much pain to talk.

"Protectorate, Enternaguard. She even had me put it on her own system! She said there would be more! Just give me the fucking Medi before I die!"

That would explain how a thug like him could afford a synth guard and be lounging around the VIP room. What did Helga have to gain from having Milos put the virus on all those systems? What did Obasin have to gain? The virus must be more than a simple scary program.

Still, it was exactly what I wanted to hear. I stepped off the wound. Blood drenched his leather jacket and turned the white shirt beneath red. I pulled down Milos's collar and pumped the Medioxyl into his shoulder.

Milos's wound knitted up at an accelerated rate. He would be sore once the painkillers wore off and should still see a doctor, but he wasn't going to bleed out. Sealing up the skin, that was Medioxyl's job.

He curled into a ball. "I don't even care, man. Life has gone to shit since that job." Deep bags sat beneath his eyes.

Both Warren and Rick had bags beneath their eyes, too. Even I was starting to develop them. I didn't consider it at the time, but Rick had mentioned bad dreams. *Is it possible I'm not the only one being kept up at night by the visions of the cave?*

I squatted next to Milos. "How has it gone to shit?"

"What do you care?" He clutched his shoulder and glared up at me.

"Because I'm a helper."

Milos growled and curled up even tighter. "It's a dream. Some cave, man. Scary shit, and it happens every single night since I did that job."

I took off my hat and ran my hand through my hair. Milos was having the same dream I was. *Does this mean I'm going to have another one tonight? And every night?* That could be why Warren and Rick looked so tired; they'd been at Glowing Future longer than I had. Obasin must be haunting people using the virus. But why? And how was Helga involved?

"I'm keeping your gun, Milos," I said, shoving it into my backpack. "If I hear you've been blabbing about our conversation, your death will be a suicide." I hurried from the trashed VIP room. I took care to leave through the back door. No telling how the bouncer was feeling at the front.

A single light cast its glow down Sparc's back alley. I returned my clothes to their normal color. Looking into the sky peeking through the high-rises of New Montreal, I couldn't see a single star.

What possible reason did a faery like Helga have for wanting to put a virus on company systems? Just some mental torture? Obasin was the key. There was one common thread through all the horrible images in the video. Like the first picture of the twisted family dinner, each image was of some kind of macabre meal. Cannibalism. Gluttony.

Feasting.

A chill sliced into me. I zipped my coat to my chin. Obasin. The Great Devourer. Its name made sense. It must be a deity of gluttony.

That didn't explain why the video was in Glowing Future's code. Or why Helga Dubois wanted it there. I had enough if I wanted to attempt to get her arrested for corporate espionage, but that wouldn't help me figure out what was going on. There was a reason Obasin kept popping up around me. And then there was the dream…

It was nearing one in the morning. Maybe I'd be able to sleep. *I should have kept the Medioxyl.*

Chapter 12

It was one short train ride before I was standing in front of my door. The familiar wood sat before me. Unlocked and ready. I knew what was supposed to be on the other side. The walls, the counter, the furniture, the circle etched into the door. I could picture it all. But a crippling fear gripped my heart. The thought of what *could* be behind the door.

The brightly lit hallway was safe. I could see everything. A stain on the carpet four feet away caused by a rampaging cat's urination. Two cracks that ran almost parallel horizontally above my door. Ten doors down the hallway — seven with the original handles and three with fancy custom ones. Six lights, three paintings, one long piece of dark red carpet with swirls. All that I could see. But whatever was behind that wooden door was unknown. Six lights, one flickering far in the distance. Three paintings, each one's eyes drilling into the back of my head. One carpet, threatening to swallow me whole.

It was insane. I was insane.

I spent a long time staring at my door, before I finally broke. I pulled out my phone and dialed the most familiar number I knew.

"Kraft, it's, like, two in the morning." Selene's voice was hoarse from sleep.

"I'm sorry. I just finished doing some research in your area; I was wondering if I could sleep there?"

"Huh? Oh, yeah, sure. I'll unlock the back. Just come into bed," she said, then hung up.

Back to the train. Great. Why was I acting like such a child? Yet, even as I questioned myself, I couldn't get those images out of my head. The video, the dream, that thing at Sparc. Obasin. It was haunting me. It wanted to break me. I couldn't let it.

~ ~ ~ ~ ~

The dark room. There was blood. Was it mine? It lay dry on the rocks. There was some light source. There had to be. The shadows surrounded me. They were moving. It lurked within. It watched. It hungered. The light was disappearing. The darkness was creeping in. It was taking over. I wanted the light back. But it was dimming...

~ ~ ~ ~ ~

"Kraft! Wake up!" Selene's hands dug into my side as she shook me.

Bright light streamed through the window. It dashed any chance of me ignoring Selene, so I forced my body to sit.

"What time is it?" I asked. My jaw was stiff but manageable. My shoulder ached when I moved it, but it didn't feel like any lasting damage was done. I blinked until the room came into focus. Selene was seated on the bed, hands pushed into my good side. She was already wearing her coveralls.

"It's two in the afternoon. Look!" She pointed at the projection across from the bed.

The news was on. Some reporter was standing downtown. Behind him was yellow POLICE holotape and plenty of flashing lights. He was talking about some kind of investigation. The headline scrolling across the bottom of the screen clued me in first: BLOODBATH AT GLOWING FUTURE TECHNOLOGIES. That snapped me snapped me awake.

"Isn't that who you're working for?" she asked.

I jumped out of bed, grasping for my jeans and tee. "I need to get downtown fast! Can I borrow your car?"

"Yeah, sure." She tossed her keys.

I snatched them out of the air and slid my shirt on. The same clothes I had been wearing for the last two days — I had bigger things to worry about than that. My bag of tricks would stay at Selene's. I wasn't about to go charging off to a crime scene with a bag full of illegal goods. I made sure to have both my guns — mine in my holster and Milos's Glock tucked into the back of my pants, before rushing out Selene's door.

———— ⟨⟩ ————

I pulled up in a deep green sedan outside Glowing Future in a record setting time. For an expert mechanic, Selene had a pretty modest car. I hid my guns beneath the passenger seat and bolted from the car. I headed for the police holotape and news reporters.

"Kraft!"

I jerked my head to Warren stomping toward me.

"What happened?" I asked.

"Rick happened! He came in this morning with a shotgun! Hit twenty people before blowing his own fucking head off!"

"Oh, shit." *Seems like the best reply.*

"Ranting and raving about demons wanting to eat him and how everyone was hunting him. He was a lunatic! This is the last thing we need!"

"Oh, shit, shit." *It still seemed like the most appropriate response.* Demons wanting to eat him — it fit with Obasin's presence. I had to be right about the insomnia; other people were having the same dreams as me. Haunted by the visions. Warren, Rick, Milos, and me. "Warren, have you been having nightmares?"

"What are you—"

"About a dark cave?"

He froze. A tremor appeared in his brow. "Who told—"

"It is quite a situation we have here," said a new voice.

Warren winced at the sound. From behind him appeared a well-dressed man. He was middle-aged, dignified, and confident in posture. A light amount of gray peppered his temples. He seemed like the kind of person who knew the power he held. Handsome, too. He had his hands behind his back and walked with a half-smile.

"Uh, Kraft," Warren spoke without looking at the newcomer or me. "This is Frank Harcourt. CEO of Glowing Future Technologies."

Oh, shit, shit, shit. I extended a hand. "Nice to meet you, Mr. Harcourt."

The man gave my hand a second-long glance, as though he was thinking about what to make of it. I thought he was going to ignore it, but he grabbed tight and shook firmly. I tried to make some polite eye contact but Harcourt's steel eyes had a coldness in them. I couldn't look for too long without feeling a squirming in my spine. His scrutiny was slightly off-putting, but his smile was still reassuring and calm.

"Mr. Kraft." He broke the shake. "So you are the one looking into our systems."

"I, uh..." I thought Warren was trying to keep this information away from the boys upstairs, now there was the CEO saying he knew? Warren refused to make any sort of eye contact with me. He looked like a child about to be scolded by his parents.

"Look." Harcourt took me by the shoulder and led me away from the crime scene. "This whole situation is terrible for all of us at Glowing Future. Rick had been my head of security for many years. It comes as a shock to anyone who knew him that he would do something like this. I guess everyone has their demons."

I nodded, still in shock by Harcourt's knowledge. Before I knew it, Harcourt had maneuvered me back to the green sedan.

"You can understand if I feel we have a bigger situation than your little technical glitch." He stopped and stepped in front of me. Both his hands were on my shoulders, squeezing kindly. "What I'm trying to say is we do not require your assistance any further."

"But I—"

With one hand raised, he stopped me. "Mr. Godwin will hold up whatever deal he agreed to, and you will be paid in full for your time rendered."

"With all due respect, sir. This entire situation is—"

"None of your concern." He never dropped his smile even while talking. It was impressive. "I applaud Warren for his innovation, but we at Glowing Future can handle ourselves. That's what our IT department is for, anyway."

He gave a hearty laugh and clapped my bad shoulder. I nearly screamed out of pain but bit my tongue.

"Put it out of your mind, Mr. Kraft." Another smaller clap and he left. Warren still stood where we had left him, bracing for some phantom impact. Harcourt took him by the shoulder and led him away from the scene.

Off the job. I could be done with that whole mess. But... I knew Obasin wasn't done with me. That cave burned in my vision, and the increasing violence and dread it evoked told me he wouldn't leave me alone. *Rick wasn't left alone.*

I snapped my gaze to the police swarming the entrance. I was hoping that Caleb might have been called in, but I couldn't see his stylish form anywhere. There was a decent number of pacers, but the detectives must be around somewhere. A flash of straw hair caught my eye, moving toward the large glass entrance. I double-checked that Harcourt had disappeared then hotfooted it across the parking lot.

I was nearing the woman when she must have seen me in the reflection of the glass — judging as she cursed and spun to face me.

"Back off, Kraft!" she ordered, with one hand solidly on her hip.

Sergeant Alexandra Thorn was a hellion of a woman. Her long blonde hair was done up in a tight bun and pierced with a spike. A light pantsuit hid her frightening muscles and tone underneath. I had once seen her take down a perp twice her size with a solid strike to the temple. In fact, the last time I'd seen her I was on my back after being tossed over her shoulder. I don't make fun of her height anymore, though I still get snickers from the cadets about that one.

"Oh, come on, Ali," I said with a smile. "We're all friends here."

She took a step toward me, making me think she was going to throw a punch. It was enough to make me stop and flinch. "This is a crime scene, Kraft. I'm not going to have you wandering around and pissing off the people who are *doing their jobs.*"

"I know how to deal with pacers — er, cops; I just have some questions that need to be answered." I stepped forward again.

She spun on her heels. "If you have any questions or concerns, please direct them toward the department."

"It's a Dark thing!"

Ali froze. I heard her sigh as she dropped her head. She stomped back toward me, stopping an inch away. She glared up, burning holes into my eyes.

"What kind of a Dark thing?" she growled. "The last 'Dark thing' ended up with me getting my ass kicked by a goddamn valkryie. The other officers still think I'm glitchy."

"You actually told them? How did that go?"

She twisted the ball of her foot into the ground. "Four months of psychiatric evaluation."

I nearly laughed in her face. "I told you not to tell them! They'd never believe you!" I'd forgotten about that fiasco. I was still with the IB at the time. It was amazing I got any work done with all the trouble the Dark got me into. I reined myself back in. "It's nothing that serious, you don't have to get involved in this one. I just have a situation I need to figure out, it's a—"

"No, no." She held up her hand to stop me. "Is this going to be another thing where I get my ass handed to me?"

"I could teach you some basic protection runes."

"For all the good it will do me."

"You might not be magical, but you can activate some runes. Simple ones at least."

"I have my gun. That's good enough for me." She sighed and looked back into the building. "You can come into the lobby and I'll answer your questions, but you can't come upstairs."

I nodded in agreement and followed Ali. She tapped on her wristscreen as we approached the holotape. It flashed white as she entered and green as I did; I was her guest. We passed by a few pacers snickering in my direction. Detectives I could handle, pacers — or beat cops — do nothing but keep pace. They don't question, they enforce. I brushed them off and we entered Glowing Future Tower.

It was grim. Half a dozen forms lay under sheets spread across the floor. Dark blots pushed against the plastic laying over the bodies. Red splattered across the walls and cool marble. Smears of a shotgun blast tearing through a body. A few trails lead away from the corpses. A pale cadet entered information into a screen, barely holding onto his breakfast. The air was somber, blood thickening it.

Ali stopped a few steps in. "He swept in, moved through the lobby, and then took the elevator to the twenty-third floor." She kept her voice as even as I assumed she could manage.

The same floor Milos worked on? "That it?" I asked.

"That's all you need to hear about it. Now ask your questions."

"The assailant. What do you know about him? Any obvious triggers?"

Ali tapped a few commands onto her wristscreen. "Rick Oslo. No prior convictions. He was apparently well liked by his coworkers, as well as upper management. No history of mental illness either." She lifted an eyebrow. "Here's something interesting. He had a red flag put on his file after a recruiter from Arno Berg came to see him."

"Arno Berg..." I knew the name. "The Iceberg" Arno was a local ne'er-do-well. One with a lot of power in New Montreal. He kept a firm hand on most of the crime northeast of Montreal Island. The police hadn't been able to do anything to him over the years, not that they were trying very hard. Since Arno came into power, the northeast had become less chaotic. At the very least, organized crime was organized.

Arno Berg was also an ogre. Not metaphorically — a real, honest-to-God ogre. A rumor was circulating the streets that he ate the bones of his enemies. I suspected that rumor might have some fact to it. He was not a fellow I was excited to tangle with.

"What did the witnesses say?" I asked.

"Almost anyone who saw him is dead. He even shut off the cameras before starting shooting. We have one guy who saw him come in, but he's... not going to be any help."

As if on cue, a loud crash echoed from the entrance of the lobby. Some man in a ragged sweater had knocked over a trash can. He babbled incessantly, and the pacer with him tried to get him under control.

"His mind is splintered," Ali explained. "Sure signs of a long-time abuser of Medioxyl. That stuff will twist your brain in knots if it doesn't have anything to heal. He's not even the worst I've seen."

The man fell to his knees. His gut wretched and heaved. He dragged his fingernails down his temple until the skin broke. His mind was going a mile-a-minute, I could tell. He had to be taking four hits a day to get where he was. *Some people have no control.*

Ali glanced to the elevator bank behind her. A pacer waited there. "Is there anything else, Kraft?"

"Did anything strange pop out about Rick Oslo to you?"

Her gaze whipped back to me. Her lips pursed and her eyes narrowed. "He was the size of a small truck, very well-maintained fingernails, and — oh yeah — was a perfectly happy man who decided to take out twenty coworkers with a shotgun before blowing his own head off. You tell me if that's odd."

She gave me a look that could peel wallpaper.

"I'm sorry," I muttered.

"You haven't seen the upper floor. He wasn't calm or methodical; he moved and fired like a man scared of everything. Maybe it was drugs, maybe a sudden onset mental illness. It doesn't really matter when it comes down to it, because twenty-one people are dead and understanding won't bring them back." Her voice was hard as she spoke. Alexandra Thorn had been on the force for a long time. She wasn't one to let things get to her.

"I said I'm sorry."

"I wish you were sorry. At least that would prove you're somewhat human. You just don't like being yelled at."

"To be fair, I don't think many people like being yell at. And what the hell do you mean by that? Proving that I'm human? Do you think I'm a synthetic or something under all this skin?"

"That might make sense. Because you know what humans do? They feel something when they walk into the scene of a mass murder."

"Do you think I don't feel anything?"

"I've known you—" She stopped and took a step back. "Tell me how many bodies are in this room."

What is she getting on about? "Seven."

"And how many shots were fired?"

I took in the blood sprays. How the bodies were lying. The shapes of the stains on the sheets. "Five."

"Then how are seven people dead?"

I laughed. "Am I supposed to do your job for you?"

She put her hands on her hips and waited.

"Fine." I pointed around. "One shot hit those two. Those four were shot individually. That's five shots and six dead. That one was beaten to death, though. What's this supposed to prove?"

"You've been in this room for two minutes and all you've thought about is blood splatters and placement of bodies. Do you know what I thought when I first walked in?"

"What?"

"These are seven people who aren't going home."

"I... thought of that, too." I rubbed my eyes. They were so tired. "People process in different ways. I'm trying to figure this out!"

"It's not about processing, Kraft! It's about feeling — no, no, your mental state is not my problem." She poked me in the chest with two fingers. Hard. "You let me know if you find anything out. Okay?"

"Yeah."

She poked me again. "Kraft."

I looked right into her eyes. "An otherworldly entity infected his brain and haunted him until he snapped."

I could tell that wasn't what she expected. She blinked once, then twice more, and shook it off. "Let me know if you find anything that *I* can deal with, then."

"I don't think I'm going to come across anything you can deal with."

She gritted her teeth. "Someday you're going to have to ask for help, Kraft."

"Is that how humans react? No, people can't handle what I do." I waved Ali off and started to back away.

"People may surprise you."

"They haven't yet." I tipped my hat and spun off. Unfortunately, people are weak, ignorant, or unreliable. I had to deal with it alone. Besides, Ali was going to have her hands full with Glowing Future. I didn't envy her.

Of course, she probably wouldn't want to go meet a bone-crunching ogre either.

Chapter 13

I parked outside the Northhill Junkyard. The field of twisted metal was Arno Berg's headquarters for his criminal empire. It was just across the river from Montreal Island. Here he could issue orders, manage fronts, and dispose of as many rivals as he needed too. All in all, it looked almost like a normal junkyard. Almost, except for the two armed guards in suits at the gated entrance.

Arno was an ogre. I'm no cryptozoologist, but from what Caleb told me that put him in the same order as other fae. The signifying feature of the fae is their aversion to cold iron, much like the spriggan in St. Rémi. The purer the iron, the better. *Yet he has no fear living in a junkyard.* I had stopped by a hardware store on the way to Northhill and picked up an iron nail. I wouldn't risk sneaking in anything larger.

The car was barely in park before one of the guards was hotfooting it to the door. He tapped the glass as I took off my seat belt. The bulge of a shoulder holster hidden under the guard's jacket sat at my eye level. I groaned, turned the key halfway, and lowered the window.

The man leaned in. From a distance, he appeared bald, but up close I could see a buzz cut of blond hair. A tribal sun tattoo peeked from within the collar of his shirt. "Junkyard is closed today," he said.

"I'm here to see Mr. Berg," I replied, putting on my Gloves.

He raised an eyebrow. The man had a stone face. I couldn't read him at all. What was clear was that he was sliding his hand toward the shoulder holster. "He's not taking visitors."

"Tell him Kraft is here."

"Kraft is going to have to come back another day."

I smiled at the guard. I snapped my fingers on my right hand, Glove flashing for a beat on contact. The gate rolled open. The second guard swung a submachine gun on a strap out from under his coat and scanned wide-eyed for a target. Tribal Sun put his hand firmly on his pistol and shot me a glare.

The silence was broken by a voice on the guard's radio.

"Send Kraft in, Mr. Gates," it said.

"Mr. Gates works the gate. You can't make this stuff up," I sneered.

Mr. Gates was obviously not happy about letting me go, but he did step back from the car so I could exit. The other guard was still pretty disconcerted by the gate spontaneously opening. I could hear Mr. Gates scold him as I entered Northhill Junkyard on foot.

I moved across the empty junkyard and into the main office. One would never be able to guess what the inside of the office looked like from the outside. While the exterior was mostly grime, the interior felt as if I'd stepped into a five-star hotel. Fine carpet covered the floor. The warmth of the ground nearly made me swoon with comfort. Soft string music played, and the room had the faint aroma of nectarines.

More of Arno's men littered the common room. They sat relaxed in the decadent chairs and couches. One jerked his head toward the large wooden door across the room, but I already knew where I was going.

I had dealt with Arno before. Our meetings were always with Arno the criminal; I never had to deal with Arno the ogre. I knew what he was due to my Beyondsight, and he knew I knew. Our relationship was tense at best. Though, I was kind of pissed he didn't let me onto the existence of faeries, considering they're ogres biological cousin or something. He was connected to Rick Oslo in some way. It was a flimsy lead, but it was the best I had. I reminded myself of the nail in my pocket and entered Arno Berg's office.

The room I came into reminded me of a more tasteful version of Warren's office. It was about one-fourth the size, but it didn't feel cramped. All wood and glass; I couldn't imagine a speck of metal would be allowed in here. It was to be expected from the home base of a fae.

Speaking of which, Arno Berg sat at his modest desk. He was a mountain. When standing, he was over six and a half feet and covered in pounds and pounds of pure muscle. He looked out of place hunched over the desk he dwarfed and dressed in a suit that could have been worn by an elephant.

Some stubble ran across his strong jaw. His face wasn't ugly — I've seen ogres who are far worse on the eyes — but he wasn't going to be modeling anytime soon. His mouth was a little lopsided, his nose was oddly turned up, and I wouldn't say his eyes were symmetrical.

He put his meat slab hands on the desk and pushed himself up from the chair with a massive creak. Standing in his shadow, I understood why ogres were seen with such fear in myths and legends. His size made me feel like a child again, looking up at all the people who were so much bigger than I was. When you are a tall man yourself, it is extremely off-putting to be the one looked down on.

Arno offered his hand to me across the desk. "Mr. Kraft," he said, "always a pleasure."

I put my hand into his paw. His fingers enveloped mine and gave a slight squeeze. I both felt and heard all my joints pop as we shook. "Hello, Mr. Berg," I grimaced.

He broke the shake first and returned to sitting, the chair creaking under his immense weight. "Would you mind placing your Gloves and firearm on the table so we may discuss why you are here?"

"Of course." I removed my Gloves and placed them on the desk, followed by my revolver and Milos's Glock. I wouldn't try shooting him anyway; I felt it wouldn't do more than tickle. I took my seat. "I always did find it a little funny that one such as you would take up residence in a junkyard. It's essentially a field full of acid for fae, isn't it?"

Arno chuckled. "I can keep out the humans that try to come in, the yard deals with the fae. Field full of acid, as you said."

"I wanted to talk to you about Rick Oslo—"

His monstrous hands flew at me. I moved to scramble out of my chair, but he was quick for his size. His grip tightened around my throat and dragged me across the desk, knocking my Gloves and guns to the floor. I was slammed into the adjacent wall, held almost to the ceiling.

Arno growled up at me. Spittle flew from his mouth and foam started forming at the corners. The room was darkening. I couldn't get any air past his fingers. I dug into my pocket and brought out the iron nail.

I drove the spike into his forearm. Arno bellowed and released my throat. My feet hit the ground and I fell to my back. I scrambled away from the seething ogre. He clutched his forearm and glared down at me. Code surrounded him, creating an aura of some massive shadow threatening to engulf the entire room.

I was frozen in place. I wanted to run or scream or maybe even cry. The horror that loomed over me. Arno panted through his growls, holding his wounded arm. It was obvious the iron wasn't having as much of an effect on him as I thought it would. He could ignore any cold iron I threw at him and snap me in half.

After what seemed like a lifetime, Arno stumbled back. He hit the adjacent wall with a thump that shook the room, and slid down. He clutched his head in his hands. His breathing slowed and the code around him subsided.

A knock came at the door. "Is everything alright, sir?" a guard yelled.

"Everything is fine!" His voice put quakes through my bones. He groaned and took another deep breath. "I am sorry, Mr. Kraft. I let myself get out of hand."

"Th— *Ahem* — that's fine." My throat burned as I spoke.

Ogres were not tame fae, not that any fae were really tame. Maybe faeries were — now that I knew they were one hundred percent real. More than anything, ogres were known for wreaking havoc wherever they went. Something was different about Arno. What I just saw — and experienced — was a taste of a true ogre.

"Mr. Kraft?" Arno's voice was weaker than before.

"Yeah?"

"Could you please remove this nail from my arm?"

I smiled slightly to myself and stood. With the tale of a lion with a thorn in its paw firm in my mind, I removed the nail from the ogre's arm. The smallest puncture wound remained. The skin surrounding only showed the slightest amount of blackening. *Ogres* are *tough*.

"I'm sorry about the iron," I said, wiping the nail off and putting it back into my pocket.

Arno heaved himself back onto his feet, straightening out his suit. "That is quite alright, Mr. Kraft," he said. "I did, perhaps, bring it on myself."

Arno Berg was an oddly pleasant man. I could almost see myself liking him. Almost. He still killed men as viciously as he'd almost killed me. Rumor said he ate them.

"You, uh," I stammered, "you weren't going to eat me, were you?"

He gave a hefty laugh. "My more vicious brethren would take joy in crunching bones. I however have found my tastes lean toward a nice steak."

The mention of steak reminded me of Rick, eating his breakfast meat just a day before. It's no wonder Arno wanted to hire him. The two big men would have gotten along wonderfully. Arno had certainly reacted badly to me mentioning his name. He had to have heard about Glowing Future on the news. Any crime boss worth his pay wouldn't fly off the rail over losing one recruit. *Unless he wasn't just a recruit. And without some of the facial deformities, Arno does kind of look like...*

"Was Rick Oslo your brother?"

Arno winced. He ran his fingers through his slicked back hair and leaned against the wall. "Half-brother, actually," he explained. "Our father was a true ogre, in all senses of the word. He... assaulted Rick's mother. I only recently found out about him. I sent Mr. Gates to try and get him to meet me, but I assume Rick thought the same thing most would — that I was trying to offer him a job."

The ogre softened, more than I thought an ogre ever could.

"I don't get along with the other ogres, obviously," he continued. "They are base creatures and I have found certain pleasures with... you humans. I was probably foolish, but the idea of a family that I could get along with was... Anyway, now he's dead."

"Do you think he succumbed to his ogre side and took it out on his work?" I asked.

Arno shook his head. "An ogre would not use one of your weapons. If he succumbed, he would have torn through those humans with his bare hands and certainly would not have killed himself at the conclusion."

"So what then?"

"Someone made him do it," growled Arno. He squeezed his hands into fists so tight that I could hear the knuckles pop in unison.

"But who w—" I was interrupted by the beep of the comm on the desk.

"Arno! Jesus Christ!" The sound of gunfire came from the radio and outside the building. "There's something here! Fuck! It tore Singh in half!"

Arno turned a hard eye to me. "One of yours?"

"I don't have things that are mine," I said, grabbing my Gloves and weapons off the ground. I threw the Gloves on and jogged out of the office, followed by Arno's hulking form.

We bolted through the now empty common room and out into the yard proper. I hardly got a step onto the gravel when half a guard spattered on the ground before me. It was the young one from the gate. His mouth was wide in horror and entrails hung from where his waist ended.

Arno arrived soon after and saw the dead man. He growled and looked toward the gate. I followed his gaze to where the action was.

The guards were firing upon what seemed like some overgrown, bipedal lizard. Actually, it looked exactly like an overgrown, bipedal lizard. It held the bottom half of the dead man in its claws. I clicked on my Beyondsight. Code rippled down its back like a frilled spine and shot out of its head like horns. *A lizard daemon? Here?*

The daemon charged the next closest guard. The man tried to pump as many rounds from his pistol into the thing's torso as he could. He might as well had been popping off BB pellets into a concrete wall. The lizard didn't falter for a second; it tossed the legs away and clenched its jaws on the guard's throat. Blood gushed from the wound, and the guard dropped. The lizard tore into the man.

"As much as I hate to say it, you're the hunter here, Kraft." Arno never broke his gaze. "What do we do?"

At least daemons I can handle. "Crossing running water would dissipate the magic that's keeping its form together in this world, but we don't have that or an exorcist," I said. Running water had a habit of disrupting Hell-magic — a special kind of Dark power. "You can't kill a daemon, but we can destroy its form and send the spirit back to Hell."

"I can do that." He started unbuttoning his suit jacket. "Consider this me paying you back for not arresting me during that brothel raid a few years ago."

"The daemon's on your property, Arno." I slammed a speedloader into my revolver's cylinder. "This is me helping you. Besides, I would have arrested you if anyone had pointed a finger."

Arno didn't even crack a smile. He threw his jacket and shirt away. I was standing next to a shirtless mound of skull-crushing muscle. I felt *very* out of shape. His biceps alone made me feel as though I was wielding two strands of spaghetti. *And that's why no one points fingers at him.*

"The Iceberg" Arno charged forward, each step pounding against the earth with a mighty thump. His men saw him coming and held their fire on the creature. Arno grabbed the lizard's throat and pulled it off the dead man. He spun like a hammer thrower and hurled the monster into a pile of cars at least twenty feet away.

The lizard hit with a grotesque crack and tumbled to the ground. That wasn't enough to stop it. It scrambled back to all fours. It looked at Arno — ogre fury unleashed — and then to me.

Something appeared to click in its mind. A low hiss came from its throat and it met my eyes. It gnashed its teeth and charged. I raised my revolver. My right shoulder was still sore, but it felt nice to use my good arm. I fired twice. My rounds were stronger than the guard's. Both shots smashed through the lizard's left foreleg.

The creature dropped — but followed with a roll and kept running on its hind legs. It was almost on me. I whipped out Milos's Glock. Both guns barked, tearing chunks out of the daemon without slowing it down.

A flash of skin caught my eye and I held back on firing. Arno shot into view and unleashed a wicked haymaker into the side of the lizard's head. The blow took the daemon right off its feet and sent it sliding across the gravel. It thrashed on its back for a second before righting itself. The lizard hissed at Arno and me before leaping into the scrap heap behind it. Its reptilian shadow disappeared into the crushed cars.

"Is it gone?" asked Arno.

"It's stalking us. It's having trouble going toe-to-toe, so it's going to wait until it can find a weakness." I never let my eyes leave the junk. Lizard daemons were always a pain, using hit and run tactics. Never know when they're gonna leap out at you.

Mr. Gates and the two remaining guards jogged up. Their faces were bone-white. One of the guards had vomit covering his jacket. *Poor guys. They probably didn't sign up for this.*

"Mr. Berg," panted Mr. Gates. His eyes were wide like dinner plates. It was the first time I had seen him show any emotion.

"What happened?" asked Arno.

"Just after *he*" — he pointed to me — "came in, we had this homeless-looking guy wander up. He was touching the car a lot then approached the gate. We told him to stop, but he kept walking. I was about to apply a little force when his skin just… split open."

"It was a shell," I cut in. "Daemons will kill someone and walk around in their skin so they don't attract attention. Fairly common actually when it comes to hunter-daemons."

"Wait… a daemon?" Mr. Gates's voice cracked with the word.

I shot a curious glance at Arno. "He's not…?"

Arno shook his head. I was surprised not more of his men were in the know.

"How long will it take for the police to get here?" I asked Arno.

"Depends who's working," Arno explained. "Some cops will ignore reports of gunfire here; others want to see if they can catch me doing something bad."

"Which of course you'd never be doing," I muttered under my breath.

Mr. Gates raised a shaking hand. He was reverting into a child, apparently. "Couldn't the cops deal with this when they get here?"

A criminal wishing for the cops help? Hilarious. "No," I said, "when the patrol gets here to investigate the commotion, the daemon will attack. It will hit hard and use the confusion to deal with whatever it came here to deal with."

"You," Arno stated. "It must have smelled you on the car."

"Yeah." I swallowed the lump in my throat. "And I noticed he came for me only after he recognized who I was."

"Then leave!" Mr. Gates yelled.

"No." Arno placed his hand on Mr. Gates's shoulder. "I want to crush this thing. Kraft knows how to hunt daemons, so he stays." He turned to me. "So what do we do?"

I thought for a second. I scanned the yard around me. There was a bunch of heavy machinery and pile upon pile of twisted metal. I let every little detail enter my brain and coalesce into a plan.

I turned back to Arno and his guards with a smile. "We let the lizard chase his prey," I said. I took a quick breath, holstered my revolver, and prepared to start. Part one, screaming. "Screw this!"

Arno was taken aback by the outburst. He was probably more confused when I pulled a one-eighty turn and took off in a dead sprint deeper into the junkyard. I left the group in my dust.

The heap to my left trembled. I pushed whatever extra energy I had through my legs as the junk exploded out and the lizard landed on my heels. It hissed and took after me on all fours. Every wound had completely healed.

It was faster than me, but I didn't have far to go. My Gloves lit up and I punched in the commands. A huge crane passed on my left, and I slapped the chassis with the activated Glove.

The junkyard crane dropped its load as the lizard was nipping at my back. A sedan flattened it against the earth.

The lizard's head stuck out from beneath the metal that pinned it.

"Too slow, ya lizard bastard," I growled with a smirk.

My smile died when I saw the head move. Its eyes opened and trained right on mine. I swear the thing somehow grinned with its reptilian lips. Claws scratched and metal creaked as it started writhing out from under the car. The metal strained. The lizard was doing it. It was escaping. I drew my revolver, reloaded, and prepared to fire.

Arno stepped in before I could squeeze the trigger and planted a big, shiny shoe onto the back of the lizard's neck. He put one beastly hand on either side of its head and began wrenching back. The lizard started screeching an unearthly cry and thrashed harder against the wreckage pinning it down. It was no use. Arno Berg's pure might hauled on its skull until the neck tore and black blood and bile soaked the ground. One last vicious tug silenced the lizard as its head popped off like a dandelion in Arno's palms.

Blood splashed over Arno's bare chest. I started to feel green in the guts. I clutched my stomach and took a few steps back.

"I probably could have been more help if you'd let me in on the plan," Arno said.

"I kinda hoped the car would kill it." I watched the code sink into the earth. The daemon's spirit was returning to Hell.

"Are you alright?" Arno asked, the decapitated head of the daemon still in his hand.

I took to looking at the sky. "This is the second decapitation by tearing I've seen in the last few days. The first was a faery. Which are real, apparently."

"Oh." Arno looked at the head in his hand then tossed it aside. "I am sorry. Did you not know faeries are real?"

"Shut up, Arno. The body will fade into ectoplasm in no time anyway. It's just... gross right now." I took a few deep breaths. A rotting smell was already reaching my nose. "There's a bigger problem. That daemon was directed, and we both know that daemons don't pop into the world and decide to attack someone. Somebody helped it through the Fade."

He growled, "Wizard."

"Exactly." Now I had a wizard gunning for me. I wasn't a fan of them to begin with, but this cemented it. Something I was doing was ruffling a whole lot of feathers. Darklings and wizards, they aren't known to be on the same team. I was getting a whole lot of questions without any answers.

"A wizard could make my brother do what he did," Arno said.

"Arno…"

"Kraft. If you find who did this, you will tell me."

The look in Arno's eyes wasn't one of rage. It was one of sadness and loss. He wanted to avenge the brother he never met. *I could always use an ogre on my side when this whole thing goes down.*

I nodded.

Arno nodded back. "The police may be here any minute. I can deal with my own. Get out and find the wizard."

I took one last look at the headless lizard daemon. Someone sent that thing after me. I took off at a quick jog back to the main gate. Arno's men were dragging away the chunks of flesh that used to be people. Mr. Gates gave me a look that bordered between fear and hatred as I left the yard and jumped into the car.

I was waist deep in waters I knew nothing of. It wouldn't be long until the wizard found out their daemon failed and tried again. The fact that they used a daemon at all was worrisome. Wizards have certain rules they follow as a group, one of which is that they frown upon the summoning and binding of daemons. If this wizard was willing to break that rule, then there was no telling what else he or she would do. Wizards are a certain kind of frightening because they're not some otherworldly being. They're just humans. Humans with power over the elements of the world. Not even me with my Beyondsight could see who a wizard was unless they told me.

I turned the engine over and peeled out from the junkyard. I had no destination in mind, just somewhere else. With all that I had been through, I still had no idea what was really going on.

Chapter 14

A few police cruisers with their sirens blaring flew past me a couple minutes after I left the junkyard. I was sure that Arno had some smooth-talking way of sending the pacers scurrying back to their cruisers. Worrying about whether or not a crime lord could fool the cops was not normally something that entered my mind. But I promised Arno I would find the wizard that possibly killed his brother. I keep my promises.

I squeezed the wheel with both hands. A wizard sent a daemon after me. *Goddamn wizards. Even the rogue ones are a pain in my neck.* I dug into my coat's inside pocket and pulled out a cloth lined with runic symbols. My wizard insurance; I might be needing it soon. I put it in my left pants pocket for easy access. I was sick and tired of being afraid or worried every time there was a twist in the case. It was time to take control again. I parked the car and jumped out.

I sat against the car's hood and watched my breath become visible in the chill air. It wasn't uncomfortably cold yet, but it was noticeable. I was reminded of Jack of Frost's job, wishing there was more I could put into it before the city froze. Instead, I pushed myself off the hood and walked into a nearby alley.

It was mostly empty, save for a few trash bins and dumpsters. I just needed a place where I could focus and talk to myself without drawing attention. It didn't need to be pretty.

I flexed my fingers and took a few deep breaths. *The facts.*

"Five companies have viruses in their systems," I started. "The virus was put there by Milos Ravinich who was hired by Helga Dubois of Orion Industries, Glowing Future's biggest competition. Milos also said Helga had him put the virus in Orion's system, though." I played with the idea of knocking down Helga's door, but thought better of it. I didn't want to go storming in with half-information. "Warren seems to believe the virus isn't doing anything but moving files and being a nuisance. However, hidden in the code was a video file showing images of gluttony, probably some tribute to this Obasin thing.

"Then there's Obasin himself. There is no mention of him in folklore when I looked, but he has at least one faery devoted to him, probably Helga as well. Then there's this wizard that is trying to kill me." I paused. "Or hell, maybe with my luck a daemon *did* just decide to take me out and there's no wizard at all. But that's more worrisome — and nearly impossible — so I'll stick with the wizard."

I paced the alley without a word, occasionally knocking the wall with my knuckles absentmindedly. Nothing was quite piecing together. I still didn't know who wrote the virus. It wasn't Milos; he was a grunt at best. It wasn't Helga; Darklings weren't known for their intricate computer skills, neither were CEOs. There was a third player involved. Plus the wizard and Obasin.

Tension crawled from my stomach to my head. I shouted and kicked a trash can across the alleyway. The crashing metal sound faded into the synth tune of my ringtone. I begrudgingly pulled my phone from my pocket and looked at the screen. INCOMING CALL. MILLIE KRAFT.

My eye twitched and I answered, "Hello, Millie."

"Well it's nice that you actually have your phone on this time," she said dryly.

"I had a meeting that day, and I forgot to turn my phone on. I'm sorry." I placed my head against the cool wall.

"And you didn't call me back about the hospital job. I'm trying to help you here!"

I rubbed the bridge of my nose. "I know you are. I have a job — er — I *had* a job. But I got paid for..." *Wait a second.* "Millie, I need to call you back."

"Don't hang up on m—"

I slid my phone back in my pocket. I was nearly vibrating with excitement; it was starting to all line up.

"I've still been thinking about this like it's corporate espionage!" I shouted to no one. "It's not about businesses, it's about people. And a faery. Forget about Glowing Future. One person gave me ten thousand eurodollars to do essentially nothing and was *very* adamant I stop my investigation. I'm so stupid!"

Frank Harcourt was a fascinating man. He could charm the spots off a leopard and knew it. But, he was a little *too* insistent I leave the job alone. He promised me my entire fee for barely half a job — the rich don't get rich by giving away money. Harcourt was hiding something.

My Gloves jumped to life. I punched Frank Harcourt's information in, clapped my hands together, and then spread them to reveal dozens of screens all about Frank Harcourt. I ran a program to find any connections between him and Helga. They were two starkly different people. However, both became the CEO of their company only two years ago. I wouldn't risk calling that a coincidence.

I shot the public system away and took a look into the private. Bank statements, real estate holdings, licenses. The projection blinked when I moved into the police records. A message scrolled across the screen:

MEET ME AT PORT DE MONTREAL.
NORTH PARKING LOT.
WE NEED TO TALK.
– CALEB

Caleb had locked up the police records *specifically* against my access. I wouldn't be able to break through without directly connecting to the NMPD system. I snorted and shut off the Gloves. Jogging back to the car, I could feel excitement bubbling up from my stomach. Things were finally moving along.

I hopped in the sedan and tore off southbound to Montreal Port. It wasn't rush hour yet, so it was easy enough to cross the city.

As I pulled up to the docks' large parking lot, Caleb stood waiting for me in one of the few open spots. He stepped back as I pulled up, looking solemnly at me. The whole situation was giving me goosebumps.

I stepped out of the car and nodded to Caleb. "What is all this?" I asked.

"This is bad, Kraft. Come on," was all he replied.

He started walking toward the docks. I took a second to build up my courage, and followed after his fleeting form. We moved past a chain-link gate and on toward one of the warehouses that littered the area. It was strange, a few dockworkers wandered by the building, but each seemed to be going out of their way to avoid it. They didn't look afraid or put off; they just appeared to prefer stepping wide around.

"A veil," I surmised.

Caleb didn't show any reaction. "Just an avoidance screen. We don't want to be interrupted."

"And who is 'we'?"

He didn't answer.

We entered the warehouse together. Tall shelves filled the space, each layer covered in crates. The lights cast an ugly florescent glow over Caleb and me, mixing with the late afternoon light streaming in. Down one of the aisles, I saw who we must have come to see.

He was an older man, probably in his fifties. A trim gray beard spread across his jaw, and his graying hair was pulled back into a ponytail. His face came into a hawkish nose arching toward thin lips. He was dressed in a white button-up and beige work pants. Oddly, he covered it all with an open black cloak and a deep purple mantle. I only knew of one group of people who would dress like that.

"Wizard," I said.

Caleb nodded, stepped toward the figure, and proclaimed, "Sir Gerard Strong, wizard of the High Circle, member of the Magi. Welcome to New Montreal." Caleb bowed deeply.

Sir Gerard Strong raised his hand, indicating for Caleb to stand. "Please, not so many formalities, acolyte."

I had to quickly reset my dropped jaw before Caleb caught on to my surprise. I spun my back to Gerard and leaned close to Caleb, never looking into his eyes.

"Kraft—" he started before I could speak.

"Acolyte," I growled, cutting him off harshly. "You're a wizard."

"In-training. Why did you think I had so much information on the Dark?"

"I didn't think it mattered."

"And I didn't think you would appreciate knowing my alignment. I know your hatred of my kind," he said, and stalked past me toward the elder wizard.

I didn't turn around yet. My stare was fixed intently on the closed door from which we had entered. It was true; I had been very upfront about my feelings toward wizards. They liked to believe themselves the alpha and the omega when it came to magical enforcement. While I agree it's important to have someone keeping an eye on the arcane criminals, wizards took to policing the underworld with extreme prejudice and violence. There was a rumor that back in the nineteenth century they had a hand in manipulating a series of fake witch trials as an attempt to deal with a supposed "Dark wizard infestation" in old Northeast America. It was only later that the wizards discovered there was no infestation.

I spun toward the wizards, my face hot with rage. "Did you send a daemon after me?"

"Kraft." Caleb stepped forward, putting himself between Gerard and me. "We'll explain everything; I just need to talk with Gerard quickly."

Gerard laid his hand on Caleb's shoulder, stepping around him. "Caleb did say you were adversarial to our kind."

"Oh, no," I said. "I love it when you send your attack dogs to harass people who haven't done anything wrong."

"Sentinels can be intimidating, I know." He stepped closer to me. "But it's their job to root out Dark-users. They have to be strong. I'll have you know I don't agree with my brethren's stance on Seers like you."

I barely resisted the urge to clap Gerard right in the face, and then give Caleb one for good measure. To wizards, someone with Beyondsight was a step from becoming a full-fledged Dark wizard. I squeezed my hand until my knuckles popped in unison. I knew now how the Sentinels found me all those years ago. Caleb told them.

Gerard sighed and offered his hand to me. "Let's try to start this fresh. It's nice to meet you, Kraft."

I glared at his calloused and weathered hand. Scars rested across his knuckles, telltale signs of a man who had been in many fistfights. There was a strange scar that started in five pieces on the back of his hand, converged into one, and then disappeared up his sleeve. It didn't look like a battle scar; it seemed like something done on purpose. Even for a wizard, that was weird. Gerard Strong. *Who is this guy?*

I let the hand hang. "So what do you want?" I had been preparing to fight a wizard ever since they first knocked my door down. If Gerard sent the daemon, I could take him down. *Probably.*

Gerard gave a small smile and returned his hand to his side. "Fair. We did not send any daemons after you. Though, I am sorry that happened. Are you alright?"

"I'm sure I'll live," I said, shooting a glare at Caleb.

Caleb rolled his eyes.

"Don't be so hard on Caleb," Gerard said. "I was the one who asked him to put the flag on Frank Harcourt's file."

"Why?"

Gerard sighed and put his hands behind his back. The cloak opened a little wider and I could see the outline of a man who took care of himself through his white shirt. "Just in case you started putting together everything during your investigation."

I cocked my head slightly. *What has Caleb been keeping from me?*

"Frank Harcourt is one of the High Circle. What complicates this is he's a member of the Magi," Gerard explained. "You know what that is, right?"

I swore under my breath. "I know all about your secret wizard club. You're telling me one of the High Circle's oligarchy is a Dark wizard?"

Gerard ran his hand over his beard. "What makes you say he's a Dark wizard?"

"Oh, please." I figured there was no reason to let them know how hard it was for me to figure out. "He practically threw money at me to stop me from investigating a Dark incident. Both he and Helga Dubois became the CEOs of their respective companies on nearly the same day. Helga who, by the way, is a faery. As I'm sure you know."

"Actually, she only came to my attention when Caleb came to me after that talk you two had. I have to thank you for that. Our spies amongst the Sidhe Courts say a noble named Orrla has been MIA for a couple years. The High Circle diviners are sure Helga Dubois is Orrla."

I turned my gaze to Caleb. "And when you sent me off to the faery circle? What was that? You know I almost got my ass killed by a spriggan, right?"

Caleb sighed. "I didn't know. I'm sorry you had to go through that, Kraft. I didn't realize at the time Helga was a sidhe. I figured that if you stayed focused on the faeries you wouldn't get in the way of investigating Frank Harcourt."

Gerard pulled an old paper file from his robes. "Harcourt is the subject of an investigation into alliances with Dark powers. This has been going on for months, and I can't have you ruining all the work the Sentinels and I have put in."

"Is this where you tell me to stop looking into him?" I asked, crossing my arms with a glare.

"Despite being a Magi, Harcourt is still very young, barely two hundred years old. The High Circle still sees him as a rebellious youth. I am trying to allow you to continue your investigation into the Glowing Future virus without ruining mine."

Harcourt certainly didn't look like a young punk. I stepped to Caleb. "How old are you?"

"Fifty-four in February."

"You have an awesome moisturizer," I sneered and rubbed my eyes. "How long do you wizards even live for?"

"A while," Gerard said. "If Harcourt knows he has been compromised, he will run and will save whatever he is planning for another decade. Benefit of living ten times longer than normal humans."

"So what do you want me to do?"

Gerard pulled a photo from the folder and held it out. Helga Dubois. "Orrla."

I must have scoffed loudly because Caleb cast me a wicked glare. "I have information that she is involved with the virus, yes. But nothing substantial and certainly nothing to prove anything supernatural."

"Then ask her." Gerard spoke as if it should have been obvious.

My face tried the best impression of shock it could manage to fake. "You think? Maybe I'll just ask her really nicely, and she'll explain the whole scheme to me." The sarcasm dripped out.

Gerard ignored the malice in my tone. He looked back to Caleb. "He really doesn't get faeries, does he?"

Caleb shook his head. "He's an odd one."

"Please don't talk about me like I'm not here," I said.

The elder wizard turned back to me. "Faeries can't lie, Mr. Kraft. It's not in their nature, nor within their power to. They can twist words and omit facts, but they can never lie."

A light bulb flashed on in my head. "That can be useful information to me." I leaned toward Caleb. "Which would have been good to know earlier."

"I forget you don't know about faeries!" Caleb protested.

Gerard chuckled. "So will you leave Frank Harcourt be?"

"Helga — or I suppose, Orrla — is back on my radar. But if this leads back to Harcourt, I *am* going after him. Understand, spellslinger?" I dug my hands into my jean pockets and glared at Gerard. I was prepared to go at him if necessary. My left hand played with the runic cloth I had moved to that pocket earlier. Wizards always underestimate other mortals, which is one of their weaknesses. Still, I hoped Gerard wouldn't take offense to my reply.

He stared at me for what seemed like forever. Caleb's eyes grew wide with fear, and I could see his hands clench.

Finally, Gerard nodded.

I didn't wait to see if he was going to say anything. I released my grip on the cloth in my pants pocket and gave a phony salute to the wizards. The smell of dirty steel started to tear into my nostrils; I needed to get out. So, I turned on my heel, pulled my hat down tight, and did just that.

Selene's car came to life and I slammed it into gear, tearing off to the street. I was incensed. Caleb knew my problem with wizards, which was exactly the reason why he didn't tell me he was one. I shouldn't be angry, I guess. If he'd told me earlier, I would have ditched him earlier — and then probably would have died earlier without his help. He was still the same guy. *Wasn't he?*

I could have overreacted. I had felt betrayed, and I lashed out. Wizards just got into my head. If I kept on being rational I would lose all my rage. I needed as much of it as I could keep.

I turned left at the next set of lights. It wouldn't be long until I was back at Orion Industries. I wasn't unprepared anymore. I was tired of being afraid of everything. And I was ready to unleash hell on a faery.

Chapter 15

The security for Orion Industries was pitiful. I was in without breaking a sweat. After the hell to get in to Tartarus Securities, Orion might as well have left its back door unlocked. As the elevator glided to the penthouse office, I planned how to approach Orrla. I briefly considered a more indirect route, easing the answers out of her through guile. But she was a faery. From what I'd heard lately, if anyone knew the ins and outs of playing around with words, it would be her. Direct route it was. I tightened the bandana over my face. *Everyone has to die someday.*

Besides, I had some anger issues to work out.

The doors opened to one elegant hallway. A desk sat empty close to where I stood. On its surface was a small screen that read DIANA FORSYTH. It was like looking at a tombstone now. I passed through a field of velvet and silk. I flipped open the wrist zippers on my coat, now black once again along with my hat. At the far end of the hallway was a set of double doors. I slid six rounds into six chambers in my gun. I hit the doors hard.

"We need to talk, Ms. Dubois!" I hollered, putting on my deepest voice.

Orrla jumped from her desk. "Who are you?" She made a lunge for the glass top. I whipped up my revolver and fired. Cracking glass flew into the air. Orrla recoiled in fear. She was still playing the human-card.

My Gloves lit up. "I prefer some privacy." I tapped on my wrist and the desk system sent out a DO NOT DISTURB message across the building.

"What do you want?" Orrla cried, pressing herself against the window.

"Stop with the act!" I slowed my gait but never took my revolver sights off her. "The whole scared-little-woman play doesn't work on me, faery."

Her expression changed. Like flipping a coin. Gone was the fearful woman pressed against the window. She stretched her back straight and stepped forward.

"Didn't your mom teach you it's rude to barge in on a lady?" Orrla taunted.

"My mom's dead," I sneered, stepping closer. "And you're no lady, Orrla."

A soft smile spread across her lips. "So, you must be the Seer. I heard that one of you was in town." She circled me like a predator.

I kept the barrel of my revolver pointed squarely to her chest. The fabric of her business suit strained as... *Were her breasts growing?* I shook my head and fired a shot just before her next step. She stopped and smiled again.

"Enough with the glamour," I growled.

She, *er*, deflated.

"Are you making fun of me?" I asked.

"Why would I?" She put her hand to her chest, mocking shock. "You're the big man with the gun, and I'm just a poor scared lady. I will admit that mask gave me a fright, but you're that journalist from earlier, aren't you? Very good. I could have sworn you were just another annoying reporter looking for a scoop." Her hips swayed with the word "scoop."

I rolled my eyes and pulled down my bandana. *What is it with these faeries and sex?*

"You hired Milos Ravinich to infiltrate and put viruses on companies' systems," I said.

"Is that really what you want to talk about?"

"It's been on my mind lately."

She licked her lips and stepped closer. "What will you do?" she asked with a voice like honey. "Threaten me?"

"Nope." I fired a round into her leg.

Green blood spurted from the wound and she dropped, screaming.

"I know. It's not iron." I crouched next to her, tapping the revolver against her head. "Those kind of bullets are a little hard to come by. But I bet it still hurts like hell."

Orrla's cries turned to a grimace. The bullet I fired spat back out of her wound and the flesh closed.

"What was that supposed to do?" she asked, returning to her feet as though she had merely stumbled.

I reached into my jean's pocket with my free hand and pulled out Diana's ID card. I tossed it at Orrla's feet. Orrla gave me a "what-are-you-doing" look and picked it up. A wash of realization came over her face, and she raised a slicing glare to meet my eyes.

"Where is she?" asked Orrla, the honey gone from her voice.

"We had a small altercation and she just kind of... lost her head."

Orrla's mouth curled into a snarl. She stepped forward until my revolver's barrel was pressed against her forehead. Her icy blue eyes never left mine.

"Do you know who you're dealing with?" she growled.

My free hand went into my pocket again. This time I felt the metal of the same nail I dug into Arno. I lashed out. I half expected her to move out of the way, but I must have really gotten under her skin — literally now, as the nail embedded deep into the front of her shoulder.

An unearthly scream emitted from her mouth and she fell back. She began writhing in pain and screeching with such fury that I thought her throat would tear. The sound dampeners in the walls better be excellent, or the entire city was going to hear her. She tried desperately to dig the nail out, but every time she touched the iron, her skin blistered and burned.

"Why the virus?" I shouted over Orrla's cries. "What is the purpose? Why on so many systems?"

"Fuck you, Seer!" She spat green fluid, staining the once nice carpet of her office.

I kicked hard at her injured shoulder. "I am not in the mood!"

She screeched again. "I'll talk!"

"Say you won't harm me."

"I won't harm you here!"

A faery can never tell a lie, I reminded myself. I dropped to my knee and dug my fingers into the putrid wound. The nail had sunken in deep thanks to my kick. Orrla groaned slightly, and I felt the iron. I yanked hard and the nail came out with a gush of green fluid. The skin around the wound had gone a pale grayish-blue, like a corpse. I gave her some distance and tossed the nail across the room. I had no intention of putting that grotesque sight back into my pocket.

"Now talk," I said.

She panted hard and clutched her shoulder. Blood still leaked from the hole; that one wasn't going to be closing as quickly as the first. Without the iron burning through her, at least she could talk.

"What do you know of Obasin?" she asked through her breaths.

"I've heard of him around."

"He's a power beyond your impotent mortal mind. The Great Devourer."

"What does this have to do with the virus?" I stepped closer, sights still trained on her. Another shot wouldn't kill Orrla, but it would hurt.

She lunged up and toward me, faster than I had ever seen anyone move. I squeezed the trigger, but she was already past my outstretched arm. The round struck harmlessly against the far wall as her hands slid to the sides of my neck, the moist blood freezing my skin. I told myself that she couldn't harm me, but it wasn't wholly reassuring. She kept moving, and her lips pressed against mine.

Frost crept up my spine. My body went numb. I reminded myself she was a monster. But she wasn't like the spriggan; no beast hid under a sidhe's skin. Her hips drove against me. She pulled me forward until I bent. Her tongue seeped forward and I could feel its icicle touch in my mouth. My body told me it should be pleasant, but my brain revolted. I couldn't feel anything but cold as my breath was drawn from my lungs.

She broke the kiss, followed by a final lick on my lips. Her hips stayed close, pressed tight against my body. I felt as though I had spent the night in a freezer; my fingers were numb and my breath came out with a mist. Something felt wrong in my brain. Her eyes opened slowly and met mine.

"You've seen his glory," she murmured.

"W-what did you do?" My voice seemed resistant to working at first.

"Relax, I can't harm you, remember? Talking is such a human act. I expedited the process."

She read my memories. There are creatures of the Dark who can drag thoughts out, but I had never met one who did it with such... horrifying pleasure.

"He promised." She placed her freezing cheek against mine and I could feel her breath against my ear. "He promised that He would eat the sins of this world. Those who do not accept Him into their souls are destined to be devoured. But we of the Endless Hunger will have our sins eaten and be finally satiated."

Her words drilled into my brain, like a worm determined to chew through the flesh. "A being of that strength would need an enormous amount of power to push through the Fade."

"It is already happening."

Something clicked. Something that I may have thought in the very recesses of my mind, but that I never really considered a possibility until now. "The virus... It's..."

"Obasin," Orrla hissed. Her hand tightened on the nape of my neck. "Or at least a part of Him."

"An actual piece of him..." That would be why the virus had been acting so strangely. Generating the FEAST.AVC file. Causing nightmares. It was the reaching finger of an aberrant horror. They found a way to put a god into a computer. "He's drawing energy through the Network."

"The Network passes through every one of you humans in every moment, every day. It holds an imprint of your sorrow, your pain, your hunger, and carries that energy to our Lord. And soon He will be born in the womb of you mortal's technology. But it's not too late for you," she moaned and shifted her hips.

A wrenching sickness grew in my stomach. Her green hands rubbed across my neck, spreading her blood around.

I threw myself back and brought the sights of my gun up to bear on her.

"I'll just shut down Glowing Future's hub. That will stop him."

She stepped forward again, brushing her hair against the gun barrel. "That won't stop all of Obasin."

"Why should I believe you?" I slid away from her. I didn't want to risk her touching me again. Who knew what she could do without technically "harming me."

She gave me a flat look.

"Because faeries can't lie, right," I sighed.

"Did you really not know faeries were real before this week?" She let out a haunting cackle.

I guess my lack of faery knowledge also transferred when she kissed me. Who knew what else she stole. Rage flooded my veins. I stopped backing up — instead, I pushed forward. "What did you take from me? When you read my mind."

"Worried about your secrets?" she asked, stepping back until she was against the wall. "I didn't see everything, but what I did see…" She mimed a shiver. "Seeing your parents get torn apart must have left quite a scar on a young body. What do you call the daemon that did it? The—"

"The Raven."

"Oh, yes." Orrla ran her fingers along the side of my revolver. "Raven daemons are vicious bastards, but they rarely do things without a reason. Do you ever wonder why? About your parents? About that blonde whore, Alexis?"

I cracked Orrla in the jaw with the side of my revolver. "My past is not your playground."

"But it is." She cracked her jaw back in place. "This world will belong to Endless Hunger."

"I'm not afraid of your cult," I said firmly.

The sidhe laughed a bone-chilling laugh. "I would not have told you all this if I wasn't sure it would come true," she warned. "Run along, little Seer. Enjoy your world while it lasts."

I contemplated shooting her again but realized it wouldn't solve anything. I could fill her with holes, but without iron, she wouldn't stay down for long. I snapped the revolver back into its holster and backed away to the exit, not allowing my eyes to drift from the gruesome faery. Green blood stained much of Orrla's body and carpet. It was a macabre sight I was glad to be rid of.

The elevator opened immediately. No one had used it since I had come up. I stepped inside and pressed the third-floor button, not wanting to pop out in the lobby covered in faery blood. At least I had finally gotten some answers. The movie file on Glowing Future's system was an image of Obasin's power. Milos probably put the same one on all those other companies' systems. The images of gluttony were a tribute to him, but adjusted by what my mind feared to see. That was why I appeared on screen at the end. I wondered briefly what poor Daniels had witnessed.

Orrla and Harcourt were attempting to summon forth Obasin as part of that "Endless Hunger" cult. A faery and a wizard working together to bring a Dark god into the world. That was why Harcourt was so intent on getting me away from the investigation — he wanted the virus to do its job. Obasin was feeding through the Network and getting stronger. That meant Harcourt was probably the one who sent the lizard after me at the junkyard.

The elevator stopped on the third floor. I peeked into the hallway, but no one was in sight. Surely, the employees were all working very hard for their faery overlord. I would need to find a bathroom to clean myself off before figuring out my next move.

I opened the door to one several feet from the elevator. The lights came on automatically in the small bathroom, and I locked the door behind me. In the mirror, I could clearly see the green substance smeared around my neck and jaw, staining my bandana. Orrla was at least a little courteous — the amount of blood on my shirt and coat was minimal. Only a dot here and there.

Using water, soap, and massive amounts of paper towel, I was able to work away at the stains. I was reminded of a case with the IB where we were chasing down a serial killer from the Asianic Collective. He was apparently inspired by a murder two hundred years earlier called "The Black

Dahlia Murder." He would slice into his victim's — always a young woman — face and bisect her at the waist. Nothing supernatural. Just normal human brutality. When we finally took him down, he attempted to bisect himself and I ended up with most of his blood on my hands. Blood is never easy to wash off, doesn't matter where it came from. After that case, I am better with gore. At least somewhat.

I watched the green blood lighten with the water and run down the drain. It didn't sound as if Obasin was ready to be released; he must still be feeding on whatever energy he could get. Still, Orrla was sure of his imminent arrival.

Orrla probably used her company's funds to pay for Milos's work. And it wasn't beyond the imagination for a wizard like Harcourt to mesmerize a board of directors into voting in whatever CEO he wanted, such as him and Orrla. That would've given them two big corporations to utilize and to separate the duties so that the always-paranoid High Circle couldn't figure it out until it was too late. That was why they hired a thug like Milos to sneak Obasin in, rather than just having Harcourt put him in himself. They couldn't risk the CEO being pulled into a scandal for sabotaging his own systems before their great god was born. Harcourt probably assisted in getting Milos past the security check. These people were playing it safe and slow.

It was starting to look more every second as though Harcourt was a mind mage. If anyone could make Rick Oslo shoot up Glowing Future, it was him. But why? Did he stumble upon something he shouldn't have? Did Harcourt have to shut him up? If so, why did Harcourt make Rick go out in such a public way?

I tossed a blood-soaked paper towel into the trash and inspected myself in the mirror. My knees gave out. I clutched onto the sink for support before dropping to the tile floor. *How dare she dig into my past?* I spent years putting my parents' deaths behind me. I hadn't thought of the Raven seriously in forever. That kitchen soaked in blood. She brought it up as if it was nothing. *That woman sends shivers up my spine.*

Actually, she literally sent shivers up my spine. I jumped to my feet and Beyondsighted myself in the mirror. Orrla's code flowed along where her blood used to be. It was the same as I saw in the elevator a couple days earlier. But I looked deeper. Something was off. Something was hiding between her lines. It was too faded to read properly. It could have been Winter energy, but in its diluted state, there was no way to tell.

It was something at least. I didn't know what kind of magic sidhe could throw out; it wasn't enough evidence on its own. Jack mentioned cold faeries, Unseelie I believe. She could have been one of those. I dug out the last bit of faery blood that had gotten beneath my fingernails in the exchange. My neck was raw from the scrubbing, but clean as a prude's browser history. I took a few extra breaths to push my past back where it belonged. I grabbed my phone from my pocket, intending to call up Caleb. As much as I was still pissed at him, the High Circle needed to know that Harcourt and Orrla were trying to summon a Dark deity. They could handle them far better than I ever could.

The line rang half a dozen times before I heard Caleb's Irish cadence. "You've reached Caleb Brennan, please leave a message, and I'll ring ya back."

I swore softly before the tone. "Caleb, it's Kraft. I need to talk to that wizard, Gerard. It's important," I said and shoved the phone back into my pocket. *Those wizards better be able to rain some fiery hell on those Endless Hunger freaks. I'm really choosing the lesser of two evils.*

The High Circle would have to wait; I was finally going home.

Chapter 16

The days seemed to be going by quicker. The sun was already set as I sat on the train that brought me home after dropping off Selene's car. She asked me if I was staying over again. I almost said yes before deciding it was probably best for me to go home. I hadn't had a hit of Medioxyl in over a day, and I could feel my body crying for some. Besides, I promised myself to not be afraid anymore.

There was almost no sound as the train glided along, but for the occasional soft hum of the electromagnets. I'd ridden this train so many times I could count the four minutes it took to cross Laval Preservation Park, though without any lights in the outside world, the view was mostly a reflection of the train's interior. Only a dozen people were spread across the car, a dwindling evening traffic of folks trying to get home.

For the first time in days, I let my mind relax and think of nothing. I ran my fingers over my bandana's fabric. The green had disappeared a couple of minutes earlier, turning to colorless ectoplasm. I could imagine my bed and how much I longed to sleep in it again. Staying with Selene had its perks, but there was nothing quite like your own home. *What was I even so worked up about last time?*

Slowly, I realized the train car had fallen silent, not even the sporadic conversations from its passengers reaching my ears. It was empty. They were there when we left the last stop, I was sure. There was an eerie, heavy feeling to the car — an otherworldly pressure squeezing me.

I turned back to the window. I froze. That flesh and sweat creature from the club was outside. Its formless face pressed against the glass. Blood and pus oozed from its body as it slid across the surface, leaving a grotesque circle. The brow of the thing cracked, sending fluid splattering against the glass. The crack spread, and I began to feel my stomach spinning. I couldn't look away out of some kind of morbid fascination.

The split had nearly bisected the fleshy mound when it began pulling apart. It was hollow, like a slimy pea pod. A black expanse — much bigger than the outside — filled the thing's body. It was as though I was looking into a starless night sky. I peered into the dripping blackness spreading out into eternity. From within the void came movement, some being tearing its way out. I tried to make out the shape as it moved closer. There, deep in the disgusting stomach of this creature, was a black shrouded figure. It had long black hair that nearly hid dead daemon eyes. It was covered in the red of my parent's blood.

I threw myself back from the window, landing hard on the train car's floor. A snicker came from behind me, and the car had passengers again. I rubbed my eyes of that final image and turned back to the window. The Raven and Obasin had disappeared. No trace of them having ever been there.

I stumbled back to my feet as the train arrived at my station. I hastily left the car behind and rushed off the platform.

Instinctively, I kept to the bright streetlights. The glow of my apartment tower entrance called for me to run. The shadows chased me. I crashed through the door and leaped into the lift. My heart rate rose with the elevator. I pressed my head against the door; it felt like something was crushing my chest.

The elevator reached the thirty-first floor quickly. I hustled out of the box and down the hallway. Everything around me was spinning and blurring together. I spotted my door down the hall. *Just one hit. The Medioxyl will calm me down.* I swore at myself for giving that last one to Milos yesterday. I needed it right now, more than ever.

"Sigmund!" came the familiar voice of Ms. Heidecker.

I snapped around to where she had called from and nearly choked on my breath. Her leash was attached to... some creature. It had the basic shape of a monstrous dog, but it was all wrong. Sores and veins covered its red and slimy body, as though someone had turned the thing inside out. It grimaced a desire that felt far too human for its form.

"Feast," it moaned.

I shoved my door open so hard it snapped the doorstop and broke the crack in the wall even wider. I barely got my body inside before I slammed the door shut behind me. My head pounded a heavy metal beat. I headed directly into my bathroom. I tore open the mirror cupboard, knocking most of the Medioxyl out. I was able to get a shaky grip on one injector. I slammed the mirror shut and was met with the grinning face of the Raven.

I threw myself back and drew Milos's Glock. I fired a shot into the mirror and crashed into the tub behind me. The shower curtain rod fell down on me. I fought with the curtain for a few seconds, trying to get my face and arm out of its twisting embrace. I finally tore it aside and pointed the pistol at the smashed mirror. The broken Medioxyl dripped into the sink below. The one I grabbed was nowhere to be found.

I went to wipe the sweat away only to find that at some point I had started crying. I was far beyond caring. I sat in the tub, pistol aimed at the broken mirror, shards covering the ground. *What does Obasin want?*

I sat in the bathroom for an hour, refusing to move, before I heard a knock at my door.

The possibility of another person being around was enough to get me out of the tub, leaving Milos's gun near the drain. Mine still sat on my hip as I walked quickly around the corner. The door was only a few steps in front of me, and I kept my eyes on the shadows as I took them. I threw the door open.

Selene stood on the other side, wearing a coat and a smile.

"Howdy," she said. "You seemed kinda down when you dropped the car off earlier so I thought I would come cheer you up."

She stepped forward and put her hand on my chest. I looked down to see a pair of purple lacy underwear hidden in her palm. She smiled and threw them into the apartment.

"I won't be needing these so—" Her eyes widened. "Jesus, Kraft. Look at your face!" She pushed me back into the kitchen area and sat me down on a stool. Looking behind her to the wall mirror, I saw what she was taking about. Protruding from my cheek a couple centimeters was a chuck of mirror. It must have lodged itself in there when I shot it.

"Whoa." It was all I could think to say.

Selene leaned in close and inspected the wound. I was slightly distracted by the view down her coat to where some sexy-looking garb waited. She seemed intent on playing nurse though. *Damn.*

"There's Medioxyl in my bathroom," I suggested, sliding off the coat I forgot I was wearing and letting it drop to the floor.

"Not for something as small as this. It's dangerous to overuse that stuff. You do know that right, Kraft?"

If she was trying to imply something, I wasn't in the mood. My brain still ached from my journey home, and the image of the Raven's grin was burned into my retinas. "Just get it out," I said, not knowing if I was referring to the shard in my cheek or the image in my mind.

Selene nodded. She backed into the bathroom before I could say anything to stop her.

"The hell?" came her voice. "Did you shoot your mirror?"

I winced with her cry. "I just tripped, that's all," I lied.

She came back in with the first aid kit I kept by the toilet. It had been used more than I would have liked, but that just made it a good investment. "There's a bullet hole in the wall behind the cabinet. Don't lie to me." She put the kit on the kitchen island and popped the latches. "I like to believe you respect me more than that."

I briefly wondered why she didn't question me on the Medioxyl. Maybe even to her, some things are not worth getting into. "I do respect you, it's just… difficult," I said.

Her fingers poked the tender area around the shard, making me wince. I hadn't even felt the glass until she mentioned it, but now a slow throb of pain was growing around the wound.

"Difficult how?" asked Selene, taking a pair of tweezers from the kit and starting to move for the shard.

"Difficult in that I can tell you won't beli— OW!" I hollered as she touched the glass.

Selene sighed and gave me a hard glare. "Don't start being a baby now."

"I'm sorry that a chunk of glass in my face hurts."

"Deep breath, babe." She smiled and tore out the glass.

I proceeded to speak in terms that would have made the more prudish blush.

"Huh, it was a little bit barbed I guess," Selene remarked, then dropped the bloodstained shard on the counter and grabbed some antiseptic spray. "Why wouldn't I believe you?"

If only she knew. "It's really crazy and, honestly, I don't want you to know about stuff like this. It's better that way."

"You're starting to worry me." She laughed half-heartedly. "Is this similar to that thing you carved into your door? I know you're superstitious and all, but you have to pull it back a little."

I looked into Selene's emerald green eyes. Her heritage had always been a mystery to me — dark hair, brown skin, and green eyes — but I felt it would be inappropriate to ask. Part of me wanted to tell her everything about the Dark. I wanted someone to talk to so I wouldn't feel so goddamn glitchy. Even if she did believe me, who knew if she would be able to handle it? How would you feel if you learned all the monsters your parents told you didn't exist were wandering around?

She finished the dressing in silence. The sealing spray that went over the gauze and tape spread warmth across my cheek. She snapped the first aid kit shut and slid it away. She gently laid her hands on my face then slid them to the back of my neck.

"You're just getting yourself worked up." She squeezed my nape. "You haven't been sleeping well; you've been killing yourself over this job. You just need to relax."

"I wish, S," I replied, removing her hands from my neck and putting them back at her sides. "But it's not that easy."

Selene sighed and kissed me lightly on my good cheek. "You stink. Go have a shower. I'll see if I can wrangle us up something to eat."

I nodded and watched Selene begin picking through my cupboards. I hopped off the stool, dropped my phone into its mount before heading back to the bathroom, and closed the door behind me. The broken mirror still laid strewn across the floor, so I used a towel to sweep the shards into the corner. I disrobed, replaced the curtain rod, and moved the gun from the tub to the counter before turning on the water.

My body ached from lack of sleep. The hot water was a godsend splashing across my skin. I checked to make sure the sealing spray was keeping the water off the dressing. My right shoulder was feeling plenty better, even though it was entirely covered in a huge bruise. It wasn't the worst injury I've ever had. I expected to be getting much worse ones in the future, unfortunately.

I shut off the water and wrapped a towel around myself. The belt with my revolver still in its holster hung over the toilet. I left it where it lay. I tossed my hat onto the floor as I returned to the main area. Some clean clothes were piled next to my bed, so I threw them on and turned back to the kitchen. Selene had just finished making pasta and was dishing it out into two bowls when the Dark code appeared.

It encircled the door, seeping in through the cracks along the frame. The code was familiar; I had last seen one like it sinking into the earth at the junkyard. Another damned lizard. Caleb's symbol wasn't meant to keep out physical threats.

Selene couldn't see the code. She smiled sweetly when she saw me approach from my bed, then stopped, raised an eyebrow, and asked, "What's wrong?"

The door exploded in. Selene shrieked as I slid to the side, the heavy door soaring past me and crashing into the adjacent wall, landing hard on my bed.

The lizard stood hunched in the doorway. Its green-black scales trembled with rage when it saw me. This one was bigger than the one at the junkyard. Its current posture put it about half a foot taller than me — its full height would be dwarfing. A black bile dripped from its crooked, razor teeth set in a grim crocodile smile.

"Kraft..." Selene's voice was weak. Her eyes were wide in fear. Something about incredible monsters seemed to revert people to a child-like state. Selene did not move an inch; she was only a few feet from the daemon. She was frozen.

Thankfully, it seemed too preoccupied with me to worry about her. I could see mine and Milos's guns sitting in the bathroom out of the corner of my eye. But if I moved to get them, the lizard would follow me in and destroy me in tight quarters.

I guess I should have been afraid, but I was pissed. That thing had entered my home. This was where I lived, and it thought it could just walk in. I was stupid enough not to think Orrla would retaliate. She must have told Harcourt about our encounter. Harcourt expected he could try again at my house where I might be taken off guard. What he forgot was that there was always something to be said for home-field advantage.

The lizard didn't let out any battle cry. It must have realized that soundproof walls were not soundproof doors. It wanted me dead without any interruption. It lunged forward, jaws ready to tear out my throat.

If you're going to booby trap your home, the entrance hall is always a good place to start. I took two steps forward and dropped to my knees. I placed one palm to the ground and poured my energy out.

It was one of those runes I'd offered to Ali Thorn. Even laypeople have a small amount of control over magic. It's not enough to summon the elements of the world to your beck and call, but usually enough to activate simple runes. I felt my power flow through the channels cut in the floor, to the symbol hiding under the rug the lizard was flying over.

Pure force ripped vertically from the rune carved into the floor, throwing the rug away. It struck the lizard hard in the chest and sent it in a line drive to the roof. The daemon impacted with a sickening thud, followed by a crunch as gravity brought it back to the ground.

That had to of hurt, but it didn't kill. I took advantage of the stunning strike and hurried to the kitchen. I vaulted over the island to Selene's side. The daemon was already shaking the cobwebs away when I pressed the small button under the island's lip. The cupboards behind me groaned slightly and slid upward. I moved to my personal occult cupboard.

"Selene, I need you to—"

Two loud cracks spun me to the fight, then two softer claps rang as bullets bounced off the lizard's scales.

Selene stood solidly with a folding, holdout pistol outstretched. She had taken some shots at the recovering daemon, but the rounds bounced off its armor-like scales. Her mouth hung open in shock at the obvious lack of effect.

"You were carrying?" I cried, ears still ringing from the gunfire.

"I wasn't going to walk around in lingerie without a piece!"

Point taken.

"What is *that*?" she yelled, never taking the weapon's sights off it.

"*That* I can deal with." I spun back to my secret nook as the daemon returned to its feet. I reached past the odds and ends, charms, and talismans. My fingers clasped around a thick, white devilbane rod.

"Kraft!" Selene screamed.

I took the rod in both hands, each at a different end and spun back. The daemon was charging, but I was ready for it. It bounded onto the island. Its teeth promised to tear me apart. I held the rod before me and Selene, then snapped it like chalk.

The lizard was midway through leaping off the island when a great light poured forth. It radiated with such brilliance that it filled every darkened corner of my apartment. I didn't feel any burn, and I didn't need to close my eyes to protect them from the light. The daemon screeched and flew back, crashing alongside where the door had flown earlier.

I didn't wait for the light to disappear. I tapped the glass on the island counter and a display projected. I selected WATER CAGE. A line depressed into the floor, bisecting the room and running along the balcony door. Water shot from the wall shared with the bathroom and flowed along the path, tracing a line of running water to trap the daemon.

The daemon saw this, and I thought it was going to go wild. Instead, it snorted and crouched low to the floor. Nevertheless, it kept a glare on me, seeing if I was going to make some kind of mistake.

"Kraft, please, tell me what that is," Selene said.

It wasn't quite being slapped with a leprechaun but it probably had the same effect. "That is a, uh, lizard daemon," I replied.

"Demon?"

"Daemon. With an 'a'."

"Okay… I guess I can see that."

She was taking it better than I thought she would.

"Why is it just sitting there? And why do you have a stream in your apartment?"

"Hellborn creatures have trouble crossing running water. It varies on the species. Vampires, for example, lose their power. But summoned daemons don't have bodies of their own, so they will disappear and their spirits are returned to Hell weaker. As for the stream, I spent a few months retrofitting my apartment for things like this. I told the building manager it was feng shui or something."

Selene nodded but I couldn't tell how much she was actually absorbing. I didn't think she had blinked since I started talking.

"And the light? What was—"

"Rod made from devilbane." I held up one half. The rod had become a dusty gray. "It's a compound made from silver and other—" Her eyes took on a glazed look. "Er, it's magic."

"Magic." Her voice made it sound as if I'd told her the sky was purple. I watched her look from me to the daemon, then back to me. Her face drained of all color and she launched herself to the sink, emptying her stomach in one large hurl.

"That's my girl," I muttered under my breath.

"What do we do?" She spoke without bringing her head up.

Giving Selene some space, I reached high over her to the armory nook. I grabbed a length of rope, a piece of chalk, and a bowl of powdered devilbane. "We could wait until the magic keeping it here dissolves," I explained. "But who knows how long that's going to be. He's a relatively low-level creature so I'm pretty sure I can exorcise him back to Hell. Normally, I would want a real exorcist to do this, but he's already bound behind that stream so I should be fine."

I think Selene nodded in agreement but I couldn't tell. She had flopped full chest against the counter, head lying on the granite. I noticed she had placed her gun next to the sink she had filled with puke. I collapsed the pistol to the size of a large lipstick container and pocketed it.

The smell of vomit wafted from the sink, so I ran the water to wash it away. Selene eased the water off again.

"I'll clean it when I'm done," she moaned.

I patted her lightly on the back. *At least I have someone to talk to now.* I took my supplies and kneeled next to the stream, making sure it stayed between me and the daemon.

The daemon crawled on all fours until it mirrored me on the other side. It never looked away. It stared across the invisible wall to where I worked. Being watched like that was unnerving, but I got down to ritualizing nevertheless.

"What are you doing?" Selene called from the kitchen.

"The secret to magic is creating connections," I replied. I might have been taking advantage of the situation a little, but it was nice to have someone to explain the stuff to. "Most of performing a ritual is the symbology of the act. In this case, I have the rope to symbolize a binding and dragging, and the devilbane to symbolize acting against a Hellborn."

I swung the rope lightly across the stream and brushed the lizard's nose. The daemon didn't move, but all I needed was the contact to lock-in. I recoiled the rope with the daemon's energy on it.

With the chalk, I drew a circle around the coil of rope and the bowl of devilbane. I strained hard to push my will into the circle and seal it shut. Magic doesn't actually come from the inside, it's an ambient energy. Wizards are people who are better at absorbing the magic around them — they have a larger magic holding bottle, as some people describe it. I didn't have a very large bottle, but more than the commoner.

Must be the Beyondsight. A wizard would be able to shut the circle with half a thought.

"The circle creates a container for magical energy," I continued. I didn't know if Selene was even listening. "Sealing it creates a vacuum of power — in this case, sealing the magic in. Ambient magic will flow in, but not out, creating a kind of battery for slowly charging my spell. It will take some time."

"Oh, God, is that smell my vomit?" Selene asked.

I was so distracted by setting up my exorcism, I had failed to notice a sickly-sweet odor fill the room. It seemed to be coming from the daemon. I couldn't imagine why a creature from Hell would emit such a stench unless...

"Selene, hide! It's calling in backup!" I whirled to the hole that used to be my front door just in time to see another lizard — this one blood red — bound into the room. It whipped past the kitchen where Selene had dived behind the island.

It coiled up and sprang forward faster than I could react, slamming into my chest and pinning me to the floor. It opened its mouth, full of razor sharp teeth and dripping with saliva. It lunged. I moved my head out of the way and its bile-spewing maw struck the ground. I could feel its hot breath on my ear.

The green daemon leaped around with joy, egging its friend on to devour me. I felt Selene's pistol in my pocket. A self-defense gun carried four rounds. She had fired two.

I tore the gun from my pocket and flipped it open as the red lizard brought its head back for another bite. *Crack-crack!* The rounds ripped into the daemon's left eye. Blackened blood dripped from the wound onto my face, but the shots didn't have the power to push it back. Instead, I had a one-eyed, pissed off daemon pinning me down.

I'd lost track of how many times I'd nearly died. One time would have been too many. The daemon scowled down at me through its one good eye, deciding where to bite first. I could feel Obasin laughing at me from across the Fade. *At least I'll make sure this lizard chokes on me.* I only hoped Selene had the good sense to run.

Light. Brilliant, brilliant light!

The red daemon flew off me and over the stream, coming apart into ectoplasmic goo. Its green friend cried out in hell-bent rage, sending black spittle back over the water and striking my face.

I rolled with the last of the strength I could muster to the exorcism circle. It sat intact, powered up. Spells need a verbal cue to fire. It didn't really matter what the words were as long as you believed they'd work. One phrase seemed to fit very well here...

"Go to Hell."

I wish I could say there was some brilliant flash or magical release of power, but one second a screaming daemon, the next nothing. All was quiet.

My heartbeat rattled my ribcage. I rolled to look at my saving light. Selene stood in the kitchen, eyes wider than I had ever seen them before. She clutched two halves of a devilbane rod.

"I swear to God," I panted, "you have never looked sexier."

She dropped the rod and rushed to my side. I slowly pushed myself to sitting, only for Selene to knock me back down, the gore on my face not putting her off, apparently. I thought she was going to cry, but no sobs came. We lay in silence.

Seconds became minutes, but we didn't move. I didn't know if she was holding me because she was worried about me, or if she was clinging on to the only thing she was sure of at the moment.

I hated myself for doing it to her. It was my fault. If I wasn't in her life, she would have been able to keep on living in innocent bliss. Maybe. Too late. There was nothing but the sound of her breathing in my ear. Then the damnedest thing happened.

The phone rang.

I sighed and started to stand but Selene held me down.

"I'll get it," she said softly.

I didn't want to fight, so I did nothing as Selene shakily returned to her feet and moved to the phone holder by the door.

She popped the cell from the holder. "Hello? Kraft's phone," she answered. She cocked an eyebrow in my direction. "Who is Harlequin?"

Aww, hell. "Um, a waitress from Sparc."

She blinked, paused, then blinked again. She covered the receiver with one hand. "The club? Why is a waitress from a club calling you? Why is her name Harlequin?"

"I have no idea." I just dealt with two beings of Hell, I didn't want to deal with Selene's jealously. It's amazing how the real world can reset your senses. Selene's gaze burned through me. I scrambled to my feet, swiped the cell phone out of her hand, and moved away. "This is Kraft."

"Uh, hey. It's Harlequin, from Sparc?" She sounded weak, as if she had been crying.

"How did you get my number?"

"My brother works for the police. Apparently, they have a file for you."

I'm going to need to deal with that.

She spoke again, quieter. "I need to talk to you."

I looked at Selene standing amused in the kitchen and stepped farther away. "What is this about?"

"Milos. He… he came in to the bar today, and he was screaming about demons and monsters and he was crying and he… he…"

Oh, no.

"He shot a lot of people. Then he… he shot himself. What did you do?" She broke into a choking weeping. She must have moved the phone away because I could hear sirens in the distance.

"I didn't do anything!" I shouted.

Selene stepped forward. I kept pace in the opposite direction.

"You were the last one to talk to him! You and that weird skinny freak."

I waved for Selene to back off. She stuck her tongue out at me and sat on the kitchen island. *She's getting back to normal quickly.* I stepped over the stream and put my back to her.

"Look, Harlequin, I didn't do—" I rewound the conversation in my head. "What weird skinny freak?"

"Wanted to talk to Milos. He came in yesterday after you left."

I was no longer tired. Finally, something to go off. "Tell me where you are."

"I'm still at Sparc. The police are here. I didn't tell them you talked to Milos yet. My brother said you were a dick but a good detective."

"That might be the nicest thing I've heard from a cop. Just stay there, everything's going to be fine. I'm coming to get you." I slipped the cell into my pocket and spun around, right into Selene's judging gaze.

"Is she cute?" she asked, arms crossed.

"Not the time, S. It's about the case." I stepped around her and into the bathroom. The blood and gunk on my face would fade like all Dark matter did, but I didn't want to pick up Harlequin looking as though I took a nosedive into a slaughterhouse.

Selene leaned against the doorframe and eyed me carefully as I washed my face. "I just watched two daemons — which are real apparently — almost kill you, I think talking is on the menu."

"Fine." I shut off the water and faced her. "What do you want to talk about?"

Her mouth twitched. She was trying to start a sentence but couldn't form the words. She steeled herself and looked me dead in the eyes. "Harlequin. Is that her stripper name or her real name?"

"What? She's not a stripper."

"Well, not yet."

I cast her a disapproving glare.

"Hey, I dated a stripper for a little while." She raised her hands in defense. "Just curious about your new girlfriend."

"Selene!" I snapped the water back on. Selene's gaze moved back to the wall. As much as she tried to hide it, the night was hitting her hard. "Are you okay?"

"Of course I am." She tossed me a towel to dry my face.

I wiped the moisture away and threw the towel into the tub. Selene's eyes were flickering in and out of focus. "Daemons, huh?" I said and touched her lightly on the cheek.

"With an 'a'." She winked and put on a strained smile. "I always thought you were weird."

She was taking the situation better than most. Selene's always been a hardy girl. I once saw her beat three robbers down with a tire iron. But, as tough as she was, Selene was still human. She was trembling almost imperceptibly, but I could feel it when I touched her.

As much as I wanted to, I couldn't figure out what to say. I could explain to her the logistics of daemons; how they crossed over or how they were different from the Christian depictions. Understanding calmed me. But, as I opened my mouth, it didn't feel right. In that moment, the thing Ali said in Glowing Future came to me.

"I wish you were sorry," she had said.

"I have to keep working," I said. I grabbed my gun belt and Milos's Glock. I looked over the Glock and handed it to Selene. "In case."

She nodded and took it.

"I just gotta meet this Harlequin girl." I slid past her and scooped my coat off the floor.

"Bring her here," she said as she threw me my hat and her keys.

I snatched both from the air. "Why?"

"I want to meet her."

I rolled my eyes, defeated once again, and turned off the stream. I gave one last look to Selene. Did she want to meet Harlequin? Or, did she not want to be alone after what happened?

I drove as fast as I could.

Chapter 17

I returned in just under an hour with Harlequin in tow and wrapped in my coat. Selene jumped from the couch at our arrival. She was wearing a few articles of my clothing. My pants were too big on her and the belt had a humorously long tail. A white *PARTY TIME* shirt hung off one shoulder, showing part of the sexy lingerie that I had no chance of seeing the rest of the night.

Selene must have spent the time I was gone cleaning. The busted door was leaning against the farthest wall. Clothes I had thrown on the floor were gone. It looked better than it had before the fight.

"Take a seat on the couch," I said to Harlequin, motioning to the living room. "Ignore the door, I'm redecorating."

She smiled. She gave Selene a polite nod.

Selene sauntered next to me. "I was cleaning up that gooey stuff the lizard turned into and it... disappeared."

"It's ectoplasm. It does that."

"Oh." She scanned Harlequin up and down. "Why is she wearing your coat?"

"Well, she was, uh..."

Harlequin removed my coat. She revealed an overflowing red corset and black leather short skirt. Her tattoo was in its eagle-mode across her chest. She sat gracefully on the couch, spine perfectly straight like a dancer. I quickly turned my gaze to the floor before Selene could see my stare.

"That," I finished.

Selene stifled a laugh. A quick punch hit my stomach before she returned to the living room and took a seat next to Harlequin. Harlequin had been silent most of the ride over. I had tried to get something out of her before returning, but she was still in shock. Now she was smiling and porcelain perfect. Putting on a show.

"Hi, I'm Selene," Selene said with a false sweetness I was pretty sure only I caught. "But everyone calls me Scoundrel. I assume Kraft has not mentioned me."

I rolled my eyes.

"Scoundrel. That's quite a name, miss." Harlequin spoke softly.

"And Harlequin, eh? That a nickname for your... club?"

"Nope! My name, since birth," giggled Harlequin. Forced happiness.

Selene turned so only I could see her face. She mouthed, "Wow" and nearly broke into a laugh. Selene was having far too much fun. I moved to intercept before Harlequin realized she was making fun of her.

Selene was quicker. "So, how do you know Kraft?"

"He came into the club last night. Gave me these." She pulled the pack of Lumos cigarettes from her purse.

"Fancy cigarettes. How old are you?"

"Just turned nineteen a few months ago."

That nearly broke Selene. She looked at me with a smile as wide as the sea. "Nineteen, Kraft. So cute." She laughed and turned back to Harlequin. "You know, in the old United States you wouldn't be allowed to drink." Then she added under her breath, "Could do porn, though."

That was my cue to jump in. I pulled Selene off the couch and directed her to the kitchen.

"Selene," I whispered. "Don't... She's a witness."

"Kraft." She stopped and put her hand on my cheek. "You hit on a nineteen-year-old set of tits in a corset. It's really funny."

"I didn't hit on her."

"Didn't you?"

"Are you drunk?"

She smiled. "I'm dealing with the situation."

On the kitchen island was a half empty bottle of gin. I planted Selene on a stool and returned the bottle to the cupboard. Selene gave me mocking finger guns as I returned to Harlequin.

"Harlequin." I stood across from her, so I could still see Selene out of the corner of my eye. "You said there was someone else who talked to Milos?"

"Uh, yeah. He came in about an hour after you."

"Describe him."

I heard Selene cough loudly. I sighed.

"Do you think you can describe him, please?"

"I think so." The shocked look she held the entire drive over was returning. Her spine bent and her breaths quickened. The facade of a carefree hostess was dropping. Even the eagle on her chest seemed to dim.

"Harlequin—"

Selene appeared. She handed a glass of water to Harlequin, and she took it down in one go. Amazing how Selene could switch from mocking to caring in the blink of an eye.

"Look." Selene kneeled before Harlequin. She swayed, and decided it was better to sit. "Don't think of everything. Be selective. Just think of the man. Cut everything else out of your mind."

Harlequin nodded that she was ready. Selene gave me a quick smile as she returned the glass to the kitchen. I pulled my Gloves from my pocket. The circuitry pulsed slightly.

"Tall, tan, skinny. He talked with this real high and mighty shit. My priest used to talk the same way."

Selene scoffed from the kitchen. "Priest." *And back to the mocking.*

I shot a disapproving glance at her before returning to Harlequin. "His face, I need you to describe his face."

"I… I can't remember," said Harlequin.

"Of course you do. You saw it, it is somewhere in your memory, hidden in your thoughts. Just close your eyes and think."

Harlequin let out an uneven exhale and shut her eyes.

"Now breathe… and think."

Harlequin inhaled deeply. Her breasts pushed even more against her corset.

Selene cupped both hands over her own chest and ballooned out. She nodded sarcastically at me, approving. I ignored her games and kept my fingers primed on my wrist display.

"I think I remember..." Harlequin said finally. "Thin. Large cheekbones. Deep cheeks though. Sharp jaw. His eyebrows were... pointed." A smile risked its way across her face. "And he had receding hair, like a widow's peak."

I let myself focus on the details given, typing away on my wrist. The description wasn't specific. I was ready for a long night of looking at mugshots, but, to my surprise, only one criminal record was found. I raised my upturned hand and a projection of a head appeared. "Like this?"

Harlequin opened her eyes. As soon as she did, they widened. "Yes! That's the freak! I remembered!"

I swept my hand across the face and it was replaced by streams of information. I threw the projection onto the TV behind me. "Al Greensmen," I read off, "arrested a couple times for hacking television stations and replacing their programming with... pseudo-religious scripture?" *Like the kind this Endless Hunger cult is spouting?* "Sounds charming. He works and owns a Lighttech repair shop. That's risky for a convicted hacker."

"So you're going to go beat a confession out of him, then?" asked Harlequin, jumping to her feet. "He forced Milos to shoot all those people, right?"

"I'm going to need a little bit more to go on," I replied. I pulled the projection back into my Gloves and brought up the website for Al's store. "His repair house closes in the next hour. I'll tail him, see if I find anything suspicious. Maybe I'll get lucky." I gave a giddy clap. My skin was tingling with anticipation as I spun to leave.

"What about me?" asked Selene. She cut me off before I could take a step.

"Hang out with Harlequin, you seem to like her."

"Kraft." She poked me in the ribs and shoved me into the bathroom, shutting the door behind us. "What are you doing?"

"I'm dealing with the situation." I started to step around her, but she slammed her hand against the wall, barring my path. "You need to sober up. I thought we dealt with this during our last bathroom talk."

"Then I had time to think and..." She looked at the shattered mirror. "It's dangerous, eh? Really dangerous."

"Yes." There was no point in lying to her now. "But I'm good at it." I've seen Selene angry many times, but worry was a new expression for her. I took her hand and pulled her close, removing my hat and laying my forehead against hers. I shut my eyes and let the closeness of our bodies fill my mind.

"This is crazy," she said.

"I know."

"I'm not emotional."

"I know."

"I've been having some fairly bad nightmares lately."

"I—" I jerked my head back and stared hard into Selene's eyes. The makeup was good cover, it nearly covered the bags under her eyes. Warren had done the same thing. She'd been having trouble sleeping. "What nightmares?"

"I'm in a cave, I think. I mean, it's probably a hall but I call it a cave. It's dark. Really dark. And it feels like—"

"Something is in there with you." My hand squeezed harder on hers.

She gave me a confused look. "Is something wrong?"

"It just sounds like a pretty bad nightmare." I guess there was a point in lying to her. My heart was playing a bass drum in my chest.

"Please be careful," Selene said. She kissed me quickly and opened the bathroom door.

"I will." I gave Selene the only smile I could muster and started to leave the bathroom.

Selene caught my wrist and hauled me back. She held out Milos's gun. "In case."

"I have a gun."

She pressed the grip into my chest. "Now you have two."

I tucked the pistol into the back of my belt. A gun wouldn't protect Selene from the monsters in her head anyway.

Harlequin was still on the couch. For a half-second I saw her overwhelmed with fear. Hands shaking, posture sloped, she looked as if she wanted to curl up somewhere and just disappear. The truth behind her act. She saw me enter the room and jumped back to her dancer's posture and porcelain smile. She didn't want to look weak. Or maybe she was too used to forcing a cheerful face for the customers.

I turned to Selene and whispered, "I hate to ask this, but could you—"

"Yeah," said Selene. She walked to Harlequin's side. "Come on, dear. I'll drive you home."

"Selene."

"Uh, in a few hours."

Harlequin nodded without breaking her smile.

My body ached to get the whole case over with. I could feel the end coming up over the horizon, and I was running to it with all my might. With Al Greensmen it might all come together.

I glanced back to Selene before I left. Obasin was infecting further and further. Somehow he must have gone through me to get to her. It was my fault. I wasn't going to let anything happen to her while I still had breath in my lungs and blood in my veins.

I swept my coat from the chair where Harlequin had laid it and headed out into the hall. I turned back and stared at the empty frame. That was going to be a problem. With great effort, I put the door back to where it should be, the lock holding it in place so it at least looked intact.

It'll do.

———— ‹‹ ›› ————

Al Greensmen stepped out from his darkened store, locking it behind him. I was across the street in the black Pandora SUV I had "borrowed," watching as he flipped up his hood and headed down the street. He moved around the side of the building and into an alley, exiting my line of sight. Light poured forth. He had started his car.

When Al turned the ignition, an indicator popped onto the map on my phone. I smiled. The tracker, standard with all vehicles, was disabled in Al's beater. I had torn one out of the SUV and put it in the car. It was working just fine.

I followed the moving dot at a distance. The dot crossed the south bridge of New Montreal and kept going. I followed Al until the tracker stopped at Mercier, another ghost town on the edge of the Dead Zone. I pulled to the side of the road and took to walking.

I found Al's car empty, parked with a few dozen more outside of a large train tunnel. The tunnel seemed ready to cave in at any second. It was part of an old initiative to connect much of North America through subway systems. The plan was abandoned as soon as the war started. Thousands of miles of underground tunnels now stretched unused throughout the earth.

The tunnel had a string of lights leading into its depths. Evidently, this section was less than abandoned. I followed the lights into the tunnel, along the rusted tracks, taking care not to crunch the gravel that lay underfoot. I was quickly deep underground and still descending.

The darkness played tricks with my eyes. Shadows appeared to dance and sway, following me as I trekked. I hugged the lights, keeping my breath steady and my mind focused. My hand began shaking violently and instinctively made a grab for the coat pocket that normally held my Medioxyl. I swore, remembering that, once again, I had never grabbed any when I left. I told myself I'd be fine and pressed on, holding my hand tightly with the other. I had to keep myself busy and the tremors would pass, they always did.

I pushed on, counting each light to keep my mind working. I reached fifty-seven before my hand calmed. Just in time, too. The flickering light of a fire shone from a large hall before me.

I pressed myself to the wall and peered into the room. It appeared to be some big underground station, disregarded and decaying. The station was filled with fifty or sixty robed individuals, holding torches and staring at the raised walkway across from me. *A cult if I've ever seen one.* From the shadows came Al Greensmen to the walkway, arms spread wide. He was topless, black tattoos spiraling up his skin in twisted and demented designs.

"Believers!" he cried from his pulpit. "Our Lord's time is nigh! Obasin will rise from the greed and sin of this world and devour those who may slight Him! He hath been given a womb in the sinful technology that this world thrives on. Soon He, the Great Devourer, will spread His fear into the minds of the heretics! And they will know that He has come!"

"Endless Hunger. Fantastic." I ducked into the shadows as a cultist peered back. I eased my head back around the corner.

"Obasin promises His followers a new world. He promises to eat our sins, so that we may be pure. He promises that those who turn their backs on Him, who do not kneel in reverence, will be punished. These promises are near fulfillment! And He shall tear his way out from the wicked halls of New Montreal and onto the Earth!"

Fanatic belief in a better world. *Gotta love a good cult.* Somehow, after experiencing Obasin personally, I didn't feel he would be the greatest leader.

The crowd cheered wildly. Al soaked in the admiration, smiling down at his rapt audience.

"We of the Endless Hunger will starve no more! We will be filled with His divine grace! His prophets have worked tirelessly doing his work. They — his chosen!"

With a great flourish, Al motioned down the catwalk to where three figures stood, dressed in the same black robes save for some red trim. Two I recognized — Frank Harcourt and Orrla — but the third was a mystery to me.

He was an incredibly drawn thing from what I could see. His neck and face bordered on emaciated, but I would hesitate to call him sick. Even from this distance I could sense the blood that stained him from head to toe.

I clicked my Beyondsight on. Harcourt was untouched. Orrla had the familiar code wings I'd recently learned signified a faery. The third figure, however, had code flowing along his face like veins that disappeared into his robes. If he wasn't wearing that foreboding cloak the code would have covered his entire body. I'd seen his kind before.

A vampire.

A cult devoted to a Dark entity run by a faery, a wizard, and a vampire. Three groups one did not normally see getting along. Obasin had found something strong enough to bring them together. A vampire could care less about getting its sins eaten. Obasin was promising something else to his chosen ones.

Evidently, Harcourt was in charge of the magic and Orrla handled contracting the criminal to insert the virus. The vampire must be pulling his own weight somehow. Al started another rant on the glory of Obasin. I raised my phone toward the vampire and snapped a photo of his face.

The connection to the Network this far underground was non-existent. I tapped a few keys at my wrist to initiate a signal burst. It wasn't long, but I got enough reception to get the information on the new mystery player. I ducked back into the tunnel to read.

"Shit," I muttered.

Dirk Humbolt. Recluse, apparent vampire, and CEO of Tartarus Securities as of two years earlier. Another entrancing use of Harcourt's mind magic, no doubt. Tartarus was the chief technologies company in charge of managing the NMPD systems. It explained why all three prophets had a long life of back stories, despite one being averse to light and the other being a real damn faery. *I was just in his building. Caleb was right, Fortune is cruel.*

Three CEOs. Three supernatural entities. Three corporations all using their systems to feed one big, bad Dark deity. It was certainly interesting information, but did little to help me solve the problem. If anything, it made it more complex. Endless Hunger had been playing much longer than I had. It was like coming into a chess game with half the pieces already moved and the other half invisible. And the opponent had a gun.

Harcourt made a slight nod to Al. The three prophets of Obasin took their leave, deeper into the tunnels. I needed some cover if I was going to get any more information. There wasn't enough time to run to Black-cloaks R Us, so I would have to ask the crowd for help.

I could fake a phone call on one of the cultist's cells, as long as they weren't going *au naturel*. Except none of their phones would have reception down here, and I couldn't signal burst them. I had no way of connecting to them to exert my control. I put my bandana over my face. There was always the old-fashioned way.

I picked my target, one cultist who was standing closest to the tunnel. I picked my tool, a small pebble from amongst the gravel. The gathering had bowed their heads, chanting some prayer to their god. There was no better time.

I aimed carefully and tossed the stone. Right on target, the pebble bounced off the back of the cultist's head. I shot back into hiding before he could see me. There were too many variables in the plan for my liking. The cultist could bring his friends. I could have alerted the others too. Maybe he just wouldn't investigate.

Gravel crunched as someone moved in the station. I had lucked out. It only sounded like one pair of feet. I held my breath and pressed myself against the tunnel wall. The entrance to the station had a lip that stuck out about a foot; I used it to give myself some cover.

The footsteps were apprehensive and slow. The anticipation was killing me. I felt the rounds on my belt and I recognized the design for a gas round. It would be stupid to fire a gun down here and not think anyone would notice. The round didn't need to be fired to be effective.

A shadow appeared on the light cast out from the station. I transferred the bullet to my right hand. I squeezed tightly and watched the shadow shrink until the figure that owned it came into my line of sight. They stopped. *Hoods should come with rearview mirrors.*

I shot forward, brought my left hand over the cultist's mouth, and struck his chest with my right. The gas round puffed its red-tinted smoke; I loosened my left hand and let my victim get a good inhale while my bandana protected me. In less than a second, he went limp.

The man was a few inches shorter than I was but plenty stockier. The rest of the cultists were chanting and it covered the sound of me dragging the poor fellow to a nearby alcove. The gas would keep him down for about twenty minutes, which was hopefully enough time to get what I needed. Once I was done, I would just clothe him, put him back in the tunnel, and maybe he'd think he just bumped his head.

Underneath the black robe was a pudgy man — probably in his early forties — dressed in a white button-up and khakis. I wondered what he was like outside of his feverish devotion to a Dark god. Did he have a family? Did they question where he went at night? Did his wife have to wash his cult cloak? I only thought the last idea because the cloak did smell summertime fresh.

I wasn't going to waste time contemplating the home life of a cultist. I replaced my hat with the hood of my new disguise, lowered my bandana, and slid into the station.

Al Greensmen seemed nowhere close to ending — Obasin is great because of this, sinners will be smote because of that. It was strangely reminiscent of when my parents would bring Millie and me to Mass — something they tried to do at least once a month before they died. Sans the black cloaks.

The crowd was too enamored with Al, and Al was too enamored with himself, to notice me moving through their ranks to where the prophets had exited. Harcourt and his crew had taken some steel steps down to the lower level and left through another lit tunnel — a smaller one, for people instead of trains. I hushed my footsteps and followed.

"I will not hear any more about him. He is not our concern," Harcourt said.

Who are they talking about?

"But," hissed Orrla, "he speared me with iron."

Oh. Me.

I followed the voices to another open area, an atrium for people to cross from line to line. Inside, the three prophets held their conference around a silver-colored box. It was a few feet high and about the same length on each side, a little fatter than it was tall. A single, thick cord winded away from the device down one of the hallways.

"I do find it funny," Dirk Humbolt finally spoke, voice like a serpent, "that you great and powerful sidhe are so cowed by a tiny nail."

"Let's take a walk in the sun and see how you feel," Orrla growled back.

"Would you two please stop bickering?" Harcourt spoke as though he was scolding schoolchildren. They weren't quite the well-oiled machine Endless Hunger thought them to be.

"Not until you accept this *Kraft* creature is a real threat." Orrla stepped to Harcourt. Her entire body shook with rage. "He is a Seer, he fought off three of your pets, and he killed my Yanswiy."

Yanswiy was no doubt the true name of Diana Forsyth. Evidently, I had made an impact on Orrla. I would be lying if I didn't say I took some pleasure from it.

"Control yourself, Orrla," Harcourt commanded. "Seers are the dime-store magicians of the arcane. I'm done wasting my time on him. Any acolyte worth his salt can take down a simple summon, and I couldn't care less about your faery consort."

Orrla looked ready to burst, but one glance from Harcourt and she settled down. I didn't know where on the power scale sidhe fell, but at least Orrla was below a wizard of the Magi.

"Now," he continued, "tomorrow night we will witness the birth of our Great Lord. I have been planning for this for a long time, and I do not wish to wait for another era because of one of you messing it up."

Tomorrow night? There was no way it could be so soon. Then again, I didn't know how long they'd been gathering power.

"Dirk, the Hunger's receivers?"

The Hunger? Another name for Obasin?

"All getting the incoming information. Each linked with fail-safes ready to go." Dirk tapped on the silver box.

A receiver. The cord must run to an antenna above ground. When Orrla spoke of the Network passing through people and taking imprints of their sorrow, this had to be where it was being sent. It must be the metaphorical "womb" they were speaking of. *Linked with fail-safes? What does that mean?*

"Orrla." Harcourt spoke without looking at her. "The feeders?"

The faery let out a loud sigh. She evidently wasn't thrilled with the way Harcourt was running things.

Still, she replied, "Milos worked perfectly. My own Orion, Infitex Communications, Protectorate Manufacturing, and Eternaguard Security are all transmitting. We sent in the human, Greensmen, yesterday to put your little mind spell on

Milos. By now he's just another drug addict who went crazy and killed himself."

"Now, Orrla." Harcourt put on a charming smile and placed a hand on her shoulder. "Do you think that with a plan like this, Kraft is anything to worry about?"

Orrla didn't say a word.

Scoffing, Harcourt spun on his heels and headed to one of the other hallways. "We shall meet tomorrow. Do not be late for the start of our new world. Your rewards are waiting." He disappeared into the dark.

Orrla's eyes turned an icy blue. She stepped toward where Harcourt disappeared, but Dirk swept his arm over her shoulder.

"Oh, darling," he said. "I have lost a hundred lovers and I know it can sting."

"She wasn't just a lover," she replied, shoving Dirk's arm off her. "She was Yanswiy."

The vampire gave a dark laugh. "Come with me, my dear."

He motioned to yet another hallway. Orrla rolled her eyes but relented, and the two Dark creatures headed into the blackness.

I wanted to follow those two, in case they were plotting something evil against me. My rational brain told me I might not get another chance at the receiver though. I let Orrla and Dirk go, hoping that whatever they came up with wouldn't be too devious.

I kept an eye to every shadow as I approached the receiver. It was plain looking; it was essentially a large hard drive after all. The only features that broke up the silver shell were the cord on one side and a screen on the top. I resisted the urge to just straight up smash the unit. In this game, information was king.

There was no security to speak of on the system. Someone wasn't expecting anyone to get this close. I investigated the command protocols. It was good I didn't just smash the thing.

The fail-safes Dirk Humbolt mentioned were two more receivers somewhere in the city. I couldn't pinpoint their exact locations; merely a phantom signal existed between the three of them. There was a command in the system that said if one went down — even if the shell was slightly cracked — all the power pulled in for Obasin would be shunted to another receiver. No doubt alerting Harcourt and his cronies when it happened. Even if I smashed one, another would just pick up the slack and I would have no idea from where.

The incoming energy was massive. The companies Milos spoke of were transmitting a seemingly useless signal to this receiver, but I could see Dark energy flowing in. Infitex, Protectorate, Eternaguard, and Orion were all sending a steady stream. Tartarus Securities, with its dozens of servers for each client that I was once so keen on breaking into, was pumping out huge amounts of energy to this location. That was why they were on such high security when I was there. Dirk was using the security contracts to create a backdoor into every company they worked for. He needed to make sure the servers weren't messed with.

However, no matter how much I scoured the system, I couldn't find a link to Glowing Future. They were the only company Milos mentioned that wasn't sending energy to the receiver. I knew they had a virus, though. I saw it myself. *What's going on? What's happening at Glowing Future?*

I couldn't get into every company and seal off their system, not before the next night. Even if I could, I was sure Harcourt could open up another feeding tube to get the last little bit in for Obasin. I couldn't destroy the receivers. I didn't have the time or means to find, much less destroy, all three.

If this is where the Network energy is going, where is the Winter energy? The underground was chilly, but nowhere near supernaturally cold enough to be filled with Winter's power. Maybe I was wrong about Orrla stealing it.

It was one of those times where you start to feel like every door is locked around you and the walls are starting to close in. I wasn't ready to give up yet. I wasn't going to let some glitchy cult win after all.

I had to get out of here. There was some way to stop Obasin. I knew there had to be. That Al Greensmen character was deserving of a little conversation. I knew exactly where he would be in the morning, too.

Chapter 18

~ ~ ~ ~ ~

*Dark. Again. That same room. The dark room. It felt more real.
The stone was cold and slimy. I couldn't feel my own body. It
wasn't there. Was I there? The light. It was barely a pinpoint.
It had warmth. Distant warmth. What happens when it runs
out...?*

~ ~ ~ ~ ~

I awoke still in the stolen SUV. Napping in a hot ride wasn't
the smartest plan, but when I got back to the Lighttech store, I
passed out. It seemed like no matter how much I slept, I never
felt rested; like punching a brick wall, it was just no use. I sat
up and lifted the handle on the side of the seat, snapping the
seatback into place. The morning sun temporarily blinded
me and I risked a look at myself in the rearview mirror.

Hell. That was what I looked like. I had a few days'
worth of beard on my jaw and deep bags under my eyes. My
bandwidth was getting strained. It was hard to believe it was
Tuesday already. I poked lightly against the bandage on my
cheek, and a small pain greeted me. My hair shot up in crazy
directions; I was able to hide it once I replaced my old cap.
The investigation was going to kill me before Endless Hunger
did, it seemed.

I let out a heavy sigh and cracked every joint I had.
Al's shop was across the street, the OPEN sign glowing in the
window.

Pushing my weary body, I got out of the car and jogged
across the street. I turned my coat red and my hat black.
Taking note of the "Protected by Eternaguard" security sticker
on the front window and pulling my Gloves tight, I entered
the building.

The walls were covered in various pieces of equipment and Lighttech devices. A few Cybertech prosthetics and neural enhancers lay under glass displays. These ones were legal, but I was sure more questionable materials sat in the back. *So much for technology being "sinful," Mr. Greensmen.* Leaning on the counter to my left was Al Greensmen, reading a technology magazine. He looked almost normal when he wasn't a half-naked cultist. He put on a big fake smile as soon as he saw me enter.

"Welcome to Emergency Repair! How can I help you?" he greeted cheerfully.

"Al Greensmen? I have a few questions." I leaned against the glass counter.

The smile instantly dropped from Al's face. Half a beat of total silence hung in the air. He shoved the magazine at me. I slapped the book away. Al was in a dead sprint toward the side door. His wares clattered to the floor.

"You didn't even wait to hear if I was a cop!" I hollered after the fleeing figure. I lifted my bandana and tapped on my wrist projection.

Al dug his feet into the floor and barreled hard into the side exit. He braced his shoulder to bash through the door, only to bounce off violently. I had dealt with Eternaguard systems before. It wasn't hard to lock it.

I risked a smirk and stepped around the counter. I stood over the moaning man. "That had to sting."

"Are you a cop?" Al asked through gritted teeth.

"No."

Al grabbed a prosthetic arm and swung it into the side of my head. I hit the ground hard and clutched my ringing ear. Al unlocked the door and disappeared. It took me a little to recover — it was one of the heavy-duty metal prosthetics, after all. I came to my feet and followed Al out with a stagger.

I stepped into the alley, and the sound of a car starting grabbed my attention. Al had already gotten in his beater. He made fierce eye contact and revved his engine. The car's wheels gripped onto the concrete and aimed straight for me.

"No time for subtlety," I muttered. I grabbed a high explosive round from my belt. I snapped out my revolver and slid the bright yellow bullet into a chamber. The cylinder shut, the electronics automatically spun, and it registered a primed shot. I took aim and fired.

I aimed for the asphalt just under the beater's front bumper. My accuracy had recovered with my healing arm and I fired true. The round detonated as it struck the earth. The front end went skyward. The intense heat cooked my skin, and I shielded my eyes. I stepped aside as the car skidded by on its back bumper. It traveled quite a distance, screeching the whole way down the alley, before it struck one of the walls and twisted to the side. It crashed hard to the alley floor and came to rest on its roof.

Fuming, I stomped to the smoking wreck. I placed my Glove on the car and unlocked the door. Al hung limply from his seat belt, barely holding on to consciousness. I tore him out of the car and slammed the door closed. I grabbed a long plastic zip tie from my coat and tied Al's hands to the door handle.

"Wake up!" I shouted, slapping Al across the face.

The man woozily gazed up at me. It took another slap for him to gain composure.

"What do you want with me?" he asked.

"You helped put Obasin into the Network."

Al perked up at my mention of Obasin. "You... you know of Obasin?"

"We are acquainted. Judging by your familiarity with Lighttech, I would even guess you figured out how to get him into a system. What? Write up a virus and do some fun little ritual?"

He shrugged. "Possibly."

"Tell me how to get him out of there."

"Ha! Why would I ever tell you that?" He rolled his head lazily on his neck.

I slammed Al's head into the car. I pointed my revolver directly between his eyes. I was in a hot rage and he could get the worst of it.

"I fear not death, nor pain, nor any earthly punishment, for in the eyes of the Great Devourer I am His chosen and I shall take my place beside Him in his pantheon." Al cracked a smile as he recited his scripture.

It only raised my ire even more. I pushed out the cylinder, dropped the expended cartridge into my palm, and drove a speedloader into the empty chambers. I snapped it shut and pressed the barrel against Al's head, still warm from firing the high explosive round.

"I have experienced Obasin! You're just a meal to him! And Harcourt? You're just a sucker to do his bidding." I pushed the metal hard into Al's forehead.

"If you are trying to shake my faith then you are sorely mistaken. I have nothing but reliance in the promises of my Lord."

I shook with fury. Al's smiling, taunting face only served to frustrate me more. In his eyes, I saw my nightmares, Rick and Milos's lives, Selene's danger. *My investigation will stop with this mortal?* I fired the revolver, shooting just past Al's head and into the inverted car.

Al didn't flinch with the gunshot. He only laughed even louder. "Enjoy your last days on Earth, heretic! The Great Devourer will rise!"

I drove my gun back into its holster and stalked toward the SUV. Any more time spent with him and I would be giving the authorities a real reason to come after me.

"Stay here, the police will come to arrest you soon," I said.

"Arrest me for what? I'm the victim here."

"Possession of an unregistered firearm." I tossed Milos's stolen gun to Al's feet. "You also may have shot a dead guy."

"What?" Al shouted, kicking at the pistol at his feet. "That will never stick!"

"Maybe, maybe not. It will give them a reason to search your store. There is sure to be something incriminating in there."

"No! Hey!"

"Have fun enjoying the new world from prison," I called back.

I left the thrashing man tied to the wreck. My body felt heavier than ever as I dropped into the driver's seat. I pulled my bandana down and let out a puff. *This investigation gets more irritating at every turn.*

I tore my Gloves off and tossed them to the passenger seat. I punched the steering wheel until my knuckles were sore. Despite all I knew, the information did nothing to help me figure out how to destroy Obasin. I knew where his power was coming from. I knew where it was going. Not even that helped. Caleb still hadn't returned my call from the day before. No help from the High Circle. They were going to sit around thinking mighty thoughts about themselves as the world started to fall apart.

I pressed my head firmly against the steering wheel. My phone began ringing. I pulled it from my pocket and saw Selene's name. I tapped the phone on the vehicle console, syncing and answering.

"Hey, Selene," I said, forehead still on the wheel.

"Kraft! Fuck, there's one of those... *things* here!" her voice screamed from the speaker.

I immediately woke up. "A lizard?"

"No. It was this older chick." Selene sniffed loudly.

She had been crying. I squeezed my free hand into a fist so tight I was worried I would cut through my palms with my fingernails.

Selene continued, "She came in all normal 'n shit but then — fuck! I don't know if Francois is alive but... there was a lot of blood..."

I slammed the SUV into drive and tore off into the city. "Where are you? Where is she?" I yelled.

"I ducked into my workshop. The wall is sealed but—"

A loud banging interrupted her. Selene screamed at nearly the same time. The sniffs started up again, and I felt my heart clench.

"She's been doing that. I'm freaking out, Kraft. Please come help me, I don't want..."

"I'm coming to get you, Selene! Get off the line and keep cover. I'll be ten minutes."

I could feel red-hot wrath boiling in the pit of my stomach. I was not going to let anything happen to her.

"I promise I will keep you safe."

"Okay, baby," she said unsteadily. It took her longer than normal to hang up. I didn't blame her.

I pushed the pedal to the floor. The drive to Total Care Auto Body would take closer to half an hour from where I was. Well, half an hour following the proper traffic laws. I was probably about to do the most obviously illegal thing I had done with my Gloves in a long time, but I wasn't about to let Selene pay for my sins.

I awkwardly replaced my Gloves — trying to get them on with my teeth while avoiding hitting a parked car. I drove at full bore with my left hand and worked with my right. Three jobs. A jamming echo to shut down any phones I went past — no police calls. All the traffic cameras had system disturbances when I crossed the intersections. Every light I hit turned green. I barely touched the brakes on the drive over. It was pretty awesome, I had to admit.

The SUV spit up gravel as I hit the brakes at Selene's shop. I left the key in the ignition and grabbed my phone from the passenger seat as I jumped out of the vehicle. *I'm not too late. I'm not too late.*

The once cracked window was now completely broken. I could make out the reception area. A lump grew in my throat. I pulled my bandana up. Slowing to a walk, I reached for the door and pulled it open carefully.

The entire room was coated in red, as if someone had tried to paint but failed terribly. I stepped inside, making sure not to let my feet touch any blood. Mushy chunks stuck to the ceiling, walls, and littered the floor. A few meat lumps had pieces of black hair poking out. I knew what it was.

Francois. Poor Francois had become a color scheme for Orrla's remodeling. I was going to tear all kinds of holes in her.

A loud banging came from the service area, Orrla still trying to gain access to Selene's workshop. That meant Selene must still be safe. I was hardly the cavalry. My gun had five rounds in its cylinder after my encounter with Al Greensmen. I also had some specialty rounds to put to use, but none too useful to this situation. I really was going to need to get my hands on steel-core rounds. I hit the service door with revolver in hand.

The closest cars looked as though something had pounded the hoods in with a cinder block. The red sports car I'd admired was flipped over onto the green sedan. Orrla stood where Selene's workshop was hidden.

Orrla looked like a wild woman. Her normally nicely done-up bun had strands pointing every which way and pasted to her sneering face. The suit she always wore was torn. Her jacket's seams were being held by a few strings. Her shirt was untucked and stained with auto-fluid in the few spots it wasn't soaked through with blood. She wielded what looked like the driveshaft of one of the torn-up trucks. She wore thick work gloves and wildly swung the makeshift club into the crumbling wall. Heavy steel was revealed behind the powdered stones.

"Orrla!" I screamed with the most warrior-might voice I could muster.

She turned, still clutching tightly onto the driveshaft. Her eyes had taken on a pure, icy blue color. The entire sight had a dangerous beauty to it. She took a step forward and the temperature in the room dropped a few degrees.

"You seem pissed," I remarked.

A frosty smile cracked across her blue-tinged lips. "I want to see your heart bleed," she said, breathy and cruel.

"This is between you and me."

"You don't know the pain of iron to the fae. It is a sickness that penetrates to your bones. You mortals throw it around with such carelessness. The memory never leaves you." The sidhe walked with such grace it seemed as though she was barely touching the ground. The temperature continued to drop. I could see the puffs of my slow breath.

"That's what this is about? The nail?" I asked, starting to circle with Orrla, never taking my gunsights off her skull.

"I want you to understand me when I say the pain of iron is nothing compared to the pain of my loss. Of the love you stole from me. I will ensure you share in it." She smiled. "Obasin is upset with you. He wants you to pay. Your blood will come later, but first he wants" — she looked back to the dusted wall — "that sweet little thing. A 'welcome to the Light' gift."

My entire body seized. I fired a shot right between Orrla's eyes. She bent back with the impact, green blood splattering from the open wound. The instant drop in temperature at the bullet's impact threatened to freeze the blood in my veins. Her body held a cranked back position for a couple seconds before she elegantly righted her spine. The hole in her head knitted until there was nothing but the green smear on her face. The bullet bounced off the concrete.

"You know," she said, "I was getting worried we would talk forever."

Before I could blink, she switched the driveshaft from her right to left hand and grabbed a nearby sedan's bumper. Her gloved grip crushed the metal and she wrenched her shoulder forward, hurling the car in a line drive at me.

I dropped to my knees in time, the car sailing just over my head and impacting with a huge, metallic crash into the wall several feet behind me. I bolted forward.

Orrla swung hard with her club. I took advantage of the slow speed of her weapon and bent low, twisted, and rolled under the swing. Orrla continued with the momentum as I ended up on my back, revolver pointed squarely up at her chin. Two shots and her lower jaw exploded in gore. The impact ripped her head back and threw her to the ground.

I flipped onto my front, scrambled up, and sprinted to the tool cabinet in the corner. A wrench, a saw, anything made of iron or steel would help. A soft sliding sound on the concrete was the only warning I had that Orrla had recovered. I felt a tug on the collar of my coat. Suddenly, my feet weren't on the ground anymore.

It was a short flight. My breath was taken from my lungs when I landed with a crunch on the front window of a big, black truck. Orrla didn't stop for a second. I looked in her direction in time to see the faery hurdling forth. Green blood coated her shirt, pasting the fabric to her torso. Her jaw had reformed. I only just saw the skin finish knitting. With one arm, she grabbed the front of the truck and flipped the vehicle with me still on it.

The sickening sensation of weightlessness was coupled with the horror of a quickly approaching floor. I pushed off the hood and rolled on my landing, the truck crashing on its roof just behind me. Not exactly cat-like, I landed with my back to the garage door, and my revolver slid away. Whether it was shock or injury — or maybe the sudden cold — that kept me down, I didn't know. All I saw was Orrla moving slowly around the wrecked truck, covered fingers dancing along its chassis.

The entire situation was getting out of hand. I remembered when I laughed about the existence of faeries. If I got out of this alive, I needed to hit some books. No more being taken off guard. *If I get out of this.*

I returned to my feet with all the grace of a drunkard, trying to come up with a way to deal with the sidhe lady strutting in my direction. I just had to put her down long enough to get Selene out of there. Get someplace highly populated where a faery wouldn't risk showing herself. Orrla's pupils faded back in and her eyes returned to normal.

"Are you thinking that you should have killed me back at my office?" she said, swaying her hips with each step. She pulled off her gloves and laid them gently onto the overturned truck.

"I do have to admit, it certainly would have made plenty of things better," I said wearily. "But all I had was a little iron nail, you see. Couldn't kill you with that."

"Or perhaps my kiss did more than read your mind." She dragged her finger from her navel to her neck, all along the blood-covered shirt.

"Don't flatter yourself. What is it with you faeries and sex?"

Orrla cocked an eyebrow. "Did it ever occur to you, we do it because it works on you humans?"

That is a good point.

"You humans are so funny. You like to believe you are free from the drag of nature and yet two little things can completely dominate you." She looked lustfully downward. "Your genitals." Her eyes rose to meet mine, hers returning to the unnatural, pure light blue. "And your heart."

My stomach twisted. I had made a terrible mistake. She never would have gotten through that door. The driveshaft was barely denting it. Orrla planned for Selene to call me. Selene would leave the room for me.

She lashed forth, and her hand clutched tightly around my mouth. I grabbed her wrist and wrenched it every way to break her grip. Air puffed from my nose in harsh breaths. Orrla didn't move an inch with my struggling. She reached forward and gently pulled my mask down.

"Let's see what the heart can do," she said, then turned to the great steel door Selene was hiding behind. "Sweetheart! You should know, I've got your boyfriend here and he isn't looking too good! If you come out I won't harm him, love!"

Orrla moved her hand from my mouth to my cheek and cracked me hard in the stomach. She might have fractured a rib, but I held my tongue and didn't make a sound.

"Mr. Kraft," she whispered, putting her face less than an inch from mine. "It would be better for all of us if you just scream for me."

She plunged two fingers into my side and her sharp nails cut through my flesh. A cold spike shot up my side from her frigid finger. The fae was trying to freeze my organs.

"Go to Hell," I muttered.

"Old news," she whispered and twisted her fingers.

I screamed, only for a second, but I knew it was enough.

"Stop!" came Selene's voice from behind the door.

My heart dropped. The wall slid open with Selene on the other side. She was dressed in the same tank top and pulled down coveralls she always wore when she was working. The red in her eyes and face told me she had been crying, but her fists were clenched tight and her stance was strong. All the strength in her couldn't stand against the Dark, unfortunately. I wanted to rain hell down on Orrla, to tear into her until only the faintest remains of a faery existed.

"Good girl," said Orrla.

I grabbed Orrla's hand that still stabbed me and leaned close. "Tell me you won't harm her," I growled.

She smiled — an icy, dead smile that chilled me even colder than the frozen temperature.

She leaned back into me and whispered, "No."

The world turned dark.

Chapter 19

I awoke on my back to the sound of my phone chime. From habit, I dug it from my pocket and answered.

"What?" I groaned. There was a cold wetness down my back. I was lying in a puddle of blood.

"You called?" It was Caleb.

I sat straight up, but immediately regretted it. My side flared angrily where Orrla had stabbed me and I laid back down with a soft splash. "Where the fuck have you been?"

"You called me yesterday, not exactly a huge delay," he said. "Gerard and I had to head out to London to bring the Sentinels up to speed on the whole Harcourt situation. I only just got back in town from the Sideroads."

The Sideroads were protected paths that ran along the Fade, used primarily by wizards to move quickly from place to place. Most of them thought themselves too high and mighty for planes. Still, Sideroads were the safest and quickest way to get around.

"What do you want?" he finished.

"Orrla took Scoundrel!" I must have looked ridiculous, lying in a pool of blood, shouting to the ceiling. "Something about a 'welcome to the Light' gift for Obasin."

Something clattered on the other end of the line. "What? Who's Obasin?"

"I was hoping you could tell me. Harcourt and Orrla claim him to be some kind of Dark deity, along with Dirk Humbolt, CEO of Tartarus Securities and apparent vampire. Word is, Obasin is going to usher in a golden era at us nonbeliever's expense."

"This is ba—"

"Do not say 'this is bad.' You always say that, and of course it's bad! I was going to tell you this earlier, but you didn't pick up your *fucking phone*. Now get me Gerard!"

There was a brief burst of chatter before Caleb spoke. "Where are you?"

"I'm at Scoundrel's body shop."

"I'll be right over. I'll meet you outside."

"Caleb?"

"Yeah?"

"I promised I would keep her safe."

He paused. "I won't be long."

We hung up. My phone displayed the time as 3:42 PM, though I couldn't remember what the time was when I arrived at the garage. I put my phone back into my pocket, pushed through the soreness of my body, stood up, and started walking. Selene could have been missing for a few minutes or a few hours.

The service area was beaten to all kinds of hell. Of the five cars in there, only two looked unscathed. There were going to be some pissed customers — I didn't know what kind of insurance would cover faery attacks.

My side burned with the steadiness of a lava flow, and blood had soaked right through the tee. My head spun from the blood loss. I was not interested in dying that way. Selene kept a first aid kit in her workshop, no Medioxyl, but it would have to do. *This is one of those situations Medioxyl was made for.*

I limped my way to the hidden room and pulled out the little red box. I threw my bloodstained coat onto a counter and lifted my shirt to examine the puncture. It was a clean pierce, thankfully, so it would be easy to get some field medicine slapped on. One cleaning, bandage, and piece of gauze around my torso later and I was ready to go.

I ducked upstairs and grabbed some spare clothes I kept in Selene's room. My bag of tricks was sitting on her dresser; it would prove invaluable in what was about to come. I grabbed it before I returned to the workshop. My coat was covered in dried blood, but I had no time to drop it off at a dry cleaner. I left it on the counter. I refilled my ammo and left the workshop. Out of respect for Selene, I closed the hidden door. The cops were sure to come around. Maybe that way, there was a chance they wouldn't stumble upon her illicit hobby.

I grabbed my revolver from the floor and left the service area. Though I held my breath when I walked through the reception, the metallic stench infected my throat. *Caleb better be here before the police arrive to this sideshow. They won't know what to make of it, but they are likely to find some way to blame it on me.*

The stolen SUV had disappeared from where I parked it. Orrla probably took it. I didn't know how she had gotten to the garage; she probably had done some faery magic that wouldn't work too well with a prisoner. That could work in my favor. I had taken over the car's systems, so I would still have some access to it in my memory. *All I have to do is activate its GPS tracker and I... tore it out to put it in Al Greensmen's beater... Shit.*

I didn't have the luxury of feeling any sort of loss for Selene. I took all forms of sadness and turned them into burning rage. Depression was a paralyzer I didn't have time to deal with. Hatred was a motivator. I had it in spades.

Hatred toward Orrla for taking her.

Hatred toward Harcourt for being part of it.

Hatred toward Obasin for commanding them to do so.

Hatred toward myself for not being strong enough to protect her.

I shivered in the cold air; the chill reminded me of how severely outclassed I was by Orrla. My earlier successes with the lesser faery and Orrla the first time had made me arrogant. Caleb had warned me about the power of the sidhe. I needed to be stronger. I needed power. I needed — something.

Caleb tore up in his shiny, black Matoro sports car several minutes later. I was already at the passenger door when the car stopped, and already inside before the dust settled. It was just Caleb and me in the car.

"Where's the wizard?" I asked. "Where's Gerard?"

"He went back to London to update the Sentinels again," Caleb said. "To see what we can figure out about this 'Obasin' character."

"Are you kidding me? Rather than helping an innocent person, he's running off to another continent to tell someone about it!"

"It's not that simple, Kraft! There are rules and protocols, we can't stop everything for one woman."

"I will!" I had to squeeze hard on to the door's handle to keep myself from slugging Caleb right in his smug face.

"Let's get back to your place." Caleb turned the engine over and reversed out from the auto shop's lot. "Maybe relax a little."

"I'm not going to relax! Do you not comprehend that someone is missing and that they will *kill* her?"

"Kraft! We are not going to help anyone by flying off the handle! The High Circle can deal with this."

"Fuck the Circle! She's going to be dead before they can even decide to help her! Obasin will be released tonight! Of the three who are in charge of this, Orrla has disappeared with Scoundrel, and Dirk Humbolt's file says he's notorious for being impossible to find. That leaves one."

Caleb cursed and turned onto the road back to Laval. "You are not going to confront Harcourt. Gerard forbid it."

"'Gerard forbid it,'" I said in my best Irish accent. "I'm not going to let your blind allegiance kill Selene."

My Gloves lit up and I punched control commands into my wrist. I clapped my hands. When I parted them, a projected steering wheel filled the dash before me. I yanked right on the wheel, the car swerving hard back into the city.

Caleb wrenched left and right on his wheel to no effect. I could see his legs trying to work the brakes, but I knew he could push all he wanted to, the car was in my control.

"Kraft," he said. "I will subdue you if necessary."

"I'm driving."

He lunged at me. I pressed an icon on the projection and his airbag deployed. Caleb took it hard in the face. The back of his head bounced off the headrest and his nose poured blood. I saw his eyes waver for a second, then go blank. At least he wouldn't bug me while unconscious.

I searched Glowing Future's records for Frank Harcourt's home address. It took me less than a minute to get through the executive level encryption — not bad for some distracted driving hacking.

I committed the address to memory and grabbed the highway heading east out of New Montreal. There was one last thing I had to do before going to meet Harcourt. I took out my phone and dialed the number of some backup.

—— «» ——

Far east of New Montreal, where the rich could still claim large chunks of land as their own, was Granby. Frank Harcourt evidently was able to get himself a few square kilometers of open space for one big ass house and its surrounding acreage. His file said he wasn't married, nor had any family, so the house just seemed even more obnoxious.

I pulled to the side of the road several meters from Harcourt's front gate. "Gate" was a little off the mark actually; it was just a sheet of selectively permeable material. When the person with the correct ID on their phone approached, a current would pass through and turn the gate into a gaseous state in which the person could enter through. Kind of like a safer version of the Ghost Goo. I remembered it once being hyped as the "future of doors." In reality, it worked just as well as a door, though I had to admit it looked cooler.

Caleb started to stir as I came to a stop. I had taken a break from driving to effectively subdue him by tying him up in his seatbelt. That fact hadn't quite reached his brain as he tried again and again to get out of his seat. Finally, he caught on and looked first at his bindings, then at me.

"Kraft," he said to me. "Don't do this. He'll kill you."

"I'm not worried," I replied. "I brought backup."

Caleb shook his head. "Not Harcourt. Obasin. I've been having dreams, Kraft. Ever since our first talk. Something was whispering in the shadows. I didn't know the name, but now I do. It's Obasin. He's strong. Now I can sense his energy everywhere. Kraft... this..." He passed out again.

I patted his shoulder. "This is bad. I know, Caleb."

First Selene, now Caleb was having night terrors. *Why these two?*

I stepped out of Caleb's car and swung my bag of tricks over my head. I was immediately hit by the cold air. Without my coat I was left shivering in a tee shirt. Every time I went back outside it just got colder and colder. The missing Winter energy was starting to hit the city hard. Judging by the freezing touches Orrla gave back at the auto body shop, it was pretty clear she stole the energy. Though there was a way to be sure.

I lifted my shirt. Blood was already soaking through the white bandage. I looked at it with my Beyondsight. Orrla's code was still staining it, but I looked deeper. Hidden between the lines was the same code I saw when I looked at myself at Orion. This time it was stronger. It was similar to Jack of Frost's code. She was steeped in Winter's energy.

That would bring Obasin's energy sources up to three: Endless Hunger's prayers, power from the Network, and pure Winter energy. But the Mercier underground was still not cold enough. Wherever the Winter power was, it wasn't being sent to that receiver. Then where? I would have to give Jack an update when I had a moment. At least I could tell him who took it, even if I didn't know where it was.

The update would have to wait, as I caught sight of a large pickup truck rumbling toward me. My backup had arrived just in time, and one hell of a backup it was. The shocks on the truck jumped back up several inches when "The Iceberg" Arno stepped out.

He appeared to have decided to forgo the classic black suit and tie combo in favor of blue jeans and white shirt under a zip-up. Where the ogre got his clothes was a mystery to me, maybe a really big and really tall store.

"Is he the one who hypnotized Rick?" Arno got right down to business.

"Mesmerized, technically," I replied, adjusting my bag over my shoulder. "And I believe so. But I have questions he needs to answer."

"I want him," he growled down at me.

"And you'll get him." I tried my best to stand tall. Dealing with ogres was never fun, but at least Arno was a little reasonable. One would have to be firm, but not unfair, lest the ogre decide you were a better meal than conversation partner. I still wasn't a hundred percent sure Arno wasn't into bone crunching. "But you'll get him after I'm done with him."

Arno eyed me up and down for what felt like an eternity. "Agreed."

I finally breathed. I looked back at Caleb napping in the car. "Arno, have you been having nightmares since we last met, by any chance?"

"I don't dream. Not many of the Dark do."

That isn't much help. "Then let's get going." I pulled up my mask and started walking to the gate.

"What are we looking at inside?" Arno made small steps to keep pace.

"Harcourt is a mind mage, but he's also one of the Magi, so I wouldn't risk thinking that he couldn't sling a few elements as well. He also has a habit of summoning and binding lizard daemons, as you would remember. A people person is not a way I would describe him, so any resistance would probably be from said daemons."

A camera high on the wall twisted and pointed at me and Arno. I waved enthusiastically.

"He's careful but pretty high on himself." I turned the wave into a middle finger. "Maybe more so than most wizards. He doesn't see me as a threat anymore, and I'm going to make sure he knows I am. So, as for a plan of attack—"

"Shock and awe," Arno finished for me.

"Exactly." I grinned as we came to the two pillars and road that signified the gate part of the wall.

"And how do you plan on dealing with Harcourt himself?" Arno asked.

I swung my bag down and pulled a silver U-shaped object out. I showed it to Arno as I tightened the bag strap again.

"And what's that?"

I put it in my left pocket next to the runic cloth I had nearly had to use with Gerard. "My plan." I inspected the gate's control panel, loosening my bag. "Just let me hack through this gate and we'll be inside in no ti—"

I wasn't able to finish my sentence before Arno brought one big ogre boot to the bricks and exploded the formerly solid wall inward. A few more kicks and we were through.

"Shock and awe, Mr. Kraft. Shock and awe," he said, stepping over the rubble and beginning the walk to Harcourt's manor.

I tightened my bag strap. "Indeed."

I followed Arno across the front lawn and drew my revolver. There was no doubt I was going to need it there. I pushed out the cylinder and checked the chambers — six rounds.

"You're bleeding," Arno said, motioning to the blood now coming through my fresh shirt.

"*Was* bleeding." I flipped the cylinder closed once again. "I'm fine now."

He grunted in reply, but seemed content with my answer.

"You seem different." Arno cracked his knuckles, never looking away from the house.

"I'm focused."

"I know loss, Mr. Kraft. You seem like a man fighting like hell against it."

Arno was more in tune with emotions than one would think an ogre would be. I wasn't in the mood to start gushing my feelings to him, though, and decided to instead take in the sight before us.

Harcourt's house was big, really big, and had a classic feel to it. I could imagine that if one would travel way back in time they would find a manor quite like this one, surrounded by farmland worked by everyone but the man who lived in the big house.

Two floors and what must have been a few thousand square feet of wood stretched before me. A long balcony ran along the entire second level, probably encircling the entire estate too. Big wood pillars ran from the ground up to the roof. Between each sat either a door or a window with elegant dressings. The manor had an eerie symmetry to it; there was even two trees mirroring each other at the two front corners.

"Trouble." Arno pointed to the second floor. One of the rooms on the right side became blazoned with a teal-colored light streaming from the windows. A classic sign of some kind of magic being performed.

"If I had to guess, a summoning ritual. We're going to have company."

I barely finished talking when the room's window blew out upon the impact of yet another lizard daemon barreling from the building. It hardly touched the balcony, one quick step across the railing, and it was lunging through the air directly at us.

Arno and I were still a dozen meters from the manor. This gave me plenty of time to aim. I shut one eye and traced an imaginary laser from the revolver's sights to the lizard flying toward me.

"Mr. Kraft," Arno said, eyeing the still charging daemon.

"Relax, Mr. Berg. I used to do this for a living." It felt nice to have my shooting arm back to full capacity. My left side was aching from Orrla's stab, but my right arm was doing just fine. The image of Orrla taking Selene from me flashed before my eyes for an instant and I fired.

The lizard could not have been more than ten feet away when half of its face exploded and its steps faltered. It skipped across the dirt. Arno took one leisurely step to avoid the scaly missile. The daemon ground to a halt a short distance behind us. I kept my eye on the motionless form, half-expecting it to jump back up and resume its attack, but nothing happened.

"I'm going to have to assume Harcourt is losing quality in exchange for quantity," I said. "They don't normally go down that easy."

"Is that good or bad?"

"Depends on the quantity."

Didn't matter either way. We were already fully invested by this point — a fact that was cemented when two more windows blew out on the first floor. Three more daemons slithered out from the busted openings.

The one coming from the rightmost window glared at me across the lawn and took off in a four-legged sprint. I felt more confident knowing that these daemons were weaker than the three I had tangled with before. Harcourt had spent less time constructing their bodies. Even in magic there were trade-offs.

I took aim and squeezed the trigger. This lizard was more on the ball than its downed brethren, and the bullet struck the dirt as my target dove to the side in a roll that barely broke its gait. I could have emptied all my chambers, but there was a distinct possibility that they would all miss. I would be left defenseless against the oncoming onslaught. I dropped my arm to my side and waited.

There had been many times like this when I was thankful for my days with the IB. My training there had curbed at least some of my impulsiveness. I knew when to stop and think. The lizard daemon must have seen it as me giving up, and buried its claws deeper into the earth, coming like a cannonball at me. It was only a few steps away when it coiled its back legs and sprang forward, jaw open and ready to take a chunk out of my flesh.

This was my time to act. I twisted my right foot and bent out of the daemon's path. My final position left my back to the manor and one surprised lizard with a gun pointed at the back of its head. *Regis Baudin taught me that move. Don't think he expected I'd use it on a daemon.* A squeeze of the trigger and the bullet ripped through its skull and out its open maw. The daemon tore up sod and dirt as it struck the ground, twitching and gurgling on its dying breath.

Satisfied that another daemon was back in Hell, I turned to Arno to see that in the time it had taken me to take down one, he had one daemon's crushed throat under his heel and another ready to be wishboned by its jawline. Arno wrenched his mighty meat hooks apart and the daemon's jaw tore off in a gory display of power. He tossed the flopping lizard and its jaw aside, letting it die in the dirt, and turned to me.

"We don't have time for this," he said. Black blood coated his once clean sweater.

"Care to knock then?"

With an ogreish grin, Arno grabbed the daemon from beneath his foot by the tail. He took a running start and, with one dominating toss, sent the body crashing through the front doors. I didn't want to wait for any more daemons to show up outside, so I dropped into a dead sprint and chased Arno into the manor.

We smashed into the elegant entrance hall of Harcourt's home. All white and gold, the hall was reasonably sized with a staircase on the left wall that led up to a balcony. Harcourt seemed to have some obsession with the medieval times. I saw at least two suits of armor polished to perfection and wielding long spears. A few kite shields and some racks displaying quite a bit of weaponry sat on the walls. Arno evidently approved, taking a large ax off the wall for himself.

The crack and groan of wood brought me back to the fight. Another lizard had perched itself on the railing directly above me, drooling black bile nearly onto my head. I snapped my revolver up and fired a shot into the wood railing under its claws. The bannister split apart, taking the daemon off guard and sending it crashing to the floor at my feet. *Crack! Crack!* Two more shots to the chest and both the daemon and my revolver were spent.

I wasn't hopeful — or foolish — enough to think that was the last of it. I slammed in a full speedloader just as the other doors in the hall blew open. Lizard daemons came crawling out of every hole. What they weren't expecting was an angry ogre with an ax to greet them. Arno unleashed his inner gladiator at the first reptilian form to come within range, bringing the great ax crashing down onto its head.

It seemed like a good idea to give Arno plenty of space, so I took some steps back and let the big guy go to work as he disintegrated each opponent into a gushy paste. A few lizards agreed, as they gave Arno a wide berth and bounded off the wall to engage me. I needed to show these Hellborns that I wasn't much better.

The first daemon still had one foot on the wall when my shot blew off the top of its head, only for the next one to come scurrying over the body of its fallen comrade. I quickly readjusted my aim and fired again. This round struck slightly off the mark and pounded into the daemon's left shoulder. It got a mouthful of hardwood when it dropped and skidded across the floor. I grabbed the spear from the closer suit of armor, lifting it from the suit's grasp, and drove the blade down and through the top of the daemon's head.

"Mr. Kraft!" Arno hollered, yanking his ax from the brain of another lizard. "What say you to letting me take care of these things while you go find the wizard?"

I eyed the three lizards that were crawling along the staircase, blocking my path to the room where we saw the light. "Sounds good," I replied.

I flipped the cylinder of my revolver out and tipped the cartridges into my hand. I slid an orange bullet into a chamber and took a shot at the front most daemon. The splinter round shattered a few feet out, sending a hundred deadly fragments that tore the three lizards apart.

"Impressive," Arno grunted.

"Thanks."

I wasn't going to say that I was more impressed by the circle of lizard daemon chunks that lay around him. Why detract from impressing an ogre?

I put the two empty casings in my pocket and loaded the four remaining. A lizard was still twitching. It reached out for my leg, so I closed the cylinder and silenced it before running up the stairs. Harcourt needed to be stopped before he inflicted any more of his tricks.

The upper floor carried on the decorating style of a medieval-themed plantation, spreading on into the tight corridors. I charged into the right hallway, leaving the sight of Arno fighting behind, though the sounds of metal cutting scaly flesh still reached me. The ritual light had come from the third and fourth windows. The second door to my right should be the one. I replaced the three shots with a white flash round as I came to inspect the door.

It was as I feared, an analog lock. Not that it stopped me; it was just... different. I squared my right shoulder, then slammed it against the wood. The door may have given, but I couldn't tell, preoccupied with the shooting pain in my left side. I gritted my teeth, clutched my left side, and kept the image of Selene in my head. I kicked hard on the door. The wood groaned on the frame and with two more boots, it broke open, swinging forcefully into the room.

Frank Harcourt stood behind a desk, with an emotion of something between shock and confusion on his face. My entrance would have probably been more impressive if it hadn't taken me so long to get through the door.

"Hello, Kraft," he said, adjusting his tie and leaning one hand casually on his desk. "Did you want to bring something up with me?"

I took a quick glance around his office. It looked almost normal, save for the numerous ritual and occult items that littered the floor and shelves. The books that lined his shelves looked worn and beaten; I assumed that, unlike Warren, he actually read them. Looking down, I saw a thin silver circle embedded in the floor and a carpet throw to the side. Silver was a huge step up from drawing one with chalk. That would be where Harcourt was bringing in his pets from.

"Where's Selene?" I said, yanking down my mask. I put my hand in my coat pocket with the silver U and runic cloth.

"I don't know what you—"

"Orrla took her! Don't tell me you weren't involved! She said she was a gift for Obasin!"

Harcourt cocked an eyebrow, honest surprise on his face. "This is an unforeseen action on her part, but not irreversible. I'll deal with her after I deal with you." He cracked his knuckles with one hand, but kept behind his desk. "You insects should know better than to come uninvited into a wizard's abode."

I took a firm hold of the fabric in my pocket and slid my foot back, ready for whatever came. "Too much Dark magic cast here, Harcourt. Your threshold is weak. You know what the problem with you wizards is?" I let my revolver arm go loose but ready. "You're arrogant."

"It is not arrogance if you can back it up." He raised his right hand, palm facing toward me. "*Inflamius.*" A basketball-sized flame formed in his palm, and he fired it in a line drive for me.

I tossed the cloth from my left pocket before me. The fireball struck the cloth and disappeared into the folds, sending the cloth flying back into my hand. Warmth radiated into my body. My right arm took the momentum and swung forward. I squeezed my eyes shut and pulled the trigger.

Even through my closed eyes, I could see the light that emitted from the barrel. I heard Harcourt gasp. I opened my eyes to see him covering his own. I bolted for him. I shoved the still warm cloth back into my pocket and pulled out the silver U.

I reached the desk and leaped forward, the sheer amount of adrenaline in my system taking me over. I drove both feet into Harcourt's chest. He flew to the ground. I followed and stumbled to a straddling position. Harcourt kicked and struggled, but I pushed his right hand to the soft carpet. I drove the silver U down, piercing Harcourt's palm and embedding it into the floor below.

He let out a bloodcurdling bellow and tried to tear it out with his other hand. I had to push his left hand down and pin it with the knife from my bag. That only made him scream louder.

I favored my left side and took a seat on Harcourt's desk, placing my revolver atop a stack of papers. "I've looked into wizards," I said, catching my breath. "I assumed I would have to tangle with one sooner or later. So, with that in mind, that" — I pointed to the silver U — "is what I have dubbed a feedback arc. It's magic-conductive. You're not flinging any fireballs until that thing is out of there. Now we can talk."

"Obasin will devour you," he spat.

"So I've heard. Where would Orrla bring Selene?"

"Why would I tell you?"

"'Cause I have a very angry ogre downstairs. Rick Oslo's half-brother."

Harcourt's eyes widened. He didn't want to meet with a vengeful ogre when he was pinned down like that.

"I did not tell Orrla to take your woman, it was probably that idiot Dirk's idea."

"But where would she bring her?"

"The birthing place. We were to meet there tonight."

I thought back to the tunnels under Mercier and the silver receiver that sat within. It would make sense, but I had to make sure. "Mercier?"

"Of course." Harcourt attempted to hide a smile.

I tapped the feedback arc with my foot and Harcourt screamed. "You're lying."

"So maybe I am." He flexed his hands from their pinned position. I doubted he could force his way out. He wasn't nearly as physically fit a wizard as Gerard. "You can't stop him, Kraft. The crossing ritual was completed a long time ago. Once all the power is collected, he'll be through the Fade."

Everybody in Endless Hunger was sure that Obasin couldn't be stopped, but until he stepped foot in the Light, there was still a chance. "Tell me about Obasin."

Harcourt laughed. "You'll learn of him when he consumes you, body and soul."

I slid off Harcourt's desk, stepping on his chest in the process. I moved along one of the walls of books. "There is no mention of Obasin in any folklore or legend. His history must have faded away long ago. However, even if it's not online, there is always a book."

I scanned both bookshelves, but couldn't find any appropriately ancient text. Something forgotten like that would have to be practically prehistoric. It had to be somewhere. Some book that tipped Harcourt off to Obasin's existence. Harcourt chuckled behind his desk. *Obviously. His desk.*

I hurried back to the desk and threw open the drawers. Sitting on top of Glowing Future's quarterly report was a sewn together bundle of what I could only assume was parchment. Across the cover was simply the word "Obasin." I carefully removed it from the drawer and opened to a random page.

"And this is not in English." I flipped to the first page.

"If you let me go I can translate for you," Harcourt said, smiling widely.

I dug in my pocket for my phone. "You wizards need to get with the times." I opened a translator app and scanned the page. AKKADIAN TO ENGLISH. *What the hell is Akkadian?* Looking through the clear glass screen, English translation hovered above the cuneiform. The book was the journal of a scribe who lived during Obasin's rule.

"'At first,'" I read, "'the beast would come and eat whenever it saw fit. Nothing could stop it. Walls would turn to dust before it. That man would appear wherever the beast was, smiling through the chaos. He claimed himself to be a ruler. I was only a child when the man who called himself Obasin took his throne.

"'He told us the beast was his Hunger, and he its Master. We would routinely sacrifice the young ones to the Hunger. The Master would stand at his palace walls, watching with those who betrayed us and stood at his side. He would smile as we hurled another poor soul down the pit. The Master would occasionally take a victim for himself. Soon it became clear to me that the Hunger and the Master were connected; for every soul the Hunger consumed, the Master grew more powerful. Yet I remember working in his palace and seeing the Master tremble at the sight of the pit where the Hunger dwelled. Perhaps he was as afraid of it as we were.'"

I leaned against the desk. Obasin used to be a god-king. Not only that, he was actually two separate — but connected — creatures. Harcourt wasn't completely lying about the Mercier receiver being where Obasin would come from. He had called it "the Hunger's receiver."

"The Hunger part of Obasin is being released in Mercier, ah?" I spoke to Harcourt without looking at him.

"Well, aren't you clever," he replied.

I resisted the urge to kick him in the ribs. "It sounds as though the Hunger is nothing but a mindless beast. You're going to let it eat those people in Endless Hunger."

"It's so easy to find fools looking for something to believe in."

Orrla said shutting off the Glowing Future hub wouldn't stop "all of Obasin." She couldn't be lying. If the Hunger was coming from Mercier, then the Master must be coming from somewhere else.

"I'm so stupid!" I smacked my head. "The virus in Future's system isn't sending power to Mercier, because it's not a transmitter. Orrla said you put a piece of Obasin in the system. You put the Master in Glowing Future's computers. That's why I'm seeing visions of him outside my dreams." I looked at my Gloves. "I still have some of the information from Glowing Future mirrored in my Gloves. I've been carrying him around with me..."

I had been right. The reason Selene and Caleb were infected by the dreams was because I brought a piece of Obasin right to them. What about Harlequin? Ali? Every man, woman, and child I passed on the street could potentially be cursed with nightmares. What about the guard, Daniels? He was standing right next to me when the video played.

Harcourt laughed uproariously. "I was curious why we were getting so much power as of late! You've been spreading the sorrow around, Kraft."

I had been unintentionally hastening Obasin's arrival.

"The Master will be summoned at Glowing Future," I said. No sense wallowing in self-pity when I could still save every person I'd cursed. "That's where Orrla will take Selene. A gift for the Master."

"That wasn't the plan." Harcourt had turned smug. "Honestly, I was going to give him Orrla and Dirk."

"You were going to feed your own people to Obasin?"

"Dirk wanted a harem of the ages. Orrla kept prattling about that Yanswiy. They thought Obasin would grant their wishes. But only I would sit by his side. See what the High Circle thinks of that."

I shook my head. "You're despicable, Harcourt."

"I do what needs to be done. You humans go around thinking you're in charge. You blew up half the world and the High Circle just sat by! A wizard could smite any one of you with half a thought. Why should we stay in the shadows when we should be ruling!" Harcourt's face turned a deep red. Pulling on his bindings turned the carpet below his hands black and wet. "I will rule with Obasin. We will purge the weak and foolish. They will learn to respect their betters. Under my rule, there will be order! I thought you would understand doing what needs to be done, Kraft. You pinned a man to the floor." He nodded his head to the arc and the knife.

"I'm doing this for her."

"Are you? Or are you terrified of living with the guilt when she dies? Guilt is for the weak. I don't let it control me. I will be stronger for it, and the world will grow stronger with me."

I couldn't stay in that room for much longer; Harcourt was sickening me. "One last thing. Rick Oslo. Why did you kill him?"

"Warren was blabbing. I was worried the High Circle would notice something before Obasin would be ready. I used Rick's rampage to generate more sorrow for the ritual."

"That's it?"

"That's it. Now get this thing out of my hand." He tried pulling his right hand up but only succeeded in hurting himself.

"No." I grabbed the journal and revolver, holstering my gun as I headed out.

"But you said—"

"I never said I would let you free."

I could hear him struggling and kicking behind me. "This won't change anything! Just let me go!"

"I made a promise." I looked ahead to where a bloody Arno Berg had appeared at the door. "He's all yours," I said, without making eye contact.

"Who is that?" Harcourt shouted from behind the desk. "Is it the ogre? Oh, God. You don't want to do this! I'm about to become very powerful!"

"No," Arno growled. "You're not."

I shut the door behind me, not wanting to hear what an ogre could do to trapped prey.

The entrance hall was covered in black blood and the remains of around thirty lizard daemons. I stepped carefully around every severed limb and clump of flesh, until I was back in the yard and heading down.

When I got back to the car, Caleb was outside and leaning against the hood. The blood from his nose had dried into a gory mask, but the airbag didn't seem to have broken it. He had his arms crossed and stared me down the entire walk from the broken gate.

"You gonna arrest me?" I asked.

"I know better than most about the difficulties between law and Dark problems," he replied, but didn't move. "This is bad, Kraft."

"You can tell the Circle that they don't have to worry about Frank Harcourt anymore."

"That's my point. The High Circle is not going to like it that you took his justice into your own hands. They like to deal with things their way."

"Then you can tell them to go to Hell!" I spat. Caleb's eyebrows rose at my outburst. I was still all riled up from the confrontation, so I paced my rage out and then leaned against the car next to Caleb. "Just tell them I took Harcourt down because he was trying to summon a Dark entity. It's true."

"I know it is, Kraft, but the Circle may be vindictive over the whole thing."

"It's great to know we have such level-headed people looking over us."

That got a small laugh out of Caleb. I had to admit, it was nice to talk friendly with him again.

"What do we do now?" he finally asked.

I rested my head in my hands. "I think it's time I asked for some help."

"I don't know if you realize this, but you're always asking for help."

Asking for information and getting weaponry was one thing. Still, I was wrong about Selene, she handled the supernatural expertly — other than the intoxication. Even though Caleb lied to me, he was still standing ready at my side. Obasin — both the Hunger and the Master — was not something I could deal with on my own.

"Scoundrel was taken to Glowing Future." I shoved off the car, looking to the distant New Montreal skyline. "I'm going to go in and get her. Stopping Obasin is going to take a little more tact though."

"You have a plan?"

Come on, Kraft, you call yourself resourceful. Look at your resources. I grinned at Caleb. "I do now."

Chapter 20

Glowing Future Technologies was still closed off by police tape and locked up tight. Not that it being locked would ever stop me. A few detours meant I didn't get there until sundown.

"Take my badge, it'll get you past the sensors," Caleb said, passing his ID over. He peered at the journal in my hands. "Nothing in there about how he was sealed away last time?"

"The writer only says one morning the palace was destroyed and Obasin was gone." I put the book into Caleb's glove box for safekeeping. "Could have been the Well of Time, could even have been the High Circle. We don't have the time to ask either of them, though. Not if Obasin is being summoned tonight."

"Just let me get this straight. They put a Dark god *into* Glowing Future's system."

"Not all of him, just a piece. Enough to make a connection. Like in a ritual."

Caleb peered out the front window, looking up at Glowing Future Tower. "I still wish you would let me clear those people out of Mercier."

"The best chance we have to save them is stopping Obasin. If the Hunger steps foot in this world, it's going to come straight for New Montreal."

Caleb bobbed his head, conceding to the logic.

I clapped him on the chest and exited the car. "Scoundrel's down there. Just wait for my signal."

"What's the signal?"

"I think you'll recognize it." I backed away from the car.

"Wait, Kraft." Caleb leaned across the center console to see me. "I'm sorry I didn't tell you I was a wizard."

"You had reasons."

"That's it?"

"I don't know if there's anything else I can say."

"Oh. That sounds like someone who's mad."

"I'm not mad!" I had hoped that Caleb and I would move on. I could see the logic behind why he kept his mouth shut, but he wanted to talk about the feelings. "I'm just about to go in there and fight a sidhe. My mind is in a different place. I'm not mad, but we don't have time right now."

"Right." He grabbed the wheel. "Good luck in there."

"It won't be luck." I waved bye and jogged toward Glowing Future, the holotape flashing white as I passed through.

Caleb peeled away into the setting sun. I walked through the eerily empty lobby as I had done so many times before. The difference this time was the splatters of blood on the floor and walls. The remnants of Rick's assault. They must have shut off the power to the elevators so I had to take the stairs to the sub-basement.

I took the steps two at a time, going at top speed, but when I opened the door from the stairwell to the basement, I nearly fell back. The area before me was shrouded in darkness — not to mention the intense cold that enveloped me. I zipped the sweater I stole from Caleb's car to my chin and brought my bandana out and around my face.

Staring into the dark, I felt my chest tighten. I shut my eyes and focused until my Beyondsight clicked on. Thousands of pieces of code, floating like snowflakes, poured out of the basement. The Winter energy. My scan hadn't caught it because the basement was heat-shielded. They had to be using it to fuel the Master's part of the ritual. I was so close to it before and didn't even realize. Though, it had grown colder in the days since I'd last been to the basement.

I extended my hand and projected a white light from my Glove to illuminate the room. I slowly slid into the ghostly white glow until I could feel the blackness surround me.

I have never had a fear of the dark before, but the last few days had left their mark. The cave, the image of Obasin, it all felt permanently etched into my brain. I was going to burn him. I was going to show him who controlled my mind.

Searching the walls, I found a light switch. The bulbs flickered on and I felt my breath return. I willed myself to keep moving.

"You must be Kraft," said a voice from behind me before I could take a step.

I turned to see Dirk Humbolt sneering at me from the elevator bank. Without the cult robes he looked even more scrawny. He was dressed in a silk button-up and black dress pants. I had a feeling he and Caleb would have had plenty to talk about when it came to fashion.

"You don't look like much," he continued, pushing himself off the wall. "Orrla is sure you're the devil though."

"Dirk," I said, as I slid my hand into my left pocket. "If you leave right now, I won't kill you."

He burst into the most obnoxious laugh I'd ever heard. "That is priceless! What cha gonna do, little mortal?"

I drew my revolver and rested it against my shoulder. "Don't think this is going to be some great battle, Dirk. You come at me, you're going down. Simple."

"You are a sheep, Kraft. I am a wolf." A smile cracked across his face, then continued along his cheeks. His mouth split open and a vicious row of fangs grew over his pearly whites. "I'm gonna drink you dry."

He rushed forward, and I brought my hand out from my pocket, arcane cloth swinging before me. The fireball it had absorbed from Harcourt flew forth. Surprise jumped across Dirk's face for half a second before it was engulfed in the flames.

His feet flew out from beneath him and he crashed to the ground. Screams resonated through the corridor as Dirk tried desperately to slap out the blaze on his face.

"See? Simple. Vampires are something I've dealt with before." I flipped out the revolver's cylinder and dropped a red incendiary round into a chamber. "You're only really scary when there are a lot of you." I flipped the cylinder closed. "Or you're not a wuss."

"You'll pay for this! My father—"

"Shut up." I set off the round into his chest. An inferno exploded out from where the incendiary round struck, and the blaze now engulfed his body. I left Dirk Humbolt to burn.

Without Warren to guide me, I had to trust my muscle memory to find the hub. It worked, and I was able to find my way back to the door to the Network hub, leaving the screams of the vampire far behind. I placed my hand on the lock, disengaged it, and pulled the door open.

The server and its many cables stood before me, and I could still smell the hint of citrus from Rick's spray, but I was more interested in Orrla and Selene. Orrla was still wearing her torn suit and looked pissed as ever. Selene stood behind her, but she wasn't focusing. Her eyes looked glazed over and her mouth hung open. I felt all the wrath I had when she was first taken swell back up.

"What's wrong with her?" I growled.

"She's fine, just more compliant this way," Orrla replied, patting Selene on the head.

"Don't touch her." I loaded my revolver with my last full speedloader.

"Kraft," sneered Orrla. "I want you to see her die, so you can feel the pain I feel."

"I'll show you pain!" Six cracks rang out and six gory chunks flew out of Orrla's face and torso, dropping the faery to the ground a few feet back. Selene collapsed to her knees. I rushed to her side and took her head in my hands, trying desperately to have her focus on me.

"Kraft..." she finally said, albeit weakly.

"I'm right here, Selene." I took her hand in mine, squeezing tight to let her know I was there.

"Why is... it so cold?" She was still wearing the tank top and coveralls. The Winter energy was freezing her alive.

I started to take off my sweater when something impacted my chest. Orrla had recovered and had kicked me hard, knocking the wind out of me and sending me skidding across the frost-encrusted concrete floor into the adjacent wall. My left side burned. I tried to scream, but there was no air in my lungs to make a sound. The wound had definitely reopened, not that it had really closed in the first place. If I didn't get some real medical attention soon I was going to bleed out.

I was finally able to take some air into my chest. I dumped the bullet casings and loaded the three loose rounds

I still had. I barely got to sitting in time to have Orrla crash into me and push my shoulder blades hard against the wall, bringing her face in close.

The once beautiful features of Orrla's face had been blown away by my bombardment. The skin and bone were recovering, but I was about an inch away from a macabre sight of exposed cartilage and green gore.

On pure reflex, I fired a shot into her gut. She yelped and loosened her grip, so I fired another shot that sent Orrla stumbling and falling onto her back. I rose to my feet and set off my last round into her cheek, blowing away whatever recovery had taken place.

"Just stay down," I sighed, pulling my bandana to my chin.

She disagreed and grabbed my ankle. With the ease of a child tossing a disc, she threw me across the room. Gray stone rushed at me fast, and I put my arms up to stop my head from cracking open. I bounced off the wall and landed hard on my upper back. I heard a sharp crack as I hit. None of the sounds I'd ever heard a monster make frightened me as much as that crack did.

I was paralyzed; I just knew it. I had broken my back. Orrla was going to kill Selene. Obasin was going to rise and take over the world, and I was going to be paralyzed. And yet… I could move my feet. I wasn't paralyzed, though that didn't necessarily put me in a better position considering I still had a homicidal faery coming at me.

Orrla was trying to ease her way onto her feet, but she must have been feeling my nine shots. I saw her falling back down out of the corner of my eye. I rolled onto my stomach and crawled to the other side of the server, hoping to find the smallest reprieve to recover. My body screamed in agony and part of me wanted to roll over and die, but I had to fight on. Saving the world sucked.

I could see Selene across the server from me. She still seemed fairly out of it — whatever faery magic Orrla had used was still affecting her — but when she saw me I noticed a hint of recognition in her eyes. The cold was making her shiver uncontrollably, but she dug into her pockets for something. She rolled a small metal object to me.

I snatched it from the floor and found myself holding onto another speedloader. This one was different. The bullets didn't look like the normal .357 cartridges I used. *The steel-core rounds!* Selene must have whipped them up at some point.

Orrla's footsteps limped toward me. I removed the empty casings, carefully but quickly, and dropped in my new steel-core rounds. Her footsteps were getting closer and closer, accompanied by the steady drip of blood to concrete. I stayed on my front, holding my weapon close to me and tapping a familiar rhythm on my chest.

Tap, tap, tap-tap, went my gun on my chest.

Drip, drip, drip, went the blood to the floor.

Orrla's presence was on top of me. Jerking onto my back, I fired into the meat of her thigh. The impact wasn't as magnificent as the hits by the softer lead rounds, but she shrieked an unearthly cry and dropped to one knee. I fired again into her chest and she flew back, landing supine.

She screamed bloody murder as I eased myself to my feet. I had to lean against the server, but I was able to stand over Orrla. Her body was healing the first set of wounds, but the steel-core rounds had punched holes into her that weren't going to go away any time soon. Her screams subsided, and she looked up at me. Pain was evidently still coursing through her, but she kept it down.

"Just kill me, Seer," she spat. "I have nothing to live for without my Yanswiy, anyway."

"I'm sorry for what happened with her," I said. I almost surprised myself by saying it.

She attempted to laugh, but green blood spurted up and turned it into a cough. "I've seen into your mind, remember? I do not want your pity. You saw her as a monster. The Sidhe Courts did too. They cried out that a sidhe could not be with a common faery, but I loved her."

I saw whatever anger was in her wash away. It was replaced with a sadness, a deep and resounding emptiness. I wondered if I looked the same when I thought of Alexis...

"Obasin promised that in His world Yanswiy and I could be together. He promised that I could make the rules and no one would look down on us or say we were wrong. But you ruined that, Seer." She looked me right in the eye. "You took my Yanswiy from me, and any future we had."

"Orrla... Harcourt, he—" I tried to find some way to explain to her what I'd learned, but it didn't really matter if Harcourt was tricking her all along. It wouldn't change anything for her. The dead would still be dead. I said nothing.

I had never imagined a faery could cry before that moment, but Orrla wept. It was easy to see creatures of the Dark as monsters who only wished to use us to their own means. Jack of Frost was right about the Light and the Dark. Orrla loved, and she fought against her people for the right to love. She was willing to tear the world apart in the name of the one she wanted to be with above all else. I thought of what I had gone through for Selene, the anger I felt when I thought I wouldn't have her anymore. Orrla and I weren't so different; we both cut and destroyed to save those we loved.

"I'm... sorry," was all I could manage to say in the end.

"You're not sorry, you're incapable of being sorry." Something bubbled in her lungs with her breath. "You've already killed me. But all fae are infinitely reborn in the next world. Make this quick, Seer. I will be freed from here and may, if Fortune pleases, join Yanswiy in the Eternal Dance."

I nodded. I could at least give Orrla some peace. I raised my revolver. "I hope you find her," I said.

"I do, too." She closed her eyes.

I pulled the trigger.

Chapter 21

Selene came woozily around the server, the spell breaking with Orrla's passing. "What was that about?" she asked.

I let out a deep sigh. "An unfortunate meeting."

Selene laid her hand on my shoulder. She looked worse for wear, tired and shivering, but still there. I wanted to just hold her close and tell her that everything was alright. Unfortunately, things were far from over. Obasin was all ready to come bursting through the Fade any minute, and I had to stop him.

"Thanks for the bullets." I waved the revolver.

"If you'd told me they were so important, I would have finished them quicker," she said, rubbing her temples. "Where are we?"

"Glowing Future Technologies' basement. And you need to get going."

Her eyes widened. "Last thing I remember I was in my workshop. That glitchy lady was outside, and I could hear you and— What do you mean, I have to go?"

"I'll explain later, but just follow the signs and y—"

"Kraft!"

"Selene! This is one of those life or death times, and I need you to listen to me and get out."

She took a threatening step forward. "I am not going to leave y—"

I kissed her. I didn't even remember what move I took to get there, just that the next second I had one hand on her waist and the other on her cheek, and pressed my lips to hers. She was cold and I wanted to warm her up. I felt her relax as I pulled tighter on her hips. Time seemed to slow to a crawl, and we finally parted.

"Please," I said. I rubbed her cheek with my thumb.

She didn't talk for a while. Her nose was lightly pressed against mine, and I could feel her warm breath on my face.

"Fine," she said softly. "But you're coming out right after me. Right?"

"I promise."

I felt her lips on my cheek and she pushed away. She took a quick glance at Orrla's body as she hurried out. She was so much stronger than I gave her credit for, after all the daemons and faery kidnappings. I couldn't have her here now, though. I had to be alone in this dusty room, hoping I didn't just lie to her.

It was no time to get lost in thought; I had a plan to put in to action. "Jack of Frost!" I cried, willing some power into the words.

"Yes?" he replied almost immediately, sauntering from around the server.

"Look what I found," I said, motioning to the cold air around us.

"Oh, yes. Winter power all around." He rubbed his hands with greedy glee.

"And you found the other receivers?"

"The one in Mercier, another in that big tower to the north, and the last one in a little warehouse in the docks."

If the one in Mercier went down, the Hunger could come popping out of any one of them. "And are the others in place?"

He nodded with a smile; he seemed to love being part of the plot. "Your Irish wizard friend is down in the docks, and that spunky blonde cop kicked her way quite expertly into the tower."

Good, both Caleb and Alexandra were in position. I was worried about rushing a plan together on the way back from Harcourt's. It had taken some work to get Ali on board, but with Caleb backing me up, we were eventually able to get her to come around.

"And Ali's ready to—"

"Someone's coming." Jack stared intently at the door.

I joined him in his gaze, expecting the door to come crashing in at any second. Selene had to be gone; there was no way she was there. I turned back to Jack. "Get in position. When I call you again, that's the cue. If you don't hear from me in fifteen minutes just go ahead anyway. That includes Ali's job."

He saluted me and disappeared into a puff of snow.

I drew my revolver. I had three more shots of steel-core in the cylinder ready to fly. Taking aim at the door, I waited. Footsteps off stonework came to a stop on the other side. My grip tightened on the gun as the door slowly opened.

"Hello? Anyone down here?" It was Daniels, the scrawny security guard.

I breathed a sigh of relief and holstered my weapon. "It's Kraft," I called out.

Daniels popped his head in. He looked disheveled and weary, though I assumed I didn't look much better myself.

"Mr. Kraft?" asked Daniels. "What are you doing here?"

I seized up for half a second, remembering the bloody corpse hiding behind the server. I prayed Daniels wouldn't go for a walk and start asking questions.

"I'm going to destroy this virus," I replied as evenly as I could.

"What do you mean?"

"It's... kind of a long process. Essentially I'm going to starve it, though." I spun to the server and unzipped my sleeves, getting ready to work.

"Oh." Daniels paused. He took a few deep breaths, as though talking was an effort. "Have you been having nightmares, Mr. Kraft?"

"Yes, Daniels."

"I didn't think they would stop." His feet dragged along the floor. "I was scared, I kept remembering that video. But, someone said they could help me."

I froze. I slowly turned to Daniels. His skin was pallid.

"Who said they could help you?" I asked, my hand sliding to my revolver.

"I don't remember. He was... I think... Obasin?"

I jumped to my feet and gripped my gun.

"Where am I? I asked him if I could sleep. I'm really tired." He grabbed his head with both hands. "Is someone screaming?"

"Daniels…"

The security guard's jaw exploded apart, sending blood splattering across the front of his uniform and the floor. Fleshy tendrils dripped from the void where his mouth should be. Daniels's body began convulsing and pulsating until his chest burst out. I jumped back to avoid being hit with gore.

Recovering, I brought my revolver up to target Daniels. My skin went pale at the sight before me, and I felt vomit attempt to make its way up my throat.

Daniels's ribs stuck straight out, moving like grasping fingers from his chest. The cavity was filled with a bloody maw of bone and sinew. Two slits cut up his wrists and split open to reveal more horrifying mouths, gnashing for my flesh.

"Feast…" The voice was not Daniels's anymore.

I unleashed the screaming of my revolver's barrel, pumping my last three rounds into the Daniels-beast's chest mouth. The wounds had no effect, and the beast charged. Willing my battered body to move, I charged forward in return, dropped down, and slid through the creature's legs as it swung its arms for me. In another fluid motion, I jumped back up and booted the creature in the back, sending the monster stumbling forward.

It all seemed to do nothing but anger it. Turning around, the Daniels-beast extended its arm and a bone spike jutted out from its palm at my face.

Dodging the spike, I had to duck quickly as another bone swung by. I felt along my belt and swore when I remembered I had used my only high explosive round earlier. Selene didn't normally make them. I had another incendiary round, but I didn't want to risk damaging the server before I did my work.

I had other options. If I played it smart enough, I might even get out alive. With a flick of my wrist, I swung the cylinder open and ejected the casings, replacing them with a flash bullet.

The monster stepped forward, mouths grinding in anticipation. I lashed out with my revolver, closing my eyes tightly. A brilliant light erupted from the mouth of the barrel, blanketing the entire room and blinding the beast.

I eased my eyes open once the light from the flash round disappeared. The monster was crying out in rage and throwing its arms about wildly. I stumbled back to avoid one such swipe and landed back first against the door. I pushed down on the handle and continued my fall to the adjacent wall outside. I took the chance to catch my breath.

Inside the room, the monster was still trying to find me so it could slice my belly open. I had heard about creatures like that, humans who gave themselves wholly to a powerful spirit of the Dark. Daniels had become an Emissary for Obasin, the embodiment of gluttony.

The Emissary started shaking. I had seen enough movies to know that never ended well. He thrust his arms wide, and I scrambled out of the way as a field of bone skewers shot from his body, thudding into the space on the wall I had just vacated. I was already disappearing into the corridors as the spikes receded back into the room.

I ran deeper and deeper into the maze of tunnels, opting to get as far from the Emissary as possible. I knew that I had to get back to the server room eventually. I also knew I wasn't going to be able to do it with a monster hunting me.

An otherworldly bellow echoed from elsewhere in the basement, distracting me enough that I almost tripped over some rebar laying across the ground. I'd evidently stumbled upon a storage area for construction supplies. Rebar, drywall, toolboxes, and a couple extension cords were littered about.

A plan quickly formulated in my head, and I grabbed a nearby pair of wire cutters. Snatching one of the extension cords, I ripped off the female head with the cutters and tore down the plastic covering to expose the wires. I jammed one piece of rebar into the broken side of the cord, making sure the wires wrapped firmly around the metal.

The sound of loud footsteps and growling soon came from the corridor behind me. I pushed myself to the wall next to the opening, gripping tightly on the rebar. My breath slowed and I focused on the approaching noises. Each step was a cue to where my foe lay.

"He lied," the Emissary moaned. "He lied. I still can't sleep. Let me sleep."

There was a stomp just around the corner.

Rushing around the bend, I drove the rebar forward. I felt it push into the flesh of the monster, hearing the cry of pain. I had speared it just below its chest mouth, barely out of reach of its horrible teeth. The beast swung its arm into my right shoulder. The aberrant mouth cut right through my sweater and bit into my skin, blood flowing quickly from the wound.

"Fuck!" I cried, yanking up on the rebar and tearing more out of the creature.

Roaring in pain, the Emissary released me. I clutched onto my shoulder and scrambled backward, following the extension cord to the wall. I turned back to see the monster bearing down on me, all three mouths ready to devour. Grabbing the cord's plug, I shoved it into the nearby socket.

Electricity sparked from the rebar and the beast seized up. It convulsed as its body became a circuit. The horrible odor of burning flesh and hair filled the corridor as electricity tore through its form. The monster collapsed to the ground, smoke trailing off it as it lay twitching and drooling in a puddle of pus and blood. The body broke down into gory remains.

Enough of this bullshit. No more people are dying. I ran back into the corridor to the server room. I favored my bleeding arm as I returned to the Network hub. Kneeling weakly before the computer, I tried to return to work.

"Seer!" a deep voice yelled, seeming to come from the server itself.

"You must be Obasin," I growled, no longer surprised by the interruptions.

"I am impressed your mind has survived my torture. But it is not over yet!"

"That's great, Obi. Why don't you shut up while I kill you?"

"I will not be defeated so easily!"

The server sparked, sending me stumbling back. My head struck the stone hard, and I slipped into the dark.

Chapter 22

My eyes opened to nothing. At first, I didn't even realize they had. I was staring into an impossibly black sky. Infinite shadows that were strangely familiar. *The cave.* I jumped to my feet and reached for my gun. The holster was empty. *It can't be real. It can't be real.*

"Seer," the voice oozed from all around.

There was only darkness in the distance. I traced a line along the strange ambient pool of light that surrounded me. I couldn't define any source. It seemed to just... be. Past the light was a Stygian hall tracing endlessly. There was something in the dark. It was Obasin. He was near.

"Welcome to my world, Seer."

This time the voice was close. I spun to the source. A figure stood just out of reach. He was barely illuminated by the pool of light.

"Obasin," I said.

He wasn't the putrid blob I saw hunting me, though. This version of him was a short, pudgy man with wisps of greasy black hair and a butcher's apron. He circled me like a hawk, never stepping too far into the light.

A wicked grin grew across his face. "Have you been having fun? Playing with my followers? My meals?"

"You're not going to win."

"Why?" he cackled. "Because you fried the vampire? Because you slaughtered the faery? Because you fed the wizard to an ogre? I have already won. This ritual was set in motion long before you came crashing in like you humans do. My Hunger will burst from its womb and into the Light. Then I follow. I will control your worm of a world and feed forever."

"That's it? You just want to eat?" I couldn't let Obasin see the shaking in my knees. He pulled me into the Dark. *What kind of power does he really have?*

"Everything wants to eat, Seer. From the largest to the smallest, all have the desire to feed. I just desire more prey. The Well locked me away because they said I was too dangerous. Too hungry." He was practically shaking with rage. "Just want to eat — do you *just* want to live? You treat it like such a shallow desire, but it is a need. I am no more a monster than the lions in your grasslands."

I turned with him. I never let his pacing form leave my eye line. "I'm not here to listen to your preaching. Harcourt is dead, your two 'gifts' gone as well. There's only me."

"Yes, you." He stopped. "You will be my first meal in the Light. You will give yourself to me."

"Not going to happen."

"You are a fool!" shouted Obasin. "You humans have no concept of how insignificant you are. Living so close to the border of absolute oblivion. Consigning us to tales of fancy and folklore. There are things in the Dark that your stories have not scratched the surface of. I am a gift compared to them."

A hundred eyes loomed over me from the shadows; the Dark beings that are too strong to push through the Fade, but the ones that would bring ruin to the Light if they did. How many more would be foolish enough to try to summon them through? The world was on a timer. I swallowed hard.

"You feel fear. Good. Fear is the most delicious of spices. I can see into your mind like an open book. You are a twisted wreck, Kraft. A knight in rusted armor. Soon you will be begging for me to end it."

He raised his hand. A cold slumber washed through me.

When I opened my eyes, Obasin was gone. There was nothing but the lightless expanse. I could stand around and wait for the next game Obasin wanted to play, or I could try to get out. I picked a direction and started walking. Whatever the light was, it followed me. It never spread far but kept pace with my footsteps on the lifeless marble. I passed by a column, spearing upward into the never-ending expanse above me. I couldn't see the ceiling, if there even was one.

Maybe I'm dreaming? It was a slightly reassuring thought. *Just let it happen and then wake up?*

The first sight to break the monotony was a massive wooden door. The sheen of the surface was pristine, though I doubted some servant was coming by to polish it every day. I passed through it and into the next room. This place risked being a copy of the last hall if not for the wood on the floor and the hint of a wall to my right. Approaching, the light revealed a series of great murals set into the wall. Scenes from a history I did not recognize.

The first mural was of a dozen black stick figures locked in some kind of combat. One figure speared another, while a third decapitated the fourth with his sword. Dark red paint shot from the wounds inflicted. A substance that looked a little too blood-like for my tastes.

I moved to the next. A dark shadow rose from the ground. It was snatching the humans and dropping them into its maw. Other humans fled in terror. At the base of the beast was another figure, this one drawn differently than the other humans. It was barely inside the normal boundary of what a person should look like. I couldn't describe it, it just seemed wrong. The Hunger and the Master. It was Obasin's history.

Each progressing mural was a chronological timeline of Obasin's rise to power. Next, the figures were praising the Master while the Hunger was fed with sacrifices. They brought the Master gifts so they would be spared, it seemed.

Then the drawing shifted. Another hand finished the story. The people grew restless and fearful. A small group confronted Obasin — the Well of Time, I assumed. They raised their hands in defense of the humans, and the beast was dragged away. The final image showed the Master fleeing, the Hunger bearing down upon him.

"You see?" Obasin's voice echoed through the hall. "I was once a king. The people worshipped me. But then, the Well decided I was too mighty in my grace and cast me into this damned realm. Now I must flee through the halls, that accursed Hunger chasing me at every turn, giving me no rest."

An unearthly growl made its way to my ears, flowing from the hall I had come from.

"It's your turn to be hunted, Seer. The Hunger comes. Run!"

I didn't wait around to see what the growl belonged too. I dug my toes into the floor and took off in the opposite direction. More murals and columns and endless black were all that met me. The Hunger kept pace, its bone-shaking footsteps pushing me forward.

My heart pumped acid, but still I ran. Everywhere I turned there was the same sound of my feet against the same ground. Wood, marble, stone. Every hall and corridor flashed past me. A corrupted statue, a torn painting, a broken chair, there was nothing about the forgotten palace that gave me the faintest sign that anyone still lived there.

"The Tomb of Hunger they called it," Obasin said. "Once my palace, but now a prison built for me. A joke, from the Well. It expands all through the Dark, each turn met with another. For many millennia I ran through its halls, my Hunger trying to make me its next meal, not understanding that by devouring me it would only be destroying itself."

My legs threatened to fail me as I crashed into the next room. I slammed the door shut behind me and found myself in a dilapidated chapel. Taking the backing to a pew that had fallen off, I slid it through the door's handles and hoped it would hold against what was coming.

Sometime between entering and barring the door, the candles on the shrine had become lit. The sanctum was unlike any I had seen before. A large, twisted statue stretched up from the top of the shrine, looming over me as I approached the pulpit. Gold and stone adorned two totems that framed the shrine. It was a dark and occult place. *Nothing good happened here.*

"They wanted me to witness my rise and fall over and over. They believed I had to be punished for my actions. Punished! I gave you humans peace!"

I touched the closest totem. It looked like stone, but as my fingers brushed it, I felt cold metal. *Strange...*

A bang against the chapel door. I instinctively reached for my gun. *Empty holster, right.* The wooden bar across the handles groaned.

"You humans crave to be ruled. Without law, you burn and destroy your planet! From the halls of my prison, I could see the ruin you brought upon yourselves. Many cataclysmic wars and with each you promised it would be the last. In the end, you had to scorch the earth so irrecoverably that not even my kind could live on it!"

The door bar cracked on the next impact, but I was already running out through another exit by the shrine. I was sprinting through the palace again. I lost track of time. It felt like hours, but there was no way I could have run that long. Time and space bled into each other.

I came bolting into the next room. I was ready to keep running when something caught my eye. The murals of Obasin's rule. *A circle, I've run in a circle.* Obasin was right, the tomb had no exit. Only more halls.

The Hunger's growl echoed. It wasn't far behind, but I couldn't push my legs any further. Even as I thought about it, they gave out and I dropped. I looked up into the empty sky above me. I wasn't ready to give up. I would just sleep for a while...

I woke up to nothing. No sound of the Hunger coming for me. Nothing.

My body felt like one large bruise. Blood trickled down my right arm from where the Emissary bit me. A wet feeling squished on my left side, and I touched my bandage to find it drenched. *How is my body staying together?* In time, I was able to roll onto my good side — not that either side was particularly good these days — and get my arms and legs beneath me.

The phantom light was still there, but the dark waited in all directions beyond it. I chose one and pushed forward.

I walked for what felt like forever. I found no columns to break up my trek this time. Only the marble beneath my feet and the steady beat of my steps against it. It was the strangest marble. When I walked across the marble in Glowing Future's lobby, it made a distinct sound. *This sounds different, though.*

"Do you know why humans fear the dark, Seer?" Obasin's voice returned. "They want to understand. They want to see all that is around them and know what rests there. With the dark, their sight is incomplete. Whatever waits beyond in the shadows is unknown. I wait in the shadows, Seer. I hunger."

I blocked his voice from my mind the best I could. He was trying to break me. It was a mental bombardment I had to withstand if I was ever going to put him in his place. *Save the world, Kraft. Why not?*

Maybe I'm dead? It seemed more and more likely. *This is Hell. Stuck here with Obasin's whispers in my head.*

The light's glow was finally broken by an object. It was wooden, a few meters high with a rusted, bloody blade set between two vertical planks, and a soft looking board to lay a head on. A guillotine. I slid closer, the only break in an otherwise endless sea of stone and black. The board looked so comfortable.

"Peace, Kraft. You will find it in death."

The top of the lunette at the base slid up. Lay down, pull the handle, and end it. That was what Obasin wanted.

It was not what I wanted. I moved around the guillotine and kept walking. There was a resounding *thud* as the blade dropped. *I'm not dead yet.*

"You're angry."

His voice penetrated my body, cutting into every fiber of my being.

"You believe your rage is your power, do you? No. It's a cover for the pain you inflict on others. You are the curse on their lives."

You can see nothing, you can hear nothing. Use your other senses, I told myself. The hall smelled like dust. Old dust. But, as I focused more, I swore I could smell something else. It was faint. It was familiar.

I almost walked smack into another door. *A door!* The wood on this one was rotted though. Dust hung on the handle. I looked from where I had come but only saw the infinite expanse — not that I was expecting anything else. I took the handle, grime pressing into my palm, and pulled. It opened with a dull groan.

Another horrid darkness greeted me. I strained to see any disruption. Any glimmer of something hiding in the distance. Far ahead of me, almost disappearing into the landscape, was a single pinpoint of light. My heart leaped. I got my second wind and ran.

The light grew like a welcome sign. All soreness was gone from my body. As I got closer, I realized it was another glowing pool, like the one around me. Two figures swirled amongst its radiant embrace. Orrla and Yanswiy. Dancing together in utmost joy.

Orrla swept Yanswiy around in some grand faery ballet. Yanswiy, glamour going at full power, laughed and took Orrla in her arms. I could nearly hear the ballad playing for them. They moved in sync, never missing a beat of their improvised frolicking. Happy. They were so very happy.

"Do you feel sorry for what you did? Do you feel anything other than anger and sadness? Fortune truly wanted to play with you."

Yanswiy dropped. Orrla clutched her hands over her mouth and fell to her side. She pushed Yanswiy lightly. The fallen spriggan didn't stir. The pushing turned to shaking, but Yanswiy wasn't reacting. She couldn't react. I watched as Orrla took her in her arms and pressed her head into the nape of Yanswiy's neck. The soft sound of weeping echoed through the void. *There's nothing I can do.*

"Then you taunted her. Because she was a monster, right? She could not truly feel for this other faery you killed. But she did. And you were shocked and enraged when she came for you? I'll ask you again. Do you feel sorry?"

"If she succeeded the world would have been in danger," I said. But I never looked away from the sight of Orrla weeping over her lover's corpse. *None of this is real. Remember that none of this is real.*

"That's not what I asked. Do you feel sorry? Or do you simply know that you should?"

A shadow of myself entered the glow, flickering like an ancient film might. It threw Yanswiy away and kicked Orrla to the ground. Orrla scrambled away but it grabbed her and dragged her back. It stepped on her neck and aimed a revolver at her chest. She struggled against its foot, but it pressed harder. Choking, whimpering breaths filled the air. She couldn't escape. I couldn't look away.

"Funny, isn't it? The faery can feel love, but you can only imitate it."

For half a second, it was Orrla with the gun and me on the ground.

"Stop!" I shouted.

The gun fired. I felt the impact. My feet flew out from beneath me and I hit the earth. Wet warmth covered my chest. I was drifting away...

I was back. I grasped for my chest wound but found no gaping hole. Orrla and Yanswiy were gone. Instead, there was only Obasin standing at the edge of the light, smiling at me.

"You have quite the past," he said. "Your sins are delectable, and they act as threads to the ones you care for. But who is closest?" He cocked his head and leaned closer. "Ah. Tell me about Selene."

From the shadows, Selene appeared. I pushed my aching body to its feet and ran for her. I didn't get past one step. A splitting pain in my leg fixed me in place. A black spear jutted from the floor and through the meat of my thigh. I went to touch it but another shot from the dark, piercing my arm. Three, four, five, six obsidian spikes skewered my limbs and held me firmly in place, as though I was being pinned to the darkness itself.

"Selene!" I cried. Every pull against my bindings sent jolts of pain through me. *I have to get to her!*

"Wasn't she ignorant before you came into her life?" Obasin teased. He swept past Selene, running his fingers through her hair. She didn't move. "Without you she wouldn't have been exposed to this loss and pain. Now you can't take it back. She puts up a strong wall, but you see how afraid she is inside. She will forever know what lurks in the world around her, and she will be marked."

The Emissary slid up behind her. Its mouths convulsed and stretched.

"No!" I pulled hard on the spikes, blood tracing down their lengths.

"She will die," Obasin said.

The Emissary whipped his arms around her. Forearm mouths gouged into her torso. Her eyes jumped wide and she screamed. Blood flowed down her front and her body began shaking. The big chest-maw's tendrils dug into her arms and began pulling her inside.

I couldn't watch. Her face begged me to help but I couldn't reach her. I squeezed my eyes tight, feeling warm tears push out.

"Is that remorse I see?" Obasin's words cut through the noise. "Do you truly feel for what you have done? Or are you just parroting the emotions you think you should have?"

Bloodcurdling screams rattled through my head. *I'm sorry.* The screams stopped with an abrupt crack. Only the grotesque slurping remained. I kept my eyes shut until the last sound left the hall and there was silence.

"What does this remind you of?"

I let my eyes open to find the Emissary and Selene gone. In their place was a familiar ivory-skinned figure. My breath caught in my throat. *It can't be.* The monster that appeared on the train. The one in my mirror. I hadn't truly seen it since the night my parents were slaughtered in our home. He stood eight feet tall and was impossibly slender. Pure black eyes stared down at me from beneath long, dark hair. A feather-like cloak draped down his form, wrapping tight against his drawn frame. The daemon that killed my parents.

The Raven.

He didn't move. Neither did I.

"Did you tell your dear little sister what you saw the day your parents died? Were there any words you could use to describe what it looked like when a raven monster tore their throats out? Before your very eyes they became nothing but skin and bone."

My entrance into the world of magic and monsters was christened in blood. My parents' blood, splattered across the kitchen floor. I had seen small things before. Little daemons and spirits, but nothing like him. I couldn't remember why I had been awake. It was late. I should have been asleep. But there they were. My parents. And there he was. The Raven.

"How long did you push it down? You told the doctors a monster killed your parents, and they said it was a robber. Some random criminal that you demonized. In time, you stopped disagreeing. But why? You saw things. You knew it was true. But they couldn't see. You were alone, child."

The Raven spread his talons and the feather cloak unfurled into expansive wings. Beneath its folds, I saw the elongated limbs that ended with blackened skin and wicked claws. Fifteen years earlier, those talons tore through my parents. *Why did the Raven come? Why did he take my parents?*

I fell back to the cold floor. A presence grew behind me. Obasin's torture never ended. *Might as well get it over with.* I took the time to catch my breath. The Raven wasn't moving to attack, so I turned to the new horror. I froze. I was on my feet without realizing it. Her hair was golden. Her eyes were a piercing steel. She smiled a glorious smile and touched me lightly on the cheek. The warmth of her hand flowed through me.

"Alexis," Obasin gurgled. "She paid for it, in the end. Could you have saved her, Kraft? Did you see what stalked her, or did you leave her alone in her time of death?"

Alexis closed her eyes. I moved to stroke her face. I needed to feel her skin against mine again. Where my fingers touched, a dead grayness grew. The rot spread from her cheeks and down her body.

"No! Alexis!" I cried, dropping to my knees. She never lost that beautiful, innocent grin. Even as her skin flaked away until only darkness remained.

"You don't fool me, Kraft. You hold that woman in your mind, locking her inside an eternal cage because when you forget about her, it'll prove you never loved her at all. Just like you never love anyone."

I pressed my head to the marble. I was numb. *He's lying,* I told myself. *He's trying to break you. He knows what troubles you. But this feeling, this proves you care. This proves I care.*

...Right?

"Are you aching?"

Plastic rattled along the floor. I raised my head and an auto-injector of Medioxyl came rolling to me. It stopped just before my face. The red and white container invited me in.

"How long has it been, Seer? How long since you last felt the lover's embrace of your drug?"

Four days. I'd never gone that long. The euphoria, the peace, the blooms. I was working so hard I forgot about it. It was all there in my little liquid devil. I took it in my hand, sitting up to kneeling. *Push to arm. Needle cuts a hole and my veins will fly.*

"You think you are a hero? Something great? You're so afraid of the void inside you that you drug your brain to ignore it. You are a junkie, Seer."

Four days. Needle cuts a hole. Push to arm. Stop shaking. *Stop shaking.*

"Go."

I seized. My body screamed at me. I flung the drug away. *It's just a little withdrawal.* Four days without it. But I felt fine without it, didn't I? When I was on it — when I thought about it — my thoughts were scattered. It helped me to forget. *Split the brain until it can't focus on what hurt you.* Without it I could think clearly. I had to think clearly. Tears burned into my cheeks. *I'm so stupid.*

"You can stop this." Obasin's voice was right in my ear.

My arm grew heavy. I felt the familiar grip of my revolver in my hand. *Obasin was right; I can stop this.*

"You are not strong, Seer."

His words traced down my brain stem, burrowing into my body.

"You are already dead. Dead from your parents. Dead from your lover. Dead from the years of pain you've analyzed. You are alone."

"How long has it been?" I whispered. "How long have I been here?"

Obasin's laugh reverberated through my body, and he appeared once again at the edge of the light.

"It must feel like an eternity, I know. But it has only been five minutes in your time. Imagine how much you will go through before I am born into your world."

How can I sustain this? Years will slide by before anyone even notices I'm gone. My revolver looked inviting in my hand. There were no bullets, I remembered, but it felt heavy with meaning.

If Obasin wanted me to be dead, then I would be dead. Ali was right, humans felt emotion. If I wanted to get out of this situation, I would have to do away with that weakness. I shut my eyes and focused on the facts. No emotion.

Obasin wanted me to take my own life, metaphorically at least. The guillotine, the drug, the gun. Why didn't he kill me himself? I ran my fingers along the marble floor. There was something weird about it. I had considered it once, but I lost it. The marble was cold. The marble was... *concrete?*

My hand tightened around the revolver, and I wiped the tears from my eyes.

"It would be easy." Obasin crept closer.

"I'm done with you."

Air sucked out of the entire tomb. Obasin had to take a second. "You don't get to choose to be done with me."

"Actually, I do," I said, returning to my feet. "I was worried you were all ready to invade the Light, but you're just stalling for time, aren't you? You don't have any real power."

"I dragged you into the Dark!"

"Not really. You've been doing well keeping me scared and distracted, but I don't see a lick of code around this place. This" — I stomped on the marble — "is concrete. The wood I was chased over was concrete. The totem in your shrine was metal because it was the hub. And that smell? The one I couldn't place. It's lemon. The same lemon that Rick sprayed around the hub to make it smell better. This world is in my head, Devourer."

I took a step toward him. Even in the shade I could see his eye tic.

"It's a suggestion, isn't it? Like a grand hypnosis. You haven't truly crossed over in any meaningful way. You haven't dragged me into the Dark. That's why you need me to let you in, like Daniels did. Even your spikes didn't leave any lasting damage!"

I spread my arms apart. The wounds left behind by the black spears had all disappeared.

"You have no idea the power I wield!" The entire room shook with his cry.

"You put me in the right mood with that whole Hunger chase, then asked the right questions so I would create my own fears. But rather than kill me with your own hands, you insisted I do it myself. Because you can't touch me physically, unless I let you. You did not bring me into your prison; you brought your prison into my head!"

"Then I will shatter your mind!" He thrust his arm forward and the black spikes returned, piercing my body a dozen times. Even if it wasn't real, it still hurt like hell. "Pity, I was hoping to consume it on my arrival!"

"Get. Out. Of. My. HEAD!" I pushed against the spears. Even the acceptance of the illusion did nothing to weaken them. How much blood would I have to lose before it equaled becoming a gibbering mess in the real world? My willpower faded. Obasin cackled in my ear.

"Die!" he cried.

"You first!" I gave one final push against his power.

Something incredible happened.

I felt an enormous energy surge out of my body. It was like water rushing along my skin. Not just on the surface. It crawled through my veins and muscles and bones before exploding out. The spears detonated. Pure force rained particles down on me and Obasin.

Obasin's jaw hung open. I doubt I looked any less confused.

"Wha— How?" he stuttered. "That's not possible." He gazed over my body. He bared his teeth. "That's mine! I'll rend it from you!"

From behind his back he drew a massive butcher's knife. The thing had to be at least four feet long with a bloody, serrated edge. He raised it high above his head and was ready to charge when a familiar bestial cry cut through the dark. Obasin froze in his tracks.

"What's wrong?" I asked with a smile. "Is that not the Hunger you sent after me?"

"How di—"

"Five minutes in here, plus the ten I spent with your Emissary. You see, Mr. Great Devourer, I may be weak, as you said. But I am not alone."

The ground trembled with massive footsteps. Obasin may have been underselling the Hunger when he made his illusionary one.

"I sent a few of my friends to the receivers meant to birth your Hunger," I continued. "They shut them all down at once, before the power could transfer elsewhere. Yet, he had to go somewhere after all that time in the Network. Like any good beast, he would follow the food. I had my good friend Alexandra send out a kill order on all outgoing signals from those companies' servers. Police can do that, you see."

Obasin was sweating. Even gods feel fear. "But h—"

"I'm not done!" I stomped my foot to the ground, a tremor shaking the hall. "You had your chance to speak, it's my turn. Now, I had her shut down all the outgoing signals from each system. But there's still one connection remaining. Can you guess which one, Obasin?"

I didn't know if he was planning to reply. An organic hook burst through his chest. I assumed he could guess at that point. I could barely see a long, fleshy tendril leading away into the growling dark. Obasin drove his knife into the ground and held tightly as the hook yanked him back.

"A funny little book implied you were afraid of your Hunger." I sauntered close to him, leaning in until I was a foot away from his straining face. "I'm here in the Light so it can't do anything to me, but you have your true body in the Dark. And that little piece of yourself that was put in Glowing Future's system? It fed the energy to you, but also left a trail for your Hunger to follow."

"No! No, please, Kraft!" Obasin cried, dark bile dripping from his mouth. "This isn't what they promised! They said I would be king again!"

Who said he would be king? "Who are 'they'?" I grabbed the giant knife's hilt. "Who are you talking about?"

Obasin started to reach for my arm, but quickly put his hand back on the handle — afraid to compromise his grip. The tendril threatened to tear his arms off at the shoulders. From the distant shadows I could still hear the Hunger growling.

"The whispers. The whispers that made promises." His shoulders cracked. "I'll tell you everything! Everything they said. Everything I know! Just help me! Please! Don't let me die like this!"

I did consider it. There was something bigger going on. Someone used Obasin like he used Endless Hunger. *The whispers? Do I release this piece of trash to discover what's really going on? Is he lying to save his skin?*

No. I stepped away from the knife. I couldn't let an entity like Obasin go free. I loaded my last incendiary round into my revolver. "Sorry, Obasin. I'm not going to let you get out of this one. If I really am here in the Light, I can end this right now. Crash your system and you'll be locked away until your Hunger can finish you."

"No! Kraft!"

"I just have to aim, and shoot."

The Emissary's bite was still tender, but I raised the weapon. The hub would have to be radiating Dark energy at this point. I raised my Sight and focused until I could see through the illusion. Code traced the floor and I swung my revolver to where it converged. Alexis stood in my way.

"Alexis!" Obasin shouted. "I can tell you what happened to her! I was kidding! You cared about her all along, clearly. You wouldn't hurt her!"

She smiled at me.

"I can answer your question! That question you are always asking!"

Why?

I gazed into Alexis's kind, familiar face.

"Maybe another day," I whispered.

I closed my eyes and fired.

Obasin's roar flooded my mind, then faded. The darkness tore away and was replaced by the server room. Heat assaulted my face from the Network hub. Fire grabbed onto anything it could. Plastic melted and metal blackened. The flames licked upward and began spreading to the wires that ran into the ceiling. A tree of fire. Smoke choked out the small room and entered my lungs. Coughing harshly, I rushed back into the hallway.

The tunnels were losing air fast as the choking smoke rolled along the ceiling. I brought my bandana back over my mouth and nose as I moved through the basement. Something must have busted the filter in my last few fights. The air I breathed wasn't getting any cleaner. I kept low, under the rolling black clouds. My wounds began to burn with pain. The world was getting dark. *Blood loss and smoke inhalation.* I pushed myself on. *I won't die in this damned pit.* I saw the elevators. Then I saw nothing.

Chapter 23

~ ~ ~ ~ ~

...

~ ~ ~ ~ ~

The light was a welcome sight when I awoke. The soreness across my body, less welcome. I was lying in a hospital room. The light was from a wall-mounted lamp hanging above me. I didn't know if I was more relieved to be alive, or that for the first night in what seemed like forever I didn't dream.

I was about to sit up when I noticed Selene sleeping on me. She was half in a chair, with her head resting on my chest. Her breaths came slow and calm.

Obasin's words echoed over and over in my mind: "Do you feel for what you have done?"

"Selene," I murmured.

Selene stirred, slowly waking up. She looked up at me, hair sticking wildly in all directions, and smiled. "Hey, Kraft," she said.

"What happened?"

"The firemen found you in an elevator at Glowing Future. The ambulance brought you here for some treatment for your... well, everything."

My good left arm ran over where Orrla had punctured me. The doctors had done their miracle work. The hole had completely healed over, though the area was still horribly tender. *They used Medioxyl.* I felt sick to my stomach.

"That wouldn't heal fully, though." She motioned to my right shoulder.

Two jagged, vertical scars branded me. The last reminder of Obasin's bite. I lightly ran my fingers over the wound.

"I figured," I muttered under my breath.

"They were worried you might die from smoke inhalation," she explained. "So, I'm your emergency contact, eh?"

"I don't exactly have a long list to choose from."

Selene let out a small laugh. "I'm glad you're alive."

"What about you?" I asked, sitting up higher on the bed.

"I'm alive too. Whatever that woman did to me didn't leave anything lasting."

"She was a faery."

Selene's eyes widened. "Wait, faeries are real?"

"Yeah." I took a deep breath. "I should tell you some things."

We talked for a while about what had happened. I told her about the nightmares and how they related to Obasin. I told her about the Dark. I explained about my ability. She was quiet for a lot of it. A nurse came in to see I was awake, giving us a momentary pause. The one thing I didn't tell her was how Obasin taunted me. That was for me to deal with alone.

After I was done, we sat in silence for what seemed like an hour. The silence was only broken when the door slammed open.

"Kraft!" Warren stomped in, eyes alive with shock and fury. "You burned down my building!"

"No, I set a small fire in your hub room. Fire suppression would make sure the entire building didn't go up. I thought about this. Oh, and I got rid of your virus problem. You're welcome."

Warren sputtered out a string of unintelligible syllables.

"How did you know I was awake? So you are keeping tabs on me?"

"Of course, I'm keeping tabs on you! You're insane!"

"Settle down." I had forgotten Warren's habit of being a drama queen. "Your insurance will cover any damages."

"And what do I tell them happened?"

"Electrical fire."

Warren looked like he was a second away from choking me out when a doctor swept in. She had long brown hair tied back in a bun and the same dark hazel eyes as mine.

"Excuse me, sir," started Millie Kraft, "I am going to have to ask you to leave my patient alone. Visiting hours are over."

Warren let out another sputtering sentence but nevertheless stomped out.

"Good working with you!" I hollered after him. I turned. "Thanks, Millie."

"Don't thank me, visiting hours are actually over," she said.

"Oh! Me," Selene exclaimed, catching on. She leaned in and gave me a quick kiss before resting her head against mine. "Everything's okay, right?"

"Yeah, S, everything is fine for now." I smiled.

She returned my smile and stood from the chair. Her hand ran along my arm as she left.

My sister watched her leave. Only once Selene was long gone did she turn to me with a sly smile. "She's cute."

"I'm not saying anything."

"Of course not," laughed Millie. "You know, when I said I better see you this month, this isn't what I meant."

It hurt to laugh.

"By the way, some police are here to see you."

I groaned and slid back to lying. "You said visiting hours were over."

"They're cops."

"Millie."

"Lawrence."

I growled slightly at the sound of my first name.

"I'm not calling you by our last name." She rested her hand reassuringly on my arm. "Just talk to them, they seem worried about you."

"Fine, bring 'em in."

She gave me that smile she always had when she got her way. Caleb and Ali entered, the former bearing a large bouquet of roses. I had to admit, I was glad to see more familiar faces.

"You have five minutes," Millie warned and shut the door behind her.

Caleb put the flowers next to me. "I don't think the old lady at the store necessarily understood they were for a sick friend and not my lover, but I assumed they would work anyway."

"They're fine," I laughed.

Caleb smiled half-heartedly. That wasn't a good sign.

Whatever was going on in Caleb's head, Ali didn't seem to have any idea. She sat in the chair Selene had vacated.

"Did it work?" she asked, taking in the cooling gauze that wrapped around my ribs. "Is it out of the Network?"

I nodded. "You all did great. If he's not dead, he at least won't be bursting through any time soon."

They both gave a sigh of relief. "That, uh, Jack came by," Ali added. "He wanted me to tell you that you're even."

Excellent, no more of that favor hanging over my head. Plus, the Winter energy was returned and New Montreal wouldn't be turning into a popsicle. At least not magically.

"Hey, Ali," I said. "I need to talk to Caleb a little bit, do you mind?"

"Of course not." She pushed herself from the chair. "But in the future, try to keep me out of all this magic stuff. It's far beyond me," she said as she left the room.

It was just me and Caleb. He dropped his scarf on the chair and unbuttoned his peacoat, taking the seat beside the bed.

"So," I said. "You look gloomy. What kind of fallout are we looking at?"

"Well." He spoke as he removed his gloves, dropping them on the sheets beside me. "The police and the fire department know you were working IT for Glowing Future, I explained that much to them. You're on file as an employee. The hub was so badly damaged that they are having trouble figuring if it's an electrical fire or not. You should be off the hook for any arson charges.

"Three CEOs are missing, of course. Tartarus, Glowing Future, and Orion are scrambling, but last I heard the boards are going to go into decisions soon. I highly doubt they're going to see any impact from it, and even if anyone finds the disappearances as more than a coincidence, they shouldn't be able to connect them."

"What about the more... magical fallout?"

Caleb sighed heavily. It wasn't a good start. "This is bad, Kraft. Gerard is trying to bring forward the evidence on Frank

Harcourt, but as far as the Magi are concerned you just killed one of their own. They want to see you."

Shit. I shut my eyes. *This is the last thing I need.*

"That's not the worst of it. Word travels fast in the underground. Everyone is hearing about the Seer who killed a Dark god. You just made a big splash in a very small pond, attracting a lot of attention in a very short time."

"Maybe they'll be too in awe of my reputation to do anything."

He grinned for half a second, but it quickly faded. "The only reason you were able to take down Harcourt, maybe even Orrla, definitely Obasin, was because they underestimated you. You're tough, Kraft, but you're nowhere near the level you're putting yourself out to be. In the future, these things aren't going to see you as a non-threat, and they're going to come hard. They say you're the Darkest Light."

I nearly burst out into laughter. "What does that even mean?"

"They think you're something dangerous. So, please, try to stay out of these things from now on." Sincerity was in his eyes as he spoke. He was sure I was in danger.

"I'll try my best, Caleb," I said. "But, to be fair, I didn't try to get involved this time. They came to me."

"I know they did." He looked out the window behind him where the sun was setting. Beautiful oranges and reds outlined the city skyline.

The sun was setting? It was night when I arrived at Glowing Future.

"Have I been asleep all day?" I asked.

Caleb cocked his head. "You've been unconscious for four days."

"Four days? From blood loss?"

"They don't know what it was. You were unresponsive, though apparently your brain activity was going wild. You must have been having one wicked dream."

I hadn't dreamed at all, at least any that I could remember. Four days. There was no way that could have been natural. Maybe some aftereffect of having Obasin messing around in my brain. He said I took something from him. I couldn't even comprehend what he meant. *What happened back there?* My right shoulder ached.

The door squeaked. Millie peeked her head in. "I'm afraid I'm going to have to ask you to leave, officer. Mr. Kraft needs his rest."

Caleb nodded first to her, then to me. "You get better," he said before heading out.

Millie smiled at Caleb as he left, then approached my bed. "You should get some sleep," she said, stepping in to flick off the lamp above my head.

I grabbed her wrist. "Just leave it on for tonight."

A smile spread across her face. "You afraid of the dark now?"

"Trust me, there's plenty to fear in the dark."

If you enjoyed this read

Please leave a review on Amazon, Facebook, Good Reads or Instagram.

It takes less than five minutes and it really does make a difference.

If you're not sure how to leave a review on Amazon:

1. *Go to amazon.com.*

2. *Type in Endless Hunger by Kevin Weir and when you see it, click on it.*

3. *Scroll down to Customer Reviews. Nearby you'll see a box labeled Write a Review. Click it.*

4. *Now, if you've never written a review before on Amazon, they might ask you to create a name for yourself.*

5. *Reviews can be as simple as, "Loved the book! Can't wait for the Next!" (Please don't give the story away.)*

And that's it!

Brian Hades, publisher

About the author:

Kevin Weir is an AMPIA Award winning writer of science fiction, fantasy, and comedy. A multidisciplinary storyteller, he has written short films, webseries, stageplays, as well as short stories. These short stories have appeared in places such as *Red Sun Magazine*, *Enigma Front*, and *In Places Between*. He lives in Alberta where he hosts *The Third Space Podcast* and lives with two dogs that he does not own, but are always around.

Need something new to read?
If you liked Endless Hunger, you should also consider these other EDGE-Lite titles:

——— < > ———

The Rosetta Man

by Claire McCague

Wanted:

Translator for first contact.

Immediate opening.

Danger pay allowance.

Estlin Hume lives in Twin Butte, Alberta surrounded by a horde of affectionate squirrels. His involuntary squirrel-attracting talent leaves him evicted, expelled, fired and near penniless until two aliens arrive and adopt him as their translator. Yanked around the world at the center of the first contact crisis, Estlin finds his new employers incomprehensible. As he faces the ultimate language barrier, unsympathetic military forces converging in the South Pacific keep threatening to kill the messenger. The question on everyone's mind is: Why are the aliens here? But Estlin's starting to think we'll happily blow ourselves up in the process of finding that out.

Praise for The Rosetta Man:

"The cover and synopsis had me expecting a light-hearted comedy. I didn't realize I was getting a geopolitical first contact thriller that somehow still managed to be a light-hearted comedy. I really enjoyed this book! The characters are rich and diverse. Estlin and Harry are great, Beth and Bomani made me cry. The story is fast paced and engaging and again, completely unexpected. Great book for fans of first contact scifi, but also fans of thrillers and mysteries. And so well-executed that I give it a solid 5 stars."
— Scott Burtness, author of Wisconsin Vamp (Monsters in the Midwest)

"This book ranks up there with many of the classic sci-fi "first contact" stories and Claire McCague's scientific background comes through in waves."
— Cameron Arsenault, Amazon Reviewer

"A completely enjoyable read. Good action, lots of humor, and a global setting. Strongly recommended."
— Diane Lacey, Amazon Reviewer

For more on The Rosetta Man visit:

tinyurl.com/edge6004

——<>——

Milky Way Repo

Book One in The Milky Way Repo Series

by Mike Prelee

Running a starship repo company isn't easy or cheap. It's just an endless string of fuel costs, ship maintenance, legal red tape, unhappy debt bailers, shady associates and uncooperative dock officials from one end of the galaxy to the other.

Nathan Teller owns and operates Milky Way Repossessions, a company that tracks down and repossesses starships. And although he's only managing to break even on his debt, he wouldn't trade it for anything. (His ex-wife holds that against him. No surprise there.)

When Nathan and his crew successfully steal a freighter from the clutches of a particularly tenacious and corrupt dock official, he earns the respect of their high profile employer. Opportunity seems a sure thing.

Nathan should be happy. But when that lucrative job op turns into a ransom delivery for a starship crew being held hostage by a cult, he suddenly finds himself pursued by a self-immolating loan shark hell bent on collecting a gambling debt.

How will it all turn out? You never know. Especially when Nathan and his Starship repo agents are up against a cult and the mob…

Praise for *Milky Way Repo*

"The debut novel of Mike Prelee is a very entertaining Sci-Fi/Noir, with vivid, likable characters and a fast pace. He's got a great handle on plot and a knack for drawing you into the story. For fans of fast-paced space adventure with a smattering of crime drama mixed in, this should do the trick. I finished it in two sittings. High praise for sure. I would definitely read a sequel (or two)."
— marc a. gayan

"Milky Way Repo is a nice, light but exciting read. With just enough action and even a bit of romance and comedy, I definitely recommend this read to anyone who enjoys a good sci-fi/blue collar space opera."

"I gave Milky Way Repo 5 stars because it provided me with a short, albeit adventurous, fun and light hearted escape for a few hours. It is well written, with well rounded characters and a wonderful storyline."

"I have to say that Duncan was my absolute favorite character. Officially starting a Duncan fan club!"
— Chaelsie Jenyk

For more on Milky Way Repo visit:

tinyurl.com/edge7003

——<>——

For more EDGE titles and information about upcoming speculative fiction please visit us at:

www.edgewebsite.com

Don't forget to sign-up for our Special Offers

91651316R00159

Made in the USA
Lexington, KY
24 June 2018